The Last Flight from Tokyo

A NOVEL

The Flight Risk Spy Series: Book Two

SHELLY SNOW PORDEA

LITTLE BLACK BOOK
PUBLISHING

Contents

CHAPTER ONE

Geneva, Switzerland: One Week After Tenerife

AMANDA FLOATED ON HER back in a saltwater pool overlooking the lake, her arms stretched wide in surrender to the silence. The warmth of the water was a welcome contrast from the crisp air, steam rising slightly from the surface, the heat making her muscles let go before her mind was ready to follow. The quiet came like fog rolling in, unspoken, and strangely serene.

She wore a black one-piece with thin, knotted straps and a plunging back. It was elegant and understated, the kind of suit that suggested she wasn't trying to impress anyone, and yet she did. The fabric clung to her perfectly, a designer statement piece, though she hadn't bought it herself. It was a gift from Tristan, like so many things lately—just her size and taste. She hadn't gotten in the habit of accepting gifts rather than rewarding herself with them, but she was learning to appreciate an important aspect of Tristan's affection.

Somewhere behind her, beyond the privacy hedges and glass walls, Tristan was on a call. She couldn't hear his words, but the rhythm of his voice carried through the air like a pulse: strong, steady, and practiced. He spoke with the kind of oration that was constantly moving and negotiating. There were moments she still didn't know what to make of the extremes in his personality. Shrewd businessman, soft lover, complex to the core.

She closed her eyes. For a moment, Amanda let herself pretend that this serene moment in the water was a vacation, a soft place to land. The stillness, the view, the passion between her and a man she was trying *not* to fall in love with. Peaceful serenity after a tumultuous storm. And maybe it was. But calm wasn't a place she had ever known how to stay. It had always felt like the fancy dress she had to borrow from Esmé—an outfit on loan, tailored for another, and never hers to keep.

Every time Amanda's eyes shut, she could see Katherine's face that night on the terrace, still hear the quiet click in Julius's voice when he said they'd been working together all along, testing her—her of all people—in the midst of some of the richest and most powerful movers and shakers in the world.

"You're thinking again," Tristan's voice called gently from the terrace. "Come inside. I have a surprise."

Amanda didn't move. "Is it another... robe... a dress... a cold drink?" she laughed, speaking playfully into the wind without opening her eyes.

Tristan had already established a habit of leaving small tokens: an engraved keyring on her nightstand, a silk wrap folded with surgical precision on the bathroom counter. The kind of gestures that said she was never far from his thoughts. Sweet, yes, and also the kind of thing a man who has obsessive tendencies would do. But she wasn't willing to entertain how that thought concerned her in the moment.

"Better than silk robes and champagne," he smiled.

"Is that a promise?" Amanda asked, still nonchalant.

"You'll have to come take a ride with me and see," Tristan teased.

She turned her head just enough to see him—barefoot and wide-grinned, holding two towels like they were an incentive to get her out of the pool.

Amanda swam to the side, resting her chin on her arms, and smirked, "So you want me to take a ride with you?"

"I do," Tristan volleyed the flirtation into her court again.

"And I suppose I should trust you for a good time?"

"Always," Tristan said, offering her a hand as she lifted herself up. He pulled her close to his bare chest without regard for the dripping water collecting at their feet. "But I think we have a few minutes before we have to leave," he smiled as she fully leaned into him.

The drive from Geneva to Interlaken unfolded like a living postcard. Amanda sat in the passenger seat, legs tucked beneath her, forehead resting briefly against the cool glass as the Swiss countryside rolled past in cinematic quiet.

Aside from the breathtaking snow-covered peaks, the lakes were the first thing she noticed—dozens of them, strung like sapphires between mountains and meadow, each one impossibly blue, as if lit from beneath. Angled surfaces shimmered even under a veil of passing clouds, mirroring sky and slope with perfect stillness.

They passed through tidy villages nestled into the folds of green hills, where terracotta roofs peeked out beneath weather-worn shutters and flower boxes spilled over with red geraniums. Some of the chalets looked centuries old, leaning slightly with time, their wood darkened to a silvery brown that blended into the land like they'd grown there.

Vineyards draped the lower slopes like patchwork, and church spires pierced the skyline in quiet, stubborn intervals. Goats and cows grazed in picturesque pastures, their bells occasionally audible even with the windows up.

As the road climbed endlessly, winding past gorges and tunnels carved through the rock, every curve revealed some new jaw-dropping vista: sheer cliffs, pine forests, waterfalls flinging themselves down from heights that defied logic. It was difficult to take in, the scenery whirring by as they drove, giving her a sense that she needed to pinch herself to see if she was dreaming.

Amanda hadn't realized how long she'd been silent until Tristan glanced sideways and said, "Beautiful, right?"

She nodded, still watching the world blur and sharpen with each bend in the road.

"I've flown into Geneva a hundred times, probably. Been over these mountains, viewing them like they were hills in a diorama. And I never knew this is what exists on the ground. It doesn't look real," she said.

"Switzerland rarely does," Tristan agreed.

And yet everything around her *was* real—the sting of pine on the wind, the way the mountains refused to apologize for their grandeur. It unsettled her, how much she wanted to place her faith in it. To believe that being here could heal her soul. Reset her mind. And maybe that was the part her brain kept circling: how could something this beautiful also be true? Beauty, to her, was always dangerous.

The landscapes that looked impossible, colors too vivid to name, air so crisp that inhalations of it went much deeper than her lungs. But what surrounded her was completely and undeniably tangible. This was the kind of place where feelings like romance, intrigue, and simple delights didn't feel foolish. They felt invited and essential, perhaps the meaning of existence itself. She spent countless mental battles trying to stay guarded. But part of her was inching toward the edge of something she was in danger of falling into, and this backdrop did her romantic skepticism no favors.

The road narrowed as they approached, coming to stop at a small station where a hanging gondola was ready to take them up the mountain. A few cars were parked in the modest lot, but otherwise, the place felt hushed, suspended, like the air just before a storm.

Amanda stepped out of the car and stretched, her sneakers crunching softly on the gravel. She inhaled deeply. Tristan opened the back door and pulled out a bag as he handed her a light windbreaker and a water bottle.

"In case it gets too chilly up there. And if we're lucky, we'll get to fill these in the fresh stream," he said, wagging the empty bottle back and forth.

"Drink directly from it?"

"Yeah, it's pretty cool. Totally safe."

"Okay," Amanda elongated the word incredulously. "So...what's the plan?" she asked, leaning her head back to see just how high up the mountain the gondola reached.

He smiled. "We're tourists. And we're going to act like it."

The gondola rose ahead of them, encased in curved glass and steel, already beginning its slow ascent up the mountain with a group of alpine explorers. Amanda watched it glide along the wire, swaying in the wind like a dangling leaf.

"That looks… unstable," she said, unable to hide her nervous energy.

"You climb the skies with just wings! This at least has a rope," Tristan smirked, brushing his hand gently against her back as they reached the ticket booth.

"A rope? And what if it gives?" Her voice sounded jovial by this point, like she was joking, but she definitely wasn't. "Does it have any wings to save us?"

He gave a low laugh, more amused than surprised. "I don't know, should we ask this guy how many fatalities they've had?"

Amanda's eyes widened, giving him a *please don't* glance without responding. She boarded the swaying cable car regardless.

As the gondola climbed steadily, its glass walls revealing layers of alpine wilderness, green pastures speckled with yellow wildflowers below, sheer rock faces streaked with snow above, and pine trees that grew in slow, stubborn spirals, Amanda stood near the edge, one hand lightly gripping the rail, the other shoved deep into the pocket of her windbreaker.

"This is unfathomably scenic," she muttered, still in disbelief about their surroundings. "You said you were taking me on an adventure, and this seems...adventure doesn't even begin to describe it."

Tristan stood just behind her, watching her reflection instead of the view. "I'm sorry, were you expecting a drop zone from thirty thousand feet?"

"I'm learning that I can't know what to expect with you," she flirted.

"Well, it's nothing so dangerous," he said, "unless you count this unstable rope swing." Tristan smiled, his delight in watching her unexpected fear come to light was too obvious to hide. "Besides, you don't think I brought you all the way to Switzerland just to impress you with the ordinary, do you?"

She cast him a sideways glance. "With you, nothing's ever ordinary." She didn't say the rest: that sometimes, that scared her. Tristan slipped his arms around her waist from behind, pressing his cheek to hers. She didn't look at him, but the heat touched her body all the same. She hated how easily he could do that—make her deeply feel things with so little effort.

Amanda kept her eyes fixated on the tiny town, watching it shrink below them until one bend of the mountain made it disappear altogether. The cable car finally came to a stop, leaving them at the perfect drop-off spot where a once untamed meadow was now a small tourist stop with gravel roads and a cafe, rocky mountain peaks still towering ahead.

As they walked from the gondola on the path, an alpine slide glinted ahead. It was a single metal track of hammered steel embedded into the mountain, winding down the green slope like a silver ribbon cutting through clusters of wildflowers. There were no helmets. No seat belts. Just small toboggan-style sleds with hand brakes, and a row of people lining up to glide one by one into the curve of the mountain.

"Oh my gosh, you want me to actually slide down the mountain?"

"Yep," Tristan said, gesturing toward the sleds, "You first."

"Is that because you're a gentleman or a strategist?"

"Both. And I want the better view on the way down."

She shot him a wide-eyed look. Trisan just smiled, bowing slightly as he pointed his palm to the empty sled on the track as if he were her host.

Amanda laughed, taking his hand and climbing in while waiting for one of the alpine slide's teenage employees to give her a "go" signal. Another staff member counted her down as Tristan gave her a thumbs up. And then she was off—coasting forward on the smooth, rounded metal, wind catching the corners of her clothes, and the track humming beneath her like a quiet song.

It wasn't just a slide, it held her like a bowl, tipping her gently toward whatever came next. She leaned into each bend, braking just enough to keep her pace steady. A hearty laugh slipped out, her breath deepening further with each second she was exposed to the crisp, thin air. Out came another laugh, a shriek of sheer delight.

At the next switchback, she glanced behind her. Tristan was in place at the top of the hill, and a second later, he was plummeting down, arms out for effect, his grin wide and boyish. When she arrived at the bottom, Amanda rolled to a stop and stepped off, brushing the wind from her hair. Tristan appeared just moments later, clearly not having used the brake nearly as much as she had. He hopped off the track with a dramatic stretch.

"I think that qualifies as reckless adventure, right?" he said.

"I didn't even use the brake much!" Amanda giggled, her hair still askew.

"You almost looked like you were flying," Tristan said with a pause, "ironically."

Amanda shrugged, smiling widely, suddenly aware of how close they were to each other. "Maybe I was."

"Careful," he whispered into her ear. "You keep letting go like that, and I'll start to think I'm really getting to you."

Amanda looked up at him, eyes soft, any guard she was trying to maintain slipping again.

"You might be," she said, flicking her head with a smile. She turned her shoulder away from him, walking toward the perfectly situated café without another word, leaving him slightly surprised, just long enough to enjoy it, before she turned back to look at him again with a wink. He hurried his pace, speeding to catch up to her.

He reached her quickly, grabbing her hand with a slight tug and intertwining their fingers seamlessly. "I know that this has been fast, and I've come on strong, but... there's something about this that feels right, Amanda." He stopped her in her tracks, placing his entire body in front of hers, leaning in with intensity.

"I am really enjoying my time with you, Tristan, and I think you know that I do care about you. But it's only been a few months, and I'm scared, to be honest. You don't know me, not really. And I don't know you..."

"Yet," Tristan interjected, breaking any tension that threatened to derail their exciting day together, and the heat obviously pulsating between them.

"Yet," Amanda parroted, smiling.

She wasn't delusional about the fact that she sometimes suspected Tristan of being more—or less—than he seemed. She knew his money and influence clouded her perception of reality, but that was only when she was analyzing things, not sitting smack dab in the middle of them.

Her skeptical view of the world had plenty of good, solid evidence behind it, and the pretty rich boy type was always a bad bet in her experience. But *she* was the one currently living a double life, something she could neither reconcile with her values nor seem to walk away from. She couldn't decide if she didn't want to fall in love with him, or if she was desperately hoping to prevent him from falling in love with her.

"Let's just enjoy the day, deal?" she said.

"Deal," Tristan agreed, pulling her in for another kiss, feeling the vibration of the earth itself as they stood pressed into each other in the vast, open expanse of the most majestic nature fathomable.

Amanda sat at the edge of the bed, brushing her hair, the scent of fresh wildflower soap clinging faintly to her skin. The windows were cracked open enough to let the morning breeze curl around the curtains, crisp and clean.

Tristan had invited her on this escape, not just from her job or the noise of life in general, but from the lingering imprint of loss. Geneva had offered its own kind of silence, a pristine order that made chaos feel far away. It wasn't meant to fix anything, but it was a pause, a breath between storms. A place where the trauma of what they'd seen—of two lives lost in rapid succession—could dull at the edges, if only for a few days.

"Let's see if the world's still standing," Tristan said, flicking on the television and flipping through channels. The sound of a British reporter rose softly, structured and calm.

"And in international headlines, British entrepreneur and philanthropist Vivian Cross has died following a diving mishap in the Canary Islands last week. Authorities report her oxygen regulator failed during a group excursion, and efforts to revive her were unsuccessful. Cross, known for her education initiatives and work with AI ethics coalitions, was forty-four."

Amanda didn't react, not visibly. But her body went still, her breath caught just behind her ribs. The broadcast played on, Vivian's name spoken with a perfect blend of reverence and distance that only news anchors could manage, but Amanda couldn't let her mind focus on the words, the vivid, gruesome scene pushing its way to the front of her thoughts.

"It's crazy, isn't it?" Tristan said, setting his phone down. "You try to get away, and life just follows you."

"Yeah," it came out as a whisper, "I think we'll forever be connected to something neither of us signed up for." Amanda met his contemplation with her own. "Did you know her well?"

"No, not really. We crossed paths a few times before Julius's party on the island."

Silence fell between them as a photo on the screen showed Vivian in evening wear, standing at a podium, mid-speech.

The kind of image that made her look iconic. Untouchable. Not like a woman pulled from the sea, gasping for her last breath.

There was no mention of Russell. No suggestion of a pattern. Just a sealed-off tragedy, sanitized and compressed into thirty seconds of polite airtime.

Amanda kept her expression neutral as she put her hairbrush down and continued getting ready for the day.

"Don't you think it's strange...how fragile life can be?" Tristan asked, breaking the quiet again, pushing the power button on the remote as if not wanting to face another moment of bad news. "Someone like Vivian, gone just like that."

"Yeah," Amanda said. "Strange." She wanted to ask him exactly *how* strange he thought it was. *How* suspicious it seemed. That there's no way she could've died from lack of oxygen in her tank without there being some other substance at play, in the tank, in her body...something. But the moment passed as quickly as it came, and Tristan reached for his jacket.

"Want to walk down to breakfast?"

"I'll meet you there. I still need a few minutes to finish getting ready."

The door clicked shut behind him, and Amanda stayed seated, eyes on the black screen as if it might flicker back to life. But it didn't. She pulled in a slow breath and let it out just as carefully. When she joined Tristan downstairs, he was standing by a stone hearth, scrolling through something on his phone, a small morning fire crackling beside him, low and welcoming.

"I've been meaning to ask you," he said without looking up. "How do you feel about Tokyo?"

Amanda paused. "In general?" She genuinely was not following his train of thought.

He smiled and glanced at her. "Yeah, you know, as a destination. I have to be there in a few days... and I'd love it if you came with me."

Her expression tightened. She felt caught off guard, and then not at all. *Tokyo?* Of course, this had been Katherine's plan. She and Julius told her that if she were to accept this mission—agree to be a spy for them, committing to a life of espionage that she had somehow inherited—she'd have to go to Tokyo. They didn't expect her to be hired for a flight or make travel plans; they knew she would secure an invite from Tristan. Of course they did. The people pulling the strings had the power to place her exactly where they needed her, without ever having to ask. It was maddening. She let out a quick breath.

"What's in Tokyo?"

"Everything," Tristan said with a proud grin. "We're debuting the Ocular Grid, finally. The team's been prepping for over a year, and this is the global unveiling. Think LED catwalks, immersive demo rooms, simulated cities—very sci-fi, very seductive," he winked. "Then, a grand ball after the main auction, and a slew of celebration events. Dignitaries. World leaders. Tech moguls. Every buyer with a stake in the future will be there."

"Sounds... low-key," she quipped.

He chuckled. "It's a bit much, I know. But it matters. There will be a lot—like a *whole lot*—of press. And I *want* you there. With me. By my side."

Amanda folded her arms. "Why?" she asked coyly.

She wasn't exactly flirting, but she did want him to say it. To spell out the reason he wanted her to be standing beside him. Because she already knew why Katherine and Julius would want her to be present. Intel only. Always intel. But she didn't know how much her heart and mind could handle, and she wanted to at least feel comfort in the fact that Tristan truly longed for her presence, her one hope of safety.

He met her eyes with a faint tilt of the head and a soft smile. "Because it's a part of me you haven't seen yet. And I want you to."

"Well, that's a better answer than: 'I need a plus-one,'" Amanda grinned. She held his gaze, her mind already working in angles Katherine had trained her to recognize: the timing, the players, the pressure. She could see the arc of it—how she'd been steered, positioned, and wooed. Just enough to say yes.

And she couldn't control the heat within her chest, begging her to lean into him.

Tokyo wasn't just a trip. It was a threshold.

And Tristan, whether he knew it or not, was standing on the other side of it, hands outstretched.

"You'll get to see Esmé again!" he continued to sell it. "You two got along so well, and I'm sure after all that went down, she'd be so happy to see your face again. So many of the people you met on the island will be there... and we'll all be surrounded by happy circumstances this time, you know?"

"Okay," Amanda acquiesced softly, contradicting the gravity of what she was saying. "I'll come."

His smile was instant and unguarded. "Good."

But Amanda suddenly felt equal parts fear, clarity, and mystery.

Chapter Two

Tokyo, Japan

Melody Drake wandered the streets of the city like a pro. She had spent enough time there to know her way around, but the truth was she had lived most of her adult life playing the part of a quiet woman at the side of a man with too many secrets.

She wasn't one to overload her spouse with nagging questions—her days were filled with managing schedules, school activities, and sports that didn't always end before dinner. She had a life to live, a family to raise, and a stacked routine built to mute suspicion as they traveled the globe after each of her husband's assignments.

Tokyo was a humming constellation of light and glass, each block folding into the next like circuitry. She didn't need a map; she had walked with Russell through these routes a dozen times before, in this exact pattern. He never said why this particular route mattered. Just that it did. And now, in his absence, she chased his ghost like a trail.

It surprised her how natural it felt. The city's pulse, sleek and sharp, reminded her of youthful ambitions. This was the kind of place where no one asked questions, where anonymity was stylish, not suspicious. In Tokyo, Melody could vanish into a crowd and become something else, and she wasn't yet aware of how profound her transformation was becoming.

She passed a woman in a slate-gray business suit talking into an earpiece, a vendor selling matcha soft serve from a neon-lit cart, and a child in a school uniform dragging a suitcase adorned with cartoon eyes. None of them looked at her twice. That was the gift of this city: its ability to swallow you whole and spit you back out reassembled.

Melody slipped into an urban art gallery tucked into the corner of a quiet building behind a tea house, its entrance framed by a pale curtain and two minimalist lanterns. She stepped inside and removed her shoes, careful not to rush, her fingers brushing the wall for balance, steadying her from the trepidation she was trying to conceal. The entry opened into a long hallway with a few stairs at the end, leading to a high-ceilinged room of white walls and silent observers.

She spotted him, the man she was looking for. Lucien Beaumont stood near the center of the room, hands clasped loosely behind his back, head tilted toward a metallic sculpture shaped like a twisted coil. He seemed older than she remembered—grayer at the temples, more polished around the edges—but still unmistakable. She let a crooked smile creep across her face, feeling accomplished.

She drifted toward the far corner of the room and paused beside a large photograph of an abandoned airfield. The date at the bottom made her stomach turn. It matched one of the last timestamps Russell had ever written down. She had scoured every document and note she could find after the news of her husband's death on a so-called business retreat had reached her. She had memorized every last clue.

Lucien approached the photo display with a thoughtful gait, coming to stop beside her. She didn't look at him. She didn't need to.

"You're following me?" He murmured without turning his face to see her.

They weren't strangers. Melody had crossed paths with Lucien over the years at international galas, tech summits, and donor receptions, occasionally appearing beside Russell, who tried with varying degrees of success to make himself seem essential in circles where he was barely tolerated. Lucien had seen it all before—his forced charm, his need to be seen. Russell had a way of showing up in rooms that weren't expecting him, clinging to connections he didn't fully hold.

Melody, by contrast, never tried. She stood with quiet grace, inhabiting the space rather than performing for it. Lucien had clocked her even then, not just as a wife, but as someone watching everything. It didn't surprise him that she'd resurfaced now, no longer trailing behind her husband's ambitions.

"I didn't come to start a war," she said quietly. "But I'll finish what Russell died for."

Lucien didn't speak until after a pause, low and measured. "What are you doing, Melody?"

She turned slowly, meeting his eyes with a false calm that made for a convincing front. She couldn't peg how much Lucien knew. And she couldn't put the pieces together yet, but she was surely going to try. "I'm here because Russell's dead, and I think you know why."

He exhaled, his expression unreadable. "I'm not involved if that's what you're insinuating. Plus, his business was never yours, Melody. Don't get in over your head."

She offered the faintest smile. "I'm not the shy twenty-year-old Russell married decades ago, Lucien."

Lucien and Melody were roughly the same age—better matched, perhaps, than she and Russell had ever been. She had only now reached the age Russell had been when he married her, much to her family's dismay at the time, but years abroad had dulled their disapproval, softened by distance and the blur of time. She had poured herself into raising their three boys, weaving her presence into their lives through schoolwork, competitions, and cross-continental moves. Kendo in Japan, tennis in Spain, soccer in Brazil—she built their foundation while Russell vanished for weeks at a time. The pride she had in her boys was enough for her, the quiet and unwavering dedication that comes with being an overly involved mother. Melody didn't need the spotlight; she was the scaffolding holding everything in place.

She hadn't been naïve–just in love. Blind to the subtle red flags—the absences she chalked up to work, the whispered late-night calls she told herself were just business, and the way his phone was always face down. Even now, standing in this pristine gallery, she could picture the way Russell used to run his hand through his hair when dodging her questions. She could hear the softness in his voice that made her believe everything he said. Love had distorted the edges until she could no longer see the outline of truth.

Melody let her eyes linger on the timestamp beneath the photograph, Russell's final breadcrumb. Her chest tightened. She swallowed hard as the taste of bile began to rise, before she forced it back. Her life—her youth—had been centered around Russell. What did people expect her to do now?

Lucien studied her face before addressing her. "I want to get—and stay—as far away as I can from the mess we all witnessed. And you should too."

Melody's eyes were full of pleas she didn't have to articulate. "I can't."

Her world, the one she had known for so long, was gone. All she could think about was the summer between high school graduation and college, when she boarded a plane in Detroit for her first transatlantic adventure to visit a friend in Germany. Airline tickets had been cheaper to Warsaw, so, operating on a teenager's budget, she flew there first, planning to take a simple train ride to Berlin.

In the early 2000s, during a post-Cold War Europe, trains still buzzed with the aura of the KGB, held memories of refugees smuggling their most prized possessions, as they crossed borders to save themselves and those they loved most. They even carried the faint, lingering scent of the occasional small farm animals that were once allowed to ride. The heavy metal trudged along the same way in liberty as it had under oppression: people sitting on banquettes in small cabins with strangers, sliding doors of glass between them, and narrow hallways. Nothing was updated or fancy. Everything still bore the scars of the cost of freedom. Travel was slower, and everyone expected it to be.

But what was supposed to be a relaxing seven hours to catch a nap or read a book became a comical fiasco when the door of the train's cabin got stuck during boarding, locking only Russell and Melody inside for five hours before a mechanic in Berlin was able to set them free. They had talked for nearly every minute of their ride, and even though she thought he was mysterious and attractive, as an eighteen-year-old, she wasn't looking to fall in love with an older man. But that day, something in her—something maternal and nurturing—knew her life would never be the same. And now that he was gone, she felt her world teetering on the edge of instability.

Lucien softened his gaze. "Alright. If you want to get close without suspicion, possibly get some answers, the person you need to talk to is Amanda Hopkins. She's new to the group…Tristan Montgomery's girlfriend. It's the only way for you to get close. No one will question if you befriend her. And it's the straightest line to Julius. If you ask me, he *has* to be the one behind it."

"Julius?" Melody's response came out in a staggered whisper.

"But you have to trust me when I say, I don't know anything. Please leave me out of any vengeance mission you're on. You must have known that Russell was at risk. He was always pushing his way in with people more powerful than him. And it cost him."

Melody did know the danger. Every single day of her life. But she'd been able to dissociate from it until danger became death.

"Give me her information. I'll talk to anyone who will help." Her voice sounded like a mix between excitement and fear, and she knew how to use it to her advantage. Melody already had suspicions about the newcomer in an exclusive group, and Lucien had just verified that she was on the right track.

Lucien stepped closer, voice low. "Be careful, please. You're underestimating how fast the world can swallow people whole."

"I'm ready for anything." Her voice cracked slightly despite her best efforts, and she glanced away, jaw clenching as she pressed her lips together. She sucked in a sharp breath through her nose, helping her maintain control.

Lucien sighed. "Here." He offered her his phone. "What's your number?"

She typed it in and handed the device back to him.

"I'll text you. I know where they're staying. The big tech summit is this weekend. Be careful," he said, already turning towards the next piece of art.

"Thank you," she whispered. After taking only a few steps away, her phone buzzed in her pocket. She turned back to give Lucien a nod of gratitude, but he had already walked further into the gallery and out of sight.

Amanda stood still as a clothing designer adjusted the shoulder of her dress, and a tailor pinned and gathered in different places. The designer stepped back with a satisfied hum, as the tailor clipped a note to the hem.

Sleek dressing suites were tucked into the forty-sixth floor of a high-rise tower, where one wall of glass offered sweeping views of the city far below—an endless sprawl of steel and motion softened by the filtered light pouring through sheer drapes. Each suite was partially enclosed, divided by minimalist panels and false walls that didn't fully seal, more suggestion than separation. The air carried the scent of pressed fabric and faint perfume, punctuated by the quiet whir of tailor's tools in motion. In the center of each room, a low, circular platform stood before tall mirrors beneath a halo of soft lighting designed to showcase and scrutinize. Multiple seamstresses moved with practiced discretion, pins on wrist cushions, voices low.

Sound carried easily: a laugh, the rustle of silk, the whispered cadence of measurements from one suite could be heard in the next. It wasn't quite private, but it was intentional, and in a way that only the art of illusion can do, created a sense of intimacy.

Amanda fixed her gaze not on the mirror, but on the city, an unbroken sprawl of concrete and glass. Tokyo had a way of feeling futuristic and paradoxically intimate all at once, like you could vanish or reinvent yourself entirely while in its mesmerizing embrace.

Amanda wasn't sure which one she was doing.

Tristan's voice drifted in from an adjoining suite. Calm, measured, charming. And on yet another call.

"We'll arrive just before the keynote, then move to the private briefing suite... Yes, he'll be there. But I want confirmation on the others. If Malonga's pulling strings behind the scenes, I want to know who he's bringing to the table."

Amanda's gaze dropped to her hands, clenched without realizing. *Malonga.* She knew the name. She had been briefed on it.

The designer fluffed the train behind her, smiling. "You're going to make headlines in this," she said, gently turning Amanda's shoulders, directing her to look in the mirror. "The woman who stole the show." She swept her hand dramatically through the air.

Amanda smiled, though it faltered at the corners. "I'm just going for the hors d'oeuvres," she said, the words dry in her throat, her eyes flicking to her own reflection—poised, elegant, and oddly remote. A version of herself she wasn't sure even she could trust.

The staff let out a laugh and returned to their handiwork, pinning fabric until it hung flawlessly. But Amanda's thoughts didn't move.

She remembered the envelope in her London flat. Katherine never offered full dossiers or concrete orders, just curated fragments meant to keep Amanda aware of only snippets of her mission, as she slipped deeper into Tristan's world. During her one-night stopover in London, just before Switzerland, the envelope had been waiting for her. Inside wasn't a briefing in the traditional sense. It was how Katherine operated, orders masked as fate. Names. Places. Phrases. Like the one with a name she just heard from Tristan's lips: *Malonga. A stabilizer or a saboteur, depending on who's watching. Still assessing.* Even before Amanda agreed to join Tristan in Tokyo and pursue the truth she desperately wanted to find, Katherine never stopped preparing her for what she might face. Perhaps the cryptic and vague communication was a tactic to string her along, but whatever it was, Amanda continued to be treated as if she were in this for the long haul.

Tristan's voice continued, lowering slightly as it cut through from the adjoining suite, "...if she suspects anything, I'll handle it."

She? Amanda took a breath.

"This should do it," the designer told her, "we can assist you with the change, so we can make sure all the pins stay in place, and you're unharmed."

"Oh, thanks," Amanda replied as Tristan entered from behind the false wall that connected their fitting sessions.

"Babe, you're stunning," he said, offering a hand as she stepped off the circular platform.

"Hey, that's not fair. I didn't get to see you in your fancy suit," Amanda protested.

"Ah, if you've seen one, you've seen them all," Tristan dismissed the notion that he could possibly have the same effect on her as she had on him. But Amanda knew that wasn't true. She'd been breathless after seeing him in his tailored silks and sharp linens.

But before she could comment, Tristan continued, "I have to head to Thailand for a meeting. You'll be okay tonight? I already let the chef know that dinner's for one. He seemed a little disappointed."

"But... what about your big launch? There are so many people coming in for the summit; you can't miss that, right? And I'm not wearing this dress without you," Amanda protested, and she wasn't kidding or exaggerating one bit.

"The presentation isn't for a couple of days. And the ball is on Sunday night, so we have plenty of time. I'll be back within twenty-four hours."

"Twenty-four hours?" Amanda's expression sharpened with disbelief. "A flight from Tokyo to Bangkok is seven hours one way!"

Tristan smiled. "I love that you know that," he winked. "All I need is an hour or two on the ground. I'm just picking up a hard drive. I'll be back before you know it."

"A hard drive? What? I mean, can't someone else just bring it to you?"

"No. This is my baby. It's what I've stuck my neck out for and convinced people to dump billions into developing. So, I am not going to trust anyone else to do this. We planned this whole summit knowing that we didn't have a working system, just a prototype. But this... this is the end product, and we made it in the nick of time. We have a team in Thailand that just finished it, and I'm not risking any missteps. Everything has to be perfect for this weekend," Tristan spoke without arrogance, just certainty.

"Okay," Amanda nodded with a grin. "I'll change fast. I can ride back to the hotel with you."

"Oh, no. I'm leaving from here. Kenji will take you back," Tristan motioned for someone to get the man who was standing just around the corner of the large viewing area. Kenji was more of a personal guide and concierge than a driver. "You'll be sure Miss Hopkins returns safely?" Tristan asked as he stepped into view.

"Of course, sir," Kenji nodded with a slight bow.

"Perfect. I just got off the phone with Julius," Tristan said, turning towards the partition that Amanda and a couple of staff members had disappeared behind to change back into her street clothes. "He's arriving later tonight, so I'm going to hire another car to take me to the airport, then wait there for Julius. I'll see you tomorrow, okay?"

Amanda's heart sank; she wasn't sure if she was disappointed that she'd have to see Julius again, or if she was sad that she'd be alone for the night. "Okay, babe. Be safe."

"I will." Tristan sounded as if he'd never seen a day of trouble in his life. "Oh, and... Amanda?" A slight nervousness flooded his tone.

"Yeah," she called, pulling a shirt over her head.

"Erm... my family is coming for the presentation. I just heard back. I... didn't want you to be surprised, and I wish we'd have had time for a formal meeting beforehand, but..."

"Oh... okay..." Amanda wanted to ease Tristan's nerves, but couldn't exactly get a handle on her own as she let the words hang in the air between them.

"Alright. I'm gonna go then?" Tristan made the statement as if asking permission.

Amanda pulled at the thin pocket door and peeked her head through before stepping out, fully dressed. "At least I have a little time to prepare myself," she smiled.

Tristan took her into his arms, slipping his hands around her with a firm squeeze. "They're gonna love you," he said.

Amanda's eyes did *not* hide her disbelief.

"Okay, they're only gonna be here for a few days!" Tristan showed a wide, toothy smile.

Amanda giggled, unable to help herself. "You're impossible."

But you love me," Tristan said playfully.

Amanda froze. The moment stretched, suspended in what wasn't said, barely perceptible, like a puff of breath in cold air.

"I mean…" he started, unable to finish.

"It's okay," she said finally, voice soft and comforting. "It's just something people say. We don't have to make it mean anything."

But even as she said it, she wasn't sure she believed it herself. Her heart thudded hard and fast, and she hated how warm she felt in the pause that followed. How much she wanted to plunge into him instead of step back.

Tristan didn't speak. He didn't need to. His gaze was steady, and when he reached for her, it wasn't rushed. His fingers brushed the edge of her jaw, trailing lightly as if memorizing the shape of her hesitation. And then his mouth met hers—deliberate, gradual, the kind of kiss that pulled her under without having to use the tiniest bit of force. Her body betrayed her once again, tilting toward him with a tenderness she couldn't resist giving.

In that moment, any practiced detachment shattered.

Chapter Three

"Miss Hopkins," the doorman said, already stepping forward with a black umbrella. "Shall I walk you in?"

Amanda glanced at the darkening sky, where rain distorted the city lights into streaks of iridescence, like watercolors bleeding across glass. "Arigatō," she thanked him, accepting the offer just as a bellhop emerged from behind, handing her a small envelope. "This was left for you at the front desk, miss."

No name. No markings. But she knew who it was from, even before opening it.

Katherine had slipped a thin piece of paper inside a blank envelope, the handwriting as spare and unmistakable as a fingerprint: *Tonight. Ten o'clock. The Ichirin Hanare restaurant. Rain or shine.*

Amanda folded the paper once and tucked it into the back pocket of her jeans, restricting her expression to studied neutrality. She had a few hours to kill, so she told Kenji to cancel dinner because she wanted to rest, claiming she needed a quiet night alone. What she actually did was order room service that she was barely able to eat, study the note, read over the papers she brought with her from London, and grab a raincoat from the hotel gift shop before heading out for her meeting.

It had been raining steadily since she was dropped off at the hotel entrance. It sheeted down in silver curtains, turning the crosswalks into a sea of black umbrellas. As she walked the streets, Amanda cinched the waist cord of her rain jacket, its damp edges clinging to her like a second skin. She moved quickly, weaving through the crowd until she spotted the unassuming entrance of Ichirin Hanare—a traditional Japanese house, its presence marked only by a subtle wooden sign and the faint aroma of spices wafting through the air.

Inside, the ambiance was serene. Shoji screens diffused warm light, and the gentle murmur of conversations blended with the soft clinking of porcelain. A host led her through the intimate space, past a small garden visible through a glass partition, and to a secluded table where her handler awaited.

Katherine sat with composed elegance, her eyes locked on Amanda with the silent intensity of someone who already knew the answers to any questions she was about to ask. No drink sat in front of her, no attempt at small talk or pretense of enjoying the ambiance. They had precious little time, and they both knew it.

"How are you?" The question came delicately, almost mothering in its delivery.

Katherine's complexity could be disarming—she could shift from icy strategist to warm confidante with unnerving ease, often leaving Amanda unsure which version to brace for. Raised in post-World War II London by a single mother who cleaned house for a British diplomat, Katherine spent her childhood listening through keyholes and reading discarded telegrams in the wastebin. Sharp, observant, and noticeably poised even as a child, she learned to imitate the upper class long before she set foot in it herself. But in scarce moments, she oozed compassion and grace, making Amanda feel off-kilter. It was oddly more comforting to her when Katherine was cold and calculated than when she seemed lovingly invested.

"I'm okay," Amanda laughed.

Katherine's brows lifted ever so slightly, a flash of curiosity passing through her eyes. Amanda caught it and shifted, clearing her throat and sitting a little straighter before restating herself. "I mean... I'm well. I... you surprise me," Amanda admitted. "I never know if I'm meeting the spy, erm, the intelligence officer," she corrected herself, "or the woman," Amanda said, curling her lip upwards with a shrug.

"Amanda, I am always both. We are not fragmented beings. We are mosaics. Always one, made up of many parts. Because I can be nurturing and caring while both facing and engaging in the dangerous part of this life does not make me one thing and not the other," Katherine spoke plainly.

"I'm learning that," Amanda let a subtle grin cross her face as she let out a quick sigh.

"You don't have to limit yourself." Katherine continued to show her softer side. "You can be whole, you *are* whole, in every moment, Amanda. No matter which part you are showing. Please, remember that," she said.

"I will," she replied, fully intending to take Katherine's words to heart.

"So," Amanda began, leaning forward with a tired but expectant look, "you asked me to come?" She shrugged, changing the philosophical discourse to the real reason she was here.

Amanda was hoping to get down to business and hurry back to her hotel for a good night's sleep. The long days of travel, constant mystery, and high-end event prep were beginning to take their toll. Even though she was used to having a rigorous schedule, the mental and emotional cost now settled deep in her bones, making her skin feel tight and her breath catch even when she was motionless. She promised herself that once she returned to the hotel, she'd book a massage—anything to coax the tension from her limbs and reset her fraying nerves before the summit.

Katherine's fingers brushed over a thin folder on the table. "I did," she nodded.

Amanda looked at the file. It had no markings. No government seals. Just her name on a thin white tab protruding narrowly at the side.

"This is for me?" Amanda asked. "Are you going to explain what it's about?" she said as she glanced down at the dossier under Katherine's palm.

Katherine exhaled through her nose with a tight release of breath. "It's about Russell Drake."

Amanda stiffened. The name was like a tripwire in her brain. She had been trying to avoid the thought—the suspicion that nagged at her, pulling her into amateur sleuth territory. She'd sneaked into his room, absurdly wondering if she could have his cup tested for poison, as though she had access to a forensic lab. It was foolish, desperate, and painfully human. The last thing Amanda wanted to do was remember watching a man writhing on the floor, struggling to take his last breath. She had hoped coming here meant moving on.

"I thought the Spanish government was taking over the investigation. Surely, you don't need me to solve a murder?"

"Of course not," Katherine said. "This isn't about who killed him, but what got him killed. He knew too many secrets about where this wealth was coming from, and he was after a prototype. Tristan's prototype. We think that he was working for Hansen off-books."

Amanda frowned. "Governor Hansen?"

Katherine nodded. "You read the notes on Malonga, right?

"Yes. But it wasn't much."

"Well, Hansen knows Malonga is holding sovereign bonds. The old kind. Physical certificates. Some of them are backing debts that the world's most powerful governments would rather pretend don't exist. If Malonga starts moving them, or worse—exposing them, demanding payment to cash them out—he could destabilize entire economies. Collapse regimes."

Amanda didn't know much about government bonds, and in reality, most governments didn't meaningfully keep track of them. But the savvy and the calculated were always keeping tabs.

There's a quirk of history that still exists—a loophole no government has ever fully closed. It's an attractive playground for men who wish to shift control of the world's richest and most powerful. Thick, cream-colored pages the size of small posters, edged with intricate scrollwork and faded national seals, still circulate in quiet corners of the world. Their parchment consists of vellum and time, their browned ink whispering of forgotten empires. At the bottom, tails of tiny perforated coupons dangle like frayed hems, still waiting to be clipped. This, the origin of our phrase, *clipping coupons*. They are relics of a past era, as tangible as gold, and just as coveted. Once upon a time, brokers had carried these by hand, tucked into leather portfolios or locked briefcases, escorted across oceans by armored couriers or diplomatic pouches.

Sovereign bonds were physical proof of a government's debt, as negotiable as any currency, and just as tempting to thieves. Today, almost all securities live in invisible ledgers and encrypted servers, but for the few ancient bonds still in circulation, the rules haven't changed: possession means ownership. Whoever holds the paper holds the power. In a world of digital surveillance, these crinkling sheets remain stubbornly and very dangerously real.

Amanda's throat constricted, a prickle running up the back of her neck as if her body sensed danger before her mind could process it.

"Collapse regimes?" Amanda asked.

"Yes," Katherine explained, "Back rooms and hushed deals have kept most bonds in existence from being cashed out. If someone demands payment based on promised interests, some governments would not be able to pay the sum owed to the bondholder. They do not possess enough cash in their federal reserves for such demands."

A pressure bloomed beneath Amanda's sternum, as if the truth itself had coiled there, warning her with each breath not to ignore it. "And you think Hansen is involved?"

"We believe Hansen wanted someone close to Malonga," Katherine went on. "Someone who could get in without raising flags. Drake was perfect—he had the right connections, with a reputation that let him fade into the background. And Malonga did trust him."

"Did trust," Amanda repeated. "Past tense? As in... he lost his trust somehow?"

Katherine's gaze hardened. "Drake found something. We think he uncovered the full list—every bond Malonga was sitting on, and every government that was implicated in the corruption tied to them. And then he ended up dead."

Amanda swallowed. "You think Malonga had him killed?"

"I think Malonga suspected Drake was playing both sides," Katherine said. "But it wasn't Malonga who could have poisoned him. He wasn't on that island with you."

Amanda stared at her. "Then who?"

Katherine slid the folder across the table. Amanda opened it to find an array of black-and-white surveillance stills. A blurred image of someone in a hallway. Another of him passing an envelope to someone Amanda didn't recognize. The next showed Lucien Beaumont watching from a distance.

"Lucien?" Amanda whispered. "But I don't get it. Who is he to any of them? I thought he was just another rich diplomat buddy."

Katherine leaned back slightly, studying Amanda as if weighing how much she was ready to hear.

"Lucien Beaumont was born into privilege—old French aristocracy, the kind that still thinks nothing but titles matter. But he carved his real fortune not with the gentle tools aristocrats are used to; he used sharper ones. Venture capital, mostly. He's charming when he needs to be, dangerously connected, and vain enough to believe the world owes him a kingdom. But don't mistake vanity for stupidity—Lucien's no fool."

She traced the outline of the empty place setting in front of her with a finger, her voice sharpening.

"Lucien's specialty isn't building companies. It's breaking them apart, dismantling them, selling off the pieces for more than the whole would ever be worth. It's a kind of art form, if you're cold enough to admire it."

Katherine's eyes flickered briefly, as if recalling old wounds.

"When it comes to Envisage, even Lucien knows that it's bigger than any one of them. It isn't just another tech company, Amanda—it's capable of becoming the blueprint for controlling entire populations. And I think Lucien doesn't just want a piece of that power. He wants to own the people who built it."

She let the words hang there, heavy in the air between them.

Amanda closed the folder, her hands trembling.

"You're telling me Lucien Beaumont had Russell Drake killed," she said. "And you and Julius both knew why. You could have kept it from happening... somehow, right?"

Katherine leaned forward. "I'm telling you what I know so far. That no one's clean in this. And that casualties happen. It's part of the job. So, keep your eyes peeled, and watch your back as you go into this."

Amanda raised her eyebrows, wide-eyed as the rain hammered harder against the window behind them. For a moment, she could only hear her own heartbeat. She didn't say a word. She didn't really have a chance to before Katherine moved on.

"For the past three and a half years, Envisage has operated four independent teams across the globe, each working on this technology. What Tristan is retrieving now is the final version, the culmination of all their work, intended for his presentation at the summit. The original prototype was kept under lock and key by Julius, the only man Tristan has ever fully trusted. But I believe it may be safer now in the hands of the only woman he does."

Amanda's eyes widened as Katherine reached under the table and produced a slim, black case, setting it gently in front of her.

"But why would I need the original if Tristan already has the final product?" she asked, shaking her head, too stunned to form a stronger objection.

"Our intel suggests there's a flaw in that version," Katherine replied smoothly. "The prototype, the one Tristan built himself, is the only model that contains the complete hardware."

Nodding towards the case, Katherine added, "Think of this as the system's brain."

Amanda sucked in a sharp breath through her nose before dropping her head into her hands.

"So, you have someone on the inside there, too? What dirt do you have on them? I seriously can't figure you out, Katherine. What is this? You're with Tristan—you're against him. You work with Julius, but you have other allegiances, including to me? Spare me."

She shoved herself back with a sharp push from the table, her chair skidding across the floor as she recoiled—not just from Katherine's words, but from the weight of everything they implied.

Without hesitation, Katherine rose, her movements unnervingly precise.

"Take it," she said, pressing the small hardshell box against Amanda's chest. "It's the safest thing to do. For you... and for him."

Amanda felt a tear bubble up in the corner of her eye. She wanted to scream, to bolt out of there and book a one-way flight home. But she knew she was in too deep now. The last thing she wanted to do was to leave Tristan there, piranhas circling, without at least keeping an eye on him and doing what she could to protect his hard work.

"Fine," she said sharply, taking the case into her hands. "But, please, let me rest a little bit. I haven't had a full night's sleep since we got here, and the one thing your expert training did not cover was how to settle my damn nerves."

Katherine didn't say another word, her quintessential nod enough to indicate she understood.

Amanda quickly exited, tightening her grip on the slim black case tucked under her arm, as she began weaving through late night crowds on the main drag. Illuminated signs buzzed overhead, painting the slick pavement in a kaleidoscope of color. Every step she took, she could feel the weight of the prototype—the first iteration of the Ocular Grid, a device that would transmit more information than humanly comprehensible—buzzing against her ribs like a live wire.

She wasn't sure why, but she ducked into a convenience store, pretending to browse a row of canned coffee while sneaking glances at her reflection in the convex security mirror. No obvious tails. No familiar shadows. Just a tightness in her chest, the faint ringing in her ears, and the raw hum of nerves gnawing at her from the inside out.

She noticed a woman outside, leaning against a vending machine, half-obscured by a cheap plastic umbrella. She caught a glimpse of her eyes; she was watching Amanda with the kind of stillness that accentuated the city's noise and hubbub. But maybe she wasn't staring with intensity. Maybe it was para-noia.

Amanda stepped back onto the street, heart pounding. "Al-most there. Hotel. Lockbox. Get it out of your hands," were the only thoughts trilling in her mind.

A sharp bark of laughter from a nearby alley snapped her attention sideways. There were two men talking, one of them shoved the other's arm as he began pulling something from his jacket. She walked faster. *Did they know?*

The case slipped in her slick hands, mist still heavy in the air and holding moisture hostage on every surface. She was nearly to the end of the street when a man in a dark raincoat stepped into her path. Amanda veered instinctively to the side, thinking she was about to accidentally bump into a stranger, but his hand shot out, grazing the empty air where her arm had been a heartbeat before. He had missed her—and the case—by a hair.

She was so tired, so enraptured with her own stupid love story, as if she were on another exotic vacation, that she was being sloppy. Not that she had years of experience to fall back on, but it was in her nature to be able to see things others miss.

It wasn't her paranoia. The man had appeared out of nowhere, not lurking in alleyways, but in plain sight.

Suddenly, the woman with the umbrella was there, mov-ing faster than Amanda could process. She hooked the man's wrist, twisted, and sent him sprawling onto the wet sidewalk with a grunt. He fell with the same force that an accidental slip on the slick pavement would create, so nothing seemed nefarious in the exchange. The woman kept moving, catching up with Amanda at a quick pace.

"Walk," she said under her breath, brushing Amanda's arm like an accidental bump in a crowd. Her voice was low, almost amused. "Now."

Stunned, Amanda obeyed. No one else around the commotion even looked twice at the women scurrying by as a few passersby began to help the man up. The two moved briskly, side by side, past blinking arcades and capsule toy shops, until the streets swallowed them whole. A sudden appreciation for the busyness of Tokyo at any hour enveloped the two women.

They ducked into a tiny izakaya, a Japanese pub, smelling the scent of charred meat, smoke, and wet coats. Amanda finally spoke. "Who the hell are you?"

The woman set her umbrella to the side, shaking off the droplets of rain, peeling off her hood, and revealing warm brown eyes and gentle features that disarmed before they challenged.

At first glance, Melody Drake looked almost out of place in the city's bustling churn, her face framed by shoulder-length hair that swayed with each step. She had the softness of a woman who had once been sheltered and therefore had believed in a kinder world. But it was the economical way she moved that told the truth: she was measured, constantly reading the space around her. There was nothing accidental in her rhythm, a quiet awareness etched into every step—too seasoned now to be careless, too scarred to be naïve. Not anymore.

"Name's Melody," she said. "Melody Drake. And if you want help with what you're about to face, you'll come with me."

There was no forced urgency in Melody's voice, just a subtle purr of gravitas that made Amanda believe she had nothing to lose.

Chapter Four

"Are you always this trusting?" Melody asked, eyeing Amanda over the rim of a sake cup.

"I'm not trusting," Amanda said. "I'm tired."

"Well, we don't have much time for rest now," Melody said, her voice low over the dull murmur of the izakaya. "You were followed."

Amanda leaned back against the splintered wall, still catching her breath. "Erm, yeah, I noticed."

Melody gave a quick, grim smile, then set a small, battered envelope between them on the table. "Good. You'll need to notice a lot more before this is over."

"And what exactly is this? Are you trying to pay me off?" Amanda laughed, picking up the envelope. "I'm not giving you the case." The black box pressed into her knees with an unforgiving heft. She almost let the word *prototype* slip from her mouth, but she wasn't sure what in the world this woman knew yet, and wasn't about to lay her cards on the table first.

"I'm not after the same thing those men want. I don't care what's in that case. All I want to know is how and why my husband is dead." Melody said, her expression morphing into something that on most faces would have looked like a snarl, but on her, it looked like a silent oath, deeply forged with every betrayal she'd survived.

Amanda drew in a slow, steady breath. The all-consuming desire to see justice was something she understood. The urge to make someone pay for what they'd done ran hot through her veins, even if she'd never seen it happen. She longed to watch in satisfaction while some coldhearted snake paid for the sins of his past. No matter how much she dreamed about seeing Governor James Hansen handcuffed in a perp walk and eventually locked away, there was something about believing justice didn't exist that was more comforting to her than hoping wrongs would be someday righted.

"I don't think I can help you with that," she lied.

"I think you can. And I think you need me," Melody finally took a sip of the fermented rice brew in front of her.

"I don't know what I need," Amanda admitted, shaking her head and tipping her small glass to Melody before slamming it back to let the sting of the liquid tickle her throat.

"Well, then let *me* help you," Melody's mouth twisted with a side grin.

"How can you help me?" Amanda didn't know the full story behind Russell's death, but what little she had gathered made her question Melody's ability to do anything. The street takedown had been impressive, yes, but it didn't make Melody an ally by default. Her skepticism ran deep, and her trust couldn't be won with a single act of valor.

"I knew you were being followed because I was tailing the man following you," Melody explained.

"But, how?" Amanda's shock was genuine.

"Lucien," Melody said.

"Lucien Beaumont?" Amanda blinked. "Don't tell me you trust him."

"Trust him?" Melody gave a short, humorless laugh. "I was married to a spy for twenty years. I don't trust anyone."

Amanda stilled, caught off guard. "Wait. Russell… was a spy?"

A cold weight settled into Amanda's chest, heavier with each word Melody spoke. It wasn't just the shock of Russell being a spy, too; it was the slow, gnawing realization that she'd been lied to by the people she was choosing to trust. Words like *acquaintance* and *associate* were tossed around as if she should have picked up on the hint. And perhaps she would have after twenty years in the game. But this felt entirely unfair to the newbie. Russell was one of them?

Pieces Amanda couldn't have known were missing suddenly appeared, warped and disjointed, and she had no idea how they fit together. She wanted to push it all away, to tell herself it didn't matter now, but it did. It mattered both because it meant Katherine had lied by omission, and because she was right. Russell hadn't just died; he was had been targeted, and what's more he was a real colleague, not just a cover story. And if he wasn't who he appeared to be, who else around her wasn't?

Melody gave a slow nod. "Russell wasn't the same kind of spy as Julius Babb; I'm sure you noticed. His was quiet work. Embedded. He played his part as the needy fool. He told me only what he had to, and even that was rare. I didn't ask. Not until recently."

Amanda leaned in, voice hushed. "So you knew?"

"I knew enough to be afraid. And not enough to stop what happened to him. And I think they sucked you into their game too." Melody's fingers tightened around the cup between her hands. "I'm here because I want answers, Amanda. I don't know who ordered the hit. I don't know why Vivian's dead, or why the whole celebration exploded into a gruesome scene. And I don't know how everyone seems gullible enough to believe it was a freak accident. But I intend to find answers. Because I know Russell was scared."

Amanda exhaled slowly, her thoughts beginning to spin. "Scared of what?"

Melody met her eyes. "Of what was coming. Of who he couldn't trust. Maybe even of Julius."

The name landed between them with a forceful thud, the accusation impossible to ignore.

Amanda rested her elbows on the table for a moment, her mind racing to connect the blur of dots taking shape. "Katherine never told me."

"Of course she didn't. She wants your loyalty clean. No ghosts." Melody's voice softened, but an underlying bite was still there.

"And Lucien..." Melody shook her head. "I know he needs something—wants something desperately, and lost someone in the process too. Just like I did."

"What do you mean?" Amanda asked.

"Lucien and Vivian," Melody said flatly.

Amanda squinted in confusion.

"Vivian Cross," Melody clarified. "She and Lucien weren't just business competitors. Their relationship lived somewhere between flirtation and chess. Neither could resist the game, and both pretended they weren't keeping score. But anyone who knew them could see it. The way the silent ledger of their accomplishments danced behind their eyes when they looked at each other. It heated everything between them, in that old-school Mr. and Mrs. Smith kind of passion."

"They were lovers? Spies?" Amanda's mouth dropped open.

"Not spies," Melody chuckled. "But lovers, yes. In the most complicated, addicted-to-each-other, and never-admitted-it kind of way."

Amanda didn't reply. Her mind was already spiraling: *Why would Lucien kill Drake instead of using him? If it had been Julius, what was his motive? If it was Lucien, why kill Vivian? Could it be as simple as being a jealous lover, the oldest story in the book? Were the murders completely unrelated?*

She narrowed her eyes at Melody, as if staring hard enough might break something loose.

"I'm not here to solve a murder, Melody," Amanda said at last. "I'm dating Tristan. That's all. I don't know what you've heard or what you think you know, but I'm just—"

"Just walking through the streets of Tokyo at midnight, clutching a black case that a strange man tried to steal from you?" Melody cut in.

Amanda dropped her gaze.

"It'd be a shame if Tristan came back from Thailand to find his girlfriend tangled up in something she couldn't explain," Melody said, one brow arching.

Amanda scoffed, her voice edged with disbelief. "Now you're threatening me?"

"Me?" Melody smiled thinly. "No. I'm telling you you're already a target. I believe Lucien's the one who hired that man to tail you. He thinks I'm some desperate widow just looking to be bought off. But here's the thing—"

Her voice lowered.

"I've learned a lot over the past two decades. And I'm not going to get screwed over the way Russell did. Or the way you might."

Amanda stiffened, but Melody pressed on.

"You haven't reacted once in a way that tells me you don't know what I'm talking about. You understand too much. You're not just Tristan's girlfriend—though maybe he believes that—you're involved. And Lucien suspects it, too. That's why he's having you followed."

Amanda's gaze didn't waver, but her throat tightened. She kept her face neutral, practiced, though her mind worked double time. Followed? By Lucien? That meant she had no idea how many people were watching.

Melody leaned in.

"If they see us meeting, it works in our favor. They'll assume my being here is because I'm exactly what they think I am—a grieving widow, desperate for hush money. And you? You're the sympathetic liaison. Julius loves appearances. Comforting a poor widow fits the image he needs. And we look like we'd be friends, don't we?"

Amanda's fingers tensed in her lap. She wasn't sure what bothered her more—how quickly Melody had sized her up, or how accurate she was. The "girlfriend" label scraped at her nerves, too neat a mask for the mess she was in. But she didn't interrupt. She let Melody spin the narrative.

Her eyes burned with intensity, hard and unflinching as she repositioned herself slightly in her seat, one leg crossing over the other. Melody was composed and calculated, or at least putting on a good show of it.

"They won't ask questions. How would it look—me showing up to one of their polished, curated events, only to be turned away? A grieving widow, unwelcome?" She gave a faint, humorless smile. "They wouldn't dare."

Melody paused long enough to let the implication settle before continuing.

"Julius gets to grant his precious goodwill. You get to play the part of protector, comforting the poor woman still mourning her husband. And Lucien? He sees exactly what he needs to: that I'm following his lead. That I'm trying to earn my way in. Secure my spot in the circle that Russell never could."

She leaned forward, resting her hands lightly on her knees, steady.

"You help me get close. I get the answers. And you stay untouched. For now."

Her voice turned crisp, stripped of sympathy. What was left wasn't anger, but resolve.

"But don't fool yourself, Amanda. If you think they won't hang you out to dry the moment it suits them, you're dreaming."

Amanda wiped her brow. The case burned against her side like a silent accusation, heavy with implication and risk. She swallowed hard, the edges of her exhaustion catching up to her as she forced a harsh breath from her lips.

"I should go," she muttered. "I need to get this thing secured before my brain gives out. I'm no good to anyone running on fumes." Amanda picked up the battered envelope Melody had presented to her and tucked it into her pocket.

"I'll come with you," Melody said quickly. "You shouldn't be alone. Not with that."

Amanda hesitated, then gave a soft, dry laugh. "Yeah, okay. Keep your friends close, right?" She slanted a look toward Melody, one that carried both trust and caution.

The two women shared a brief smile, the moment of humor a kind of dark camaraderie forged under unthinkable circumstances.

They didn't speak another word, just exited the space in a string of moves that looked like well-practiced choreography. By the time they made it out of the izakaya, the rain had picked up again. Amanda pulled her hood over her head more to ensure she wasn't easily identifiable than to keep herself dry, as she gripped the case tucked into her jacket, clutching it close to her body. Melody walked beside her, casual, but more alert than ever.

They reached the quiet hallway near the guest lockers, and Melody lingered by the corridor's edge, eyes flicking toward the elevator like she belonged there, casual but alert. Amanda slipped the case into a narrow locker, turned the key, and stepped back as the latch clicked shut. It felt louder than it should have been.

Melody met her gaze as she rejoined her, and Amanda nodded. She had no backup plan. No escape hatch. Just the woman beside her, watching her like she already knew what would come next.

She hated how much she needed to trust her. "I don't know what the hell I'm doing here," Amanda blurted.

Melody glanced at the closed locker, then at Amanda. "It's okay," she said quietly, "I promise you're not alone in this... whatever your battle is. I don't know what they have on you, and I can't pretend to be an expert, but I see it in you. It's the same fire that keeps me going. And I have to believe the good guys win in the end."

Amanda scoffed, "Believe what you want, Melody. But you're wrong about me."

Melody didn't have to insist that she did, in fact, know how right she was about Amanda. The look she met her eyes with gave voice to a thousand unspoken words that laid Amanda Hopkins out like an open book.

"Good night, Amanda," Melody grinned.

Chapter Five

Amanda found Katherine already seated in the small reading lounge off the hotel's private library, across from the twentieth-floor lounge, her legs crossed, with a linen-bound book resting open in her lap.

Soft light filtered through floor-to-ceiling windows, catching on the fine steam of Amanda's tea as she stepped inside. Her movements were slow and deliberate, like someone reacclimating after a brisk descent, still waiting for the ground beneath them to feel steady again. Fatigue blurred the edges of her thoughts as she set her cup down on the table.

Katherine didn't look up. "You slept?"

Amanda couldn't tell if it was concern, habit, or manipulation. Part of her wanted it to be compassion—some remnant of trust she could cling to—but Katherine's tone, as always, was unreadable. Calm to the point of being sterile. The woman slipped between warmth and strategy like they were stitched from the same thread.

Amanda gave a quiet snort as she sank into the chair opposite Katherine, placing her tea on the tall round table between the high-backed chairs.

"I closed my eyes for a few hours. My mind didn't quite get the exhaustion memo," she muttered.

Silence fell between them, a moment long enough for Amanda to narrow her focus. "Can I ask you something?"

"Of course," Katherine replied, looking up for the first time since Amanda had arrived.

"You told me once, when I was in that training in London, in your office, that if I ever really wanted out," Amanda said slowly, "there'd be a way."

Katherine tilted her head, but said nothing, waiting for the question part.

Amanda exhaled. "So why does it feel like I'm being drawn in deeper? Why did you give *me* the case?"

Katherine looked at her with unsettling calm. "I trust you," she said.

Amanda choked on her sip of tea, trying to keep from spitting it anywhere. "Since when?"

"Since you chose not to run. Since you agreed to follow us into Tokyo, knowing what might be waiting on the other side."

"Knowing?" Amanda laughed with an unintentionally ominous tone. She looked down at her drink, curing her fingers around it again, subconsciously begging the warmth of the cup to ground her. Against what, she wasn't entirely sure. Perhaps it was Katherine's words, the uneasiness of Melody's involvement, or the unsettling truth that she might be the only person in this tangled web without a long game. Whatever it was, the playing field kept shifting beneath her feet.

"I just don't understand why," she said softly. "Why not someone more trained, more connected? You're putting too much on me. Because this still doesn't make sense, you know."

Katherine leaned back in the plush armchair, folding the book closed with a soft thud.

"It makes sense because you're neither loyal to anyone, it would seem, nor in love with power. Because you still hesitate before you lie, and you haven't learned to mask the weight of your decisions. You're messy, Amanda. And that's the most dangerous kind of person to men like Hansen and even Julius. Because they can't predict you. Which means, in my experience, that they can't outwit you."

Amanda let her gaze drift to the window again, to the streaks of early morning condensation blurring the edges of Tokyo's skyline. For a moment, neither of them spoke. The silence wasn't uncomfortable; it was the kind Amanda had come to associate with Katherine—methodical and expectant, like they were both being timed, but only one of them held the clock.

Amanda traced the rim of her teacup. The heat seeped out. Dissipated into the air, visibly disappearing like a version of herself she was trying to hold onto.

"I keep wondering," she said quietly, "if this is the phase where I'm supposed to fall apart. Where I tell you I have to go back to who I was before you dragged me into this. But I don't think I can. I don't think that version of me exists anymore."

Katherine tilted her head. "Would you want her back if she did?"

Amanda gave a tired smile, not answering. She didn't know. Not really. The woman who was carefully measured, fiercely independent, and happily solitary felt distant now, like a sketch of someone drawn in another life. Part of her did want that old self back. But another part of her wasn't sure she'd survive as that person again. She glanced down for a moment, then back up at Katherine.

"I was followed last night," she said. "Melody intervened."

"I know."

Amanda widened her eyes, not angry or even surprised, just tired of being a few pages behind in Katherine's carefully-plotted script.

"Okay. I sometimes forget you're still watching. But I wouldn't have known I was in danger if Melody hadn't stopped the guy following me. That's the part that scares me.

I thought I was getting better at this—at watching, reading, reacting. But if she hadn't been there…"

Katherine raised a brow, but Amanda didn't finish the sentence.

"Well, I'm happy you're alright. And that the prototype is safe. She's not just a widow, you know."

"No," Amanda agreed.

"She's what happens when someone like Russell dies and leaves behind a woman smart enough to start asking the right questions," Katherine said.

"She's asking the same ones I am. And then you keep showing up with half the answers." Amanda followed a lazy arc of dust drifting through the morning light, caught in the air, suspended in motion like her entire life.

Katherine's smile was faint, as if it couldn't mask the deep sadness behind her eyes. "That's because the full answers come with a cost."

Amanda looked at her intensely.

"And you think I'm not ready to pay it?"

"I'm not sure you should have to."

Amanda let that sit between them for a moment. The quiet of the small library seemed to deepen, the air thinning as if straining to listen to their weighty conversation. She leaned forward, feeling the gravity of the prototype still overcrowding her thoughts.

"But you've trusted me with something that could alter the future of global security," she said. "So tell me, just tell me. Why?"

"You know that Russell was Melody's husband. And you've gathered by now that he was one of ours. But what you may not know is how far back he and Julius go."

Amanda leaned in slightly. "We were actually talking about him just before..." she couldn't finish the sentence. She coughed slightly as if clearing her throat would allow her to expel the memory itself. "Esmé told me he was one of Julius's oldest associates."

"Older than most. Times were different then. The way our governments recruited young men back then was less... tactful, shall we say."

Katherine shifted in her chair before continuing. "They were both brought in around the same time—young, bright, and entirely too confident. Julius was the tactician. Cool under pressure, always angling for the long game. And Russell... well, he was brilliant in his own right, but less polished. He could slip in and out of places most men wouldn't dare walk. He was the sort of asset they'd send in when deniability was more important than outcome."

She gave a slight shake of her head, wishing she could bury more memories than she was forced to dig up.

"It wasn't just one moment—it was years of being passed over, shut out of meetings he'd earned a seat in, being sent halfway across the world while Julius stayed close to the corridors of influence. A thousand paper cuts, mostly. Until the last one."

She drew a breath.

"He tried to leave it all behind once—resign quietly, disappear with some dignity—he found the doors locked. His clearance revoked. Contacts ghosted him. He'd become inconvenient. Not because of what he'd done, but because of what he *knew*."

A crease formed between Amanda's brows. The words left her lips slower than usual, as if speaking them might make her surprise unnoticeable. "Julius didn't help him?"

"Oh, he helped, in that maddening way men with power often do. A seat at the back of the room. An occasional check-in. Nothing that would dare tarnish Julius' illustrious veneer."

Katherine's voice was mellow, but her eyes flicked with a hint of animosity. "Russell had done too much. Knew too much. And yet, he was always just outside the circle. Still loyal to the cause and his country. But bitterness has a way of settling into purpose, doesn't it?"

Amanda said nothing, but a strong sense of a word neither one of them yet spoke hovered between them: betrayal. She nodded her head, signaling for Katherine to continue.

"So Russell began appearing at functions—board meetings, charitable events, barely tolerated, but present all the same. He played the part, as charming as ever. But he wasn't there for the drinks or the nostalgia. He was watching. Waiting. And then came the yacht."

Katherine's tone changed, just slightly. Not softer, but slower.

"It wasn't Russell making a scene. It was Russell making a move. He had something—I don't know what—but I'm rather confident that he came prepared. It wasn't bluster. It was intent. He either meant to sabotage the summit or to gain control of the Grid somehow. And I'm not sure who figured it out before I did."

She folded her hands in her lap, gaze briefly dropping before meeting Amanda's again.

"I used to think I knew the difference between leverage and loyalty. But Russel had a way of making me doubt, and with Julius... I'm not so certain anymore either."

"I used to think I knew the difference between leverage and loyalty," Katherine said quietly. "But Russell had a way of making me doubt. And with Julius... I'm not so certain anymore either."

She didn't say *Julius probably had him killed.* She didn't need to. The space between her words, the way her gaze dropped for half a second, said it for her.

Amanda sat back, letting the tornado of facts settle in her mind before reacting. She could have felt clarity, or at the very least, a direction forward, but instead, the picture only jumbled.

"But you said before that Lucien was the one who had Russell killed, right?"

"I said I wasn't convinced he wasn't involved."

Amanda studied her. "So you think he did have a hand in it?"

"I think Lucien plays the long game, and rarely shows the board," Katherine said coolly. "He doesn't build. He dismantles slowly and profitably. That's why we tolerated him."

She paused, the flicker of an old memory catching in her voice before vanishing.

"Years ago, he and I found ourselves on the same side of a complicated negotiation—sovereign bonds, Eastern Europe, post-crisis market manipulation. We were meant to be observers, not actors. But Lucien was never content to spectate."

She took a beat, adjusting the ring on her index finger with quiet precision.

"Still, my gut tells me he's not a killer. Not directly. But men like Lucien—men who collapse systems for a living—rarely come away clean. Whether he dealt the final blow or simply looked the other way... I've yet to decide."

Katherine's tone held steady.

"He's the sort who insists he's one of the good guys—a philanthropist at heart, because he gives away hundreds of millions each year to hospitals, scientific research, even infrastructure in his quiet little hometown. So his shrewdness in business is easily forgiven, at least in the public eye. There was a time I might've staked everything on Lucien. I'm not sure I would now."

There was so much to untangle. A thousand threads knotted in all directions—Lucien, Julius, Russell, Vivian. If Amanda left soon, she could still make her massage appointment. One hour of quiet before having to face the world. One hour to lie still and pretend, just for a short while, that she wasn't being dragged deeper into a war she hadn't meant to join. But something in her couldn't let it go. A part of her needed to continue trying to solve the twisted puzzle.

She looked down at her hands. She hadn't even realized that she'd be squeezing her cup so tightly that her knuckles had gone white. She set it back down on the table. She settled her back against the tall chair, shoulders aching. Reaching into her pocket, she pulled out the battered envelope Melody had passed across the izakaya table. The paper was soft at the corners, creased from being folded and refolded, handled with the kind of compulsive reverence only grief could explain.

"Melody's been carrying this around," she said, laying it on the table between them. "It's full of notes Russell left behind. Not the originals—just her copies. Numbers and words, things she couldn't decipher, I think. But it's hard to make sense of."

Amanda paused, watching Katherine closely. There was no flicker of surprise on her face, but it's not like she could expect that from Katherine.

"Melody said Russell had started keeping records. That he would obsessively write things down. Nothing official. Just scribbled notes. She's been carrying these papers around like they'd tell her something new if she stared long enough."

Katherine reached for the envelope, but Amanda didn't hand it over; she just opened it and let a few worn pages spill onto the small table between them. The handwriting was cramped and uneven, trailing off in spots like it had been jotted in a hurry. A few were dated. Amanda tapped her finger on one.

"August ninth. Nagasaki."

The date had been circled twice with pencil marks darker and more deliberate than anything else on the page. Amanda held the paper between them, waiting for a reaction.

Katherine said nothing at first. Her gaze settled on the note, still and focused, like she was weighing more than just the words.

Amanda reached for another scrap from the envelope. "Here's another. Oak Ridge, with this arrow... see? Pointing to 'Sapphire.'"

She laid it flat, then sat back slightly. "Melody said she couldn't make sense of any of it. I didn't press her. But I figured you might've seen something like this before."

Katherine's gaze lingered on the papers. "These aren't names. They're references."

"References to what?"

Katherine exhaled slowly through her nose. "He must have been tracking something... and these clues are linked to nuclear weapons. Old bomb sites and links to new development."

She pointed to another place: *Nizhny Novgorod Oblast.* "This is in Russia. It's what Julius was referencing in Tenerife. What we all fear—the possibility of new warheads, of reactivated ones that haven't been destroyed or repurposed to provide energy to power grids. But these notations... they're old. Coded references from decades ago."

Amanda sat back. "So Russell wasn't just trying to get out of the espionage game, or like Esmé treated him—a man desperate to get into the inner circle for the money and clout. He was tracing something deeper."

"It would appear so." Katherine's voice was low, sounding as if she was speaking only to herself. "I wasn't fully briefed on Russell Drake's movements—not all of them. And Melody was never meant to be involved."

She paused, her eyes growing distant. "But he knew things were beginning to slip. He must have left behind more than we imagined."

Amanda leaned forward. "So, am I supposed to sit on a dead man's trail of breadcrumbs and hope they lead somewhere before everything burns down? All while Tristan walks into a summit with a device that, in the wrong hands, could implode worldwide financial institutions, and potentially lead to wars?"

Katherine shook her head silently as Amanda gathered the papers, sliding them back into the envelope, her hands slow and deliberate as she spoke. "I don't think Melody knows what she has. But Russell... I think he was *trying* to tell someone. Maybe not her. But someone. And it got him killed."

Katherine was silent for a moment, then shifted forward. "So it's good that 'the someone' his intel ended up with is you. We've got to stay sharp."

Amanda glanced up. "That's not exactly a plan."

"No," Katherine agreed. "But it's a start."

Amanda exhaled, her voice low. "So what happens now?"

"Now," Katherine said, "we keep the prototype secured and well out of reach of anyone eager to fold it into a global surveillance network. Let Tristan give his presentation with the upgraded version. Let him believe he's in control."

She paused, eyes narrowing slightly. "It's easier to redirect something in motion than to stop it cold."

"And then?"

"Then we wait for the system to show its first fracture. It's the only insurance worth holding."

Amanda looked down at her hands. "And it's in my hands."

"For now." Katherine inhaled an extended breath. "Each build site had its own iteration of the hardware, deployed across the globe. But anytime one neared completion, the others began to fail—drives corrupted, frameworks dismantled. I don't believe it was a coincidence."

Amanda frowned. "So, you're saying someone is sabotaging?"

Katherine nodded. "It's always a virus, precisely deployed, clean and devastating. Each time a model approached full functionality, the system collapsed. And according to our contacts, it wasn't the work of an outsider. It came from within—someone with deep access, careful timing, and an agenda. It was deliberate and methodical."

Amanda's eyes widened. "And the one Tristan's picking up..."

"It could already be compromised, or may never have been clean to begin with. That's why the prototype matters now more than ever. The one you placed in the locker is offline, and it has been for months. Untouched. It retains the original architecture. And at this point, it's the only version we can verify."

"And he has no idea," Amanda breathed in deeply, surprised at how much pain her heart felt at the thought.

Her gaze drifted toward the window. The image of Tristan standing on a brightly lit Tokyo stage hovered at the margins of her thoughts, his voice steady, his belief in the Ocular Grid unshaken.

He trusted this system. Trusted Julius. Trusted *her*. And that was the part she couldn't untangle, where loyalty to him ended and responsibility to something greater began. She forced air out of her lungs slowly, willing herself to keep a tear from forming in her eye. A clear understanding of what she needed to do was setting in.

"So we hold it. Quietly," she finally whispered.

Katherine nodded. "Until we know who's behind the sabotage, we watch. We track who surfaces and who begins bidding on the version Tristan brings back. That's why Malonga matters. If he arrives with funds in hand, it means someone has finally bought the bonds he's been trying to convert. And if that's the case... he may not be the saboteur at all. It means he, too, trusts the technology."

Amanda exhaled. "But he's still hungry for power." She paused. "And I'll be the one holding the key to it."

"Yes," Katherine said quietly.

Amanda brought her hands to her head, pressing her fingertips into her temples. It was less an effort to soothe than to keep the pressure pulsating between her ears from exploding outward. Her shoulders sagged forward, the weight of what she now carried impossible not to feel. Somewhere between resistance and reluctant resolve, she felt herself inescapably drawn to this crazy mission. Katherine's request hadn't landed like a command—it echoed like a call of the wild that Amanda couldn't ignore.

She looked back up at Katherine. "So am I just your backup plan?"

"No," Katherine said. "You're my safest bet."

CHAPTER SIX

Tokyo: Three Days Before the Summit, 3:18 p.m.

THE SUITE SMELLED FAINTLY of bergamot and fresh linen, evidence of the housekeeper's recent pass-through, but the air was still warm from the steam of Amanda's shower after her massage. Near the balcony windows, curtains stirred gently in the breeze, as a mild day overtook the city after the heavy rain. A tray of tea sat untouched on the low table, its delicate porcelain still faintly steaming beneath a crisp white napkin.

Amanda had managed a short nap and made herself a cup of her favorite tea, but it had done little to quiet the swirl of thoughts behind her eyes. She sat on the bed with her legs tucked beneath her, robe loosely belted, hair pinned back in the effortless way that only comes with trying to look put together without spending too much time. She heard the click of the door behind her and turned.

"Hey," she smiled.

"Hey, there," Tristan said as he stepped inside, duffel slung over one shoulder, his blazer rumpled just enough to suggest a long day in motion. His hair curled slightly from the lingering humidity, and his presence carried the same quiet charge as the weather. Their eyes met in an unspoken desire.

Amanda knew she had to look like the version of herself he expected to find. The one who had spent the afternoon resting. Resetting. Not the one with coded documents hidden in the lining of her overnight bag. The massage had helped with that.

But when she looked at Tristan, any performance fell away. With him, she didn't have to pretend. Whether she liked it or not, he quieted something in her, a steadying presence in a world that had grown too loud, and too layered. It wasn't logical, and it certainly wasn't safe, but the ease he carried disarmed her.

He made her feel secure, seen, and unguarded in ways she hadn't dared to feel since her first and deepest love. That part of her—the one she thought had hardened past repair—softened in his presence, as if memory and possibility could, for a brief moment, hold the same space.

"No complications?" she asked, rising to meet him.

He let the duffel fall near the console and crossed the room, loosening the top button of his shirt.

"Nothing I couldn't smooth over," he said.

Amanda gave a faint smile. "So... yes," she murmured, drawing closer, her arms naturally slipping around his neck as he found himself resting his hands lightly on her hips, pulling her into him.

He nodded. "Definitely a yes," he answered before pushing back slightly, and brushing a kiss against her cheek as he reached into his coat pocket. "But that doesn't matter now. And before I get *too* distracted..." his smile teetered on the verge of evil. "I got you something."

He opened the palm of his hand, revealing a small wooden box. He blinked, hating that he had to remove both hands from her body to show her. He cupped the box in one hand and lifted the lid with the other, revealing a pair of gold hoop earrings. Sapphires glistened, inset along the curve, and each catchpoint was marked with a single diamond. They were dainty, both striking and sophisticatedly understated.

"I passed a boutique in Bangkok. These stopped me cold," he said with a crooked grin. "Something about them felt like you. Like the version of you that walked into that garden party in Tenerife and made me forget why I was even there."

Amanda turned the box in her hands. The earrings shimmered, an echo of a night that had once felt like possibility—a quiet moment before this new life of hers began to reveal itself fully. The memories weren't exactly comforting, but they were real. And so was he.

She pushed the conflict down, choosing to focus on the man standing in front of her. "They're beautiful."

"Will you wear them to the summit ball?"

She hesitated for a millisecond, then nodded. "Of course, I will."

Tristan secured one, then the other, his fingertips grazing her skin with precision. She inhaled reflexively and unguardedly.

"You always do this," she said, her voice barely above a breath.

"Do what?"

"Make the ordinary feel like something cinematic."

He smiled. "Only because you keep showing up like the leading lady."

Amanda laughed, genuine and sudden, the kind of laugh she didn't realize she needed. "You big cheeseball. You're impossible."

"But persuasive," he winked. He wasn't about to make the mistake of joking about that pesky l-o-v-e word again. He stepped back and pulled his phone from his pocket.

"Okay, get dressed," he said, already texting. "We've got special dinner reservations."

Amanda raised an eyebrow. "What? I thought you were buried in prep for the summit."

"I am. But I moved a few things around."

"You moved your pressing Tokyo schedule for us to have a special dinner?"

"I didn't have to do much. I had help," he said with a wink. "And I only pull strings for the big things." Tristan lifted his eyebrows up and down with a comical flair, causing them both to laugh and fall into each other's arms again.

After a few phone calls in the room, Tristan kissed her temple and whispered something about final prep, disappearing again—one of his signature exits, leaving her with a vague timeline and a promise that a car would be waiting.

He liked it that way. The drama of having her arrive where he was already in place, as if the scene had been curated just for her, was a bit of a game to him. Tristan Montgomery never met a woman who didn't appreciate his attention to detail and planning efforts, but Amanda appeared to be uncomfortable rather than impressed by these skills. Of course, this gave Tristan even more incentive to win her approval, if not amazement.

Once alone, Amanda slipped into a black dress and pinned her hair with a steadier hand than she had used before, her elegant messy bun looking more intentional than carefree. She caught a glimpse of the earrings in the mirror, refracting the light as they swayed. A few touches of mascara, a dab of scent behind her ears, and by the time the car pulled up to the hotel entrance, she looked ready. *"I am ready,"* she told herself.

As she walked out onto the rooftop garden, a breath caught just behind her ribs. It felt like stepping into a dream carefully stitched above the skyline—twinkling lanterns casting soft halos, a glassy pool rimmed in floating petals and flickering candles, and beyond it all, Tokyo Tower glowing like an ember suspended in mist. The air smelled of jasmine and rain-slicked stone, sweet and alive.

A translucent canopy blurred the boundary between sky and space, and at the garden's center, a single table waited, draped in white linen, candles burning slow and steady, their flames undisturbed by the soft breeze. Everything felt deliberate. Intimate. As if time had paused just long enough to make room for this one, storybook scene.

Tristan stood smiling, jacket set aside, and sleeves rolled neatly to his forearms. A vintage record player spun low near the far edge, notes of decades-old French jazz melodies drifting through the air like smoke. When Amanda stepped forward, the sapphires at her ears caught the light and held it captive. Tristan's smile widened.

"This place does *not* even exist," she murmured, eyes sweeping the scene.

"It does," he said, motioning towards her chair. "It just doesn't belong to anyone else but us tonight."

She drifted toward the table, her dress brushing softly at her ankles, a hush of fabric sweeping lightly against the stone. Tristan pulled out her chair without ceremony, and Amanda let herself ease into the moment.

The chef arrived moments later, a tall man in tailored whites, his presence as composed as the meal he carried. With the elegance of choreography, he placed the first course before them. Behind him, the sommelier poured a pale gold wine into their glasses with practiced ease, pausing just long enough to introduce it.

"A junmai daiginjo sake—light, aromatic. It complements the brightness of the scallops."

The chef gave a short bow, then gestured toward the dish. "This evening's tasting menu moves from sea to land. Each course is designed with subtle contrast. Texture, temperature, restraint. Nothing here will overpower."

Tristan grinned at Amanda. "Thank you, chef."

The chef nodded, smiled without comment, and stepped back as the first bites began.

For several minutes, the world softened. The food melted delicately on their tongues. Conversation flowed easily as they shared stories about their first failed attempts at using chopsticks, a sommelier in Sicily who'd lectured Amanda for drinking red wine too sweet and too cold, and Tristan being mistaken for a server at a gala in Madrid.

Amanda found herself laughing, not just politely but freely. The kind of laughing that came from a place deep within, loose and unguarded. The wine warmed her chest, and for the first time in days, she allowed herself to simply enjoy a perfect evening. The glow felt intoxicating, the spice tingled every tastebud, and the smooth ease of Tristan's company settled on her with every glance, every touch that left hot pricks of desire on her skin.

He leaned back, his voice quiet. "Do you want to ask me about it?"

Amanda set her glass down, her smile dimming just slightly. "About the Ocular Grid?"

Tristan nodded. "Yes."

She tilted her head, maintaining a casual, almost curious tone. "What part?"

He didn't hesitate. "The part no one gets to see on stage."

His voice dropped a shade, not conspiratorial, but weighted, like he finally didn't care about the warnings others gave him of being guarded with this part of his life. His excitement to talk to his lover, friend, and confidant about his most prestigious accomplishment was exhilarating. It was as if he had been waiting to open a floodgate.

Amanda nodded. "Sure, if you want to tell me. I don't have a top-level security clearance."

Tristan grinned. "Well, I may have to kill you after this, but it's been a fun ride, right?"

Amanda felt his leg press up against hers, the table so intimate that they couldn't avoid bumping limbs all evening. She'd had enough wine to ignore the unthinkable dangers surrounding them, wishing that they would only spend the evening getting lost in each other.

"It has been fun knowing you," she agreed with a wry smile.

Tristan, mistaking her flirtation for genuine curiosity, leaned in closer, his voice dropping to a near-whisper.

"It's not just about connection. It's about foresight. Most systems up until now have reacted. They pull inputs, cross-check from separate data streams, then wait for human decision-making to catch up. But this..."

He paused, as if savoring the moment before sharing something sacred.

"Our model is anticipatory. It learns patterns across networks: energy grids, transportation routes, communication systems, and flags anomalies *before* they ripple into disruption. It self-prioritizes data, reroutes traffic, and adjusts permissions in real time. No human interference needed. No lag."

Amanda raised her eyebrows slightly, giving a nod she hoped would read as impressed, not concerned.

"It's a live feed with predictive depth," Tristan went on. "The Ocular Grid sees across systems: geographic, digital, and even behavioral patterns in online spaces. It decodes intent from infrastructure. Imagine it like an eye that never blinks—watching, adapting, rebalancing the whole system second by second."

Amanda tilted her head, her voice dry. "Hence the name."

Tristan's satisfied grin lit up his entire face. "Hence the name," he nodded.

Amanda reached for her glass again, if only to give her hand something to do. Her pulse had quickened, not from the wine or the view or the soft jazz, but from the sheer enormity of what he was saying. Her mind began forming connections faster than she could sort them. The system site failures.

Russell. Melody. Lucien. Katherine. Julius. *Hansen.* And God knows who else.

Tristan sighed. "I look at it as a global infrastructure product, like a new form of internet or cloud-based surveillance system that governments, corporations, and high-level institutions can buy into—or more accurately, license access to. It's like teaching a mirror to see into the future. That's the simplest way I can describe it."

"But if it's making those decisions on its own," she said, letting her tone stay light, "who decides what counts as a threat? Doesn't that put a lot of trust in the system's... judgment?"

Tristan didn't miss a beat. "That's the beauty of it. The Grid doesn't rely on hard-coded parameters. It evolves. It absorbs enough data to form its own logic based on context, environment, and even real-time shifts in public sentiment. We're not just training a watchdog. We're building a living lens. It learns what to look for and adapts faster than any human ever could."

Amanda gave a small, thoughtful nod, masking the chill that ran through her spine.

"So basically," she murmured, "it watches everyone... and decides who's safe?" She hadn't meant it to sound like a question. Not one she expected him to answer.

He angled his head to the side, studying her as she lifted her eyes to his. The tenderness between them still held—but Amanda's voice had changed, just enough. "I just mean..." Her voice trailed off before saying what she really wanted to. "Have you ever considered what one of these governments or companies with bad intentions might do with it?"

Tristan didn't answer right away. He set his glass down gently, the movement precise, and leaned forward.

"That's the point. They can't." He smiled, but there was a flash of doubt behind his confidence, and Amanda could see it. "We've made it foolproof. Air-gapped. Ethically guarded. The systems self-limit. I've designed it to recognize misuse and reroute it internally before damage can occur."

Amanda arched an eyebrow, not even trying to hide her skepticism.

She didn't look at him when she asked, "So... does the Grid differentiate between users?"

He turned his head, a faint smile tugging at his mouth. "Of course it does. That's the whole point. Every access point is authenticated—retinal scans, voice patterns, behavioral markers. You can't fake your way in."

"Even if someone has the credentials? The passwords, the protocols... even the voice?"

Tristan straightened a little. "It's not just voice. The system analyzes cadence, pitch fluctuation, and stress markers. It measures how you move—your typing rhythm, blink rate, and reaction time. It doesn't just know *who* you are. It knows *how* you are. The Grid recognizes intention."

She let that sit for a moment, watching the candle flicker softly. "But what if someone figures out how to spoof all that?" she said quietly. "What if they teach the system to *believe* they're someone else?"

That made him pause.

"To do that, someone would have to compromise the root algorithm. That's not possible without the original biometric key. And those are under lock, literal and neural. Three layers deep." He hesitated. "There are only a handful of people who can even get close."

The wind shifted, bringing with it the sound of distant traffic and the ghost of unspoken doubts between them.

"So, you trust the architecture," she said.

"I trust the code," he replied a little too quickly.

She folded her hands loosely in her lap. Her voice stayed soft, but the words landed sharply.

"And what about the people who already control nuclear warheads? Economies? Populations?" She shook her head slightly. "What happens when someone with more ambition than conscience gets close enough to manipulate its rules? If you license it out, don't they get control access?"

The breeze stirred the lanterns above them, creating shadows that danced across their faces. Tristan looked at her plainly.

"You can't build something like this with fear," he said finally. "You build it with clarity. You set the parameters, then trust the machine to uphold them."

Amanda nodded slowly, as if she understood. But deep down, she knew too much about people in power. Men who sat behind glass boardroom doors and silent arsenals.

She picked up her glass again. "And if the machine decides the wrong person is right?"

Tristan looked at her longer this time. His expression didn't darken, but his posture tightened, almost imperceptibly.

"Then I've built something I can't control."

Tristan's fingers traced the stem of his wine glass. Amanda watched him, not drinking, not moving, just watching. The hard lines of his jaw became more visible in the dimness of the evening. She didn't have to beg her thoughts of impending doom to flee; his glance, the way the edge of his mouth flicked upwards when she asked an annoying question, and a little help from free-flowing wine, made it easy for her to push it away.

She stood, letting the night breeze catch her dress as she stepped toward the edge of the rooftop. The city stretched out beneath them, alive and indifferent.

He joined her a moment later, standing close enough that the sleeve of his shirt brushed her bare arm. She moved closer, silently begging him to draw her close.

"Did you plan the wisteria?" she asked.

"I made a suggestion."

She looked up. "Of course you did."

Tristan turned toward her, ignoring the romantic ambience, keeping nothing but her in his view. His voice dropped. "You know I'm not playing, right?"

Amanda's pulse slowed. It happened every time she landed a plane. No rush of adrenaline, just an abatement of seconds that dragged on like minutes, everything in sharp focus before gliding a multi-ton chunk of metal onto asphalt as smoothly as a bee landing on a fluttering leaf. It's what she was known for. Her soft landing.

"I know you're not," she said, still hungry for him, but unwilling to make the first move.

He reached out slowly and deliberately, tucking a loose strand of hair behind her ear. His hand lingered, palm warm against her cheek. Amanda's fears melted under the steaming caresses of his fingers. Their mouths found each other. Not rushed. Not tentative. Just... certain.

His hands slid to her waist, drawing her closer, yet never close enough. Her fingers found the buttons at the collar of his shirt, undoing one, then two, and then just resting there, against the steady rhythm of his heart. She didn't want to think about Katherine, or the prototype, or how this night would dissolve into strategy and secrets the moment it ended.

Tristan pulled back just enough to look at her. "Tell me if this isn't what you want."

Amanda's breath caught.

"It is," she said. "Just... don't ask me to define it."

"I wouldn't dare," he smiled, taking off his jacket and putting it around her shoulders.

She drew the blazer tighter around her shoulders, not for warmth, but to sharpen the contrast—soft wool over bare skin. Then she shifted, letting one leg slide forward until the high slit of her dress opened like a secret invitation. Her body curved into his, molding to the heat of him, arms sliding up around his neck, fingers threading through the back of his hair.

The city disappeared as their mouths found each other with no preamble, lips parting with a heat that made her dizzy. His hands were already at her hips, anchoring her, pulling her closer. She kissed him deeper, opening to him, her breath hitching as his fingers slid along the edge of her thigh, just beneath the fabric.

He bit her bottom lip, just enough to draw a gasp. She answered with a moan, low and involuntary, then dragged her nails down the length of his torso, feeling the muscles shift beneath her touch.

This wasn't curiosity or performance. It was escape. She wanted to drown in him, to forget what she knew or what she feared. She just needed to feel.

He pressed her against the glass, one hand cupping the back of her neck, the other slipping under the blazer. Her body arched into his, unthinking now, ruled by heat and longing and the sharp need to lose herself for just a moment.

But Tristan broke the kiss, forehead against hers, his breath ragged. "Should we go?" he asked, voice husky and thick with restraint.

Amanda hesitated, chest rising and falling with every racing breath. The answer was obvious, but she smiled instead, a little unsteady. "Sure. Thank you for dinner."

She laced her fingers through his as they turned back toward the table, flushed and breathless. The spell hadn't broken—it had simply been paused.

As if summoned by the shift in air, the chef emerged, triumphantly carrying a flaming dessert. Amanda blinked, then met Tristan's eyes, a laugh caught in her throat.

"Perfect timing," she murmured, lips still tingling from the fire they hadn't finished.

"As if there weren't enough heat on this rooftop," she mumbled.

"Thank you," Tristan said to the chef as he again gave a short bow before returning to somewhere behind the glass and concrete.

"I was thinking of a different kind of dessert," Tristan smiled.

"Same," Amanda agreed.

"This first?" Tristan gestured to the bananas foster.

"Begrudingly," she replied with a wink.

But, as if pulled back into reality when sitting at the tiny table, she looked at him and said, "So...you mentioned that the Grid will make the world more *manageable.*" She accentuated the word.

Tristan's brow lifted. "I did."

"Manageable," she echoed again. "Streamlined. Efficient. Those are all very... corporate words."

"I'm a very corporate man," he teased, trying not to lose the moment they had just shared, but an edge in his voice revealed that he could definitely sense where she was going.

Amanda kept her voice soft. "Do you think about the people on the other end of that efficiency? The ones who don't get to consent?"

"I think about all of it," he said. "I have to. But intention matters. What we're building—what I'm building—it's meant to protect."

She nodded slowly, watching him. "And if someone uses it to control instead? If it's co-opted?"

He didn't flinch. "Then we build safeguards. We work harder. We adapt."

Amanda let her eyes fall to her lap. "You always sound so certain," she murmured.

"I'm not."

She looked up at him, bewildered. It wasn't that Tristan hadn't let her see him vulnerable. Yet even when he seemed exposed, he felt secure, sure that everything in life inevitably did go his way. It wasn't a mantra or an affirmation that he tried to convince himself of; it felt embodied in him.

He leaned forward, elbows on his knees, hands clasped loosely. "Amanda, it's not that I don't see what this could become. I do. But if I stop now—if I let fear shape it before it's even born—then I lose the only chance I have to make something better. Something... lasting. I want to leave the world functioning better than I found it—smarter, more stable. Less guesswork. Less chaos. And hopefully... safely out of the hands of bad actors."

They sat in silence, the city still humming below. When Amanda finally spoke, her voice was soft and low. "You always know how to sound like a visionary."

He twisted his mouth into a crooked smile. "Only when you're around to challenge me."

She reached across the table, fingers curling around his. "It's something I'm pretty good at."

"And I like it," he said, lifting her hand to his lips. "Even when you make me squirm."

Amanda stood slowly, the jacket slipping from her shoulders. He rose to meet her.

"Come with me," he said.

They walked to the entrance of the top floor of the glassy tower, turning to an elevator that took them to a hallway of luxurious suites.

"Oh, when you said you pulled some strings..." Amanda's mouth fell open.

"I like to keep you on your toes," he grinned.

The door closed behind them with a soft click as he gently tugged her fingers, pulling her to his chest. The quiet inside the room was heavy, tinged with electricity and longing.

Tristan pulled her closer, fingers grazing her waist, then slipping behind her neck, guiding her mouth back to his. She moved with him in rhythm, a dance unrehearsed but undeniably in sync. Every shift of his body against hers felt like memory and electricity, both familiar and charged.

The way his hands framed her—one splayed across her lower back, the other tangled in her hair—felt instinctual, but not practiced. Like he was discovering her shape in real time.

His mouth claimed hers again, deeper this time and without hesitation. Amanda's breath caught as she slid her fingers beneath his shirt, exploring him with a hunger that made her thighs tighten. He groaned softly against her lips as she pressed closer, her hips meeting his in a slow, deliberate grind that made it clear: she wasn't just present. She was *starving* for him.

Her thoughts threatened to rise—about Katherine, about the prototype, about Melody and Russell—but she had to compartmentalize. Whatever truths they'd been dancing around moments ago dissolved into heat and want. She didn't care who might see, didn't care what tomorrow would ask of her. Right now, there was only this—his hands, her skin, and the electric pull between them that refused to be ignored.

Tonight, her mind taunted her with spy games, but her body had already chosen, drawn to the heat of him, to the illusion, and to the dangerous comfort of his touch.

Chapter Seven

Bangkok, Thailand: Two Days Before the Summit

"Was the module sealed before transport?"

A razor-sharp voice drifted in from the side of the lab's perimeter. It wasn't forceful, but it landed like a command.

A technician at the console looked up at the man, spine straightening as he reached to key open the security log. The soft blue glow of data projections reflected off his lenses, the sweat on his temples catching in the halogen light. Bangkok's heat never truly left, not even behind glass and chilled filtration systems.

"Yes, sir. Vacuum-sealed. Double compression confirmed. No anomalies since containment."

Tucked behind the façade of a mid-rise logistics company on the outskirts of the city, this lab looked like little more than a concrete shell; a building caught between progress and neglect. But once inside, fluorescent lights hummed low over polished black floors. Glass partitions divided workstations where modular screens twinkled with cascading code and predictive models that updated in real time.

The air was cool and dry, scrubbed clean by a silent filtration system. A synthetic calm hovered just beneath the surface, the kind of quiet that came not from peace, but from control.

At the center of the main chamber sat the core testing console for the Ocular Grid—a monolithic workstation wrapped in matte steel, glowing faintly at its base. It resembled neither a weapon center nor a network hub, but something in between, a hybrid of surveillance and command. Cables ran from its base like veins, feeding into the walls, the ceiling, the grid of satellite terminals mounted across the lab like sentries.

Everything was automated. Observed. Logged. A hidden camera tracked eye movement at the entrance. Another one scanned a person's gait.

This was where the latest version of the Grid had been perfected—not in a government facility or university think tank, but in this curated shadow-space where engineers were nameless, everything was recorded, and no one asked the real question: *who was watching?*

The man didn't step forward, but his presence did. "Show me the test window," he said.

The technician complied, fingers darting across the interface. On the monitor, the graphs unfolded—tight response curves, clean packet compression, adaptive feedback within expected tolerances.

"It performed better than projected," the tech said. "Stable under strain. Neural mapping remained clean, and auto-correction held for twenty cycles without user override."

Beyond the observation deck, the cradle sat empty—an unassuming core of black and silver, emitting a faint, rhythmic whir. Its energy signature blinked in near-perfect cadence with the heartbeat-like metronome on the screen. One would never guess the compact system missing from its core had the capacity to trigger or suppress a cascade of global systems.

The man exhaled softly through his nose. "And these results are from the unit Tristan Montgomery will present in Tokyo?"

"Yes, sir. It's already en route via private transport. He came for it himself."

The man studied the screen again. Shifting lights moved across his features, as his calculating face held no obvious emotion.

"Will it hold up under scrutiny in Tokyo?"

The technician hesitated. "It's never been tested under optics that sharp. Not without the actual mechanics of a fully-operational grid. But technically? It should."

The man tipped his head abruptly. "That's not a guarantee." He sounded like he was scolding a toddler.

"No, sir. But it's close."

Outside, Bangkok swam in the dense blue of early evening, traffic thickening along the expressways like slow-moving circuits.

"Keep the backups isolated," the man said. "No uplinks, no mirrors, no passive network pinging. Air-gap everything."

"Yes, sir."

"And if the system hesitates—if even a whisper of interruption presents itself during that demonstration—I want the failover unit live before the lights shift on the main stage."

The technician nodded quickly, already tapping in the lockdown protocols.

"Who do we have on the ground there besides Montgomery?" the man asked, moving to the door.

"Rafael," the technician replied confidently, knowing that was the only answer he'd given that wouldn't be scrutinized.

"Perfect," the man said, and as quietly as he'd arrived, he was gone.

Tokyo, Japan: Two Days Before the Summit

Amanda's phone vibrated against the hotel vanity. She and Tristan had left the little rooftop paradise and luxury suites before breakfast was served, knowing a major entourage would be arriving before noon at the summit hotel, and they'd be expected to greet them. Not to mention his parents would be among them.

She had just finished dressing and was slipping on her shoes when she heard a low and persistent buzz beside the neatly rolled hand towel and an untouched glass of cucumber water. She reached for her phone with one hand while the other was busy attempting to clasp the tiny strap on her heels.

Lyla's texts came through in quick succession.

Babe. You good?

Turn on the news.

Governor Hansen just landed in Tokyo.

For your man's presentation. Wtf?

Apparently, the entire U.S. press is combusting in real time.

Amanda's brows lifted as she tapped a link that came in the next text. A video opened to a sharp-featured anchor standing in front of sleek summit graphics, his voice brimming with manufactured awe. Tristan's face filled the next frame, calm, confident, and composed. Headlines followed like a ticker parade: Tech Visionary. Global Innovator. The World's Most Eligible Billionaire.

The camera cut to a jet taxiing toward a motorcade at Haneda Airport. Stepping off, Governor Hansen looked every bit the part: designer trench, composed stride, a faint nod to the cameras as if they were expected. Amanda's stomach pulled tight.

Her phone vibrated again, lighting up with a new message.

Forbes just said Tristan's part Elon, part Bond, part messiah. Good God.

I just threw up in my mouth a little.

I mean, you know I love him, but c'mon with the hyperbole.

She then sent a GIF: Cher from *Clueless* blows a kiss, flips her hair, then checks an imaginary watch with exaggerated flair.

Amanda cracked a smile, still listening to the news coverage. The press was already calling Tristan the man of the future. It wasn't that she didn't expect this, but she tended to agree with Lyla. Messiah? Really?

The screen shifted again, Lyla having decided to call.

"Please tell me you're calling to say it's all been canceled and we're running away to Mexico together for tequila and denial."

"Tempting," Lyla said. "But no, hon. I'm calling to remind you that you don't have to do any of this alone."

Amanda stood, letting her forehead gently rest against the wall, holding still for a beat she hadn't planned to take. The words had landed harder than she'd anticipated.

"What makes you think I'm *doing* anything?"

"Oh, I don't know. Maybe the fact that your boyfriend is currently being called the most important man in tech, with global AI and defense headlines trailing in his shadow. The press is comparing him to Elon Musk, for God's sake. They do say he has better stage presence, so there's that. But your face is definitely going to end up in some side column about what it means to date power."

Amanda stayed quiet.

"You don't have to say anything, you know," Lyla continued, a little more gently. "This is me being absolutely serious. If you want me there, I can be on a flight tonight. I'll land in time for the presentation. I'll bring the shoes you left at my place, the fancy headache patches, and a bag of special chocolate that customs can *not* stop me from smuggling in."

Amanda snickered. "You'd cross the world just to make sure I don't panic under pressure?"

"I'd cross the world because you're Amanda Jane Hopkins, and I know the difference between when you're fine and when you're *performing* fine."

The pause stretched, soft and familiar like a silent gap between two heartbeats. Amanda didn't rush to fill it. She didn't have to. With Lyla, silence had always been safe. It had been that way since they were fifteen, when a glance across a crowded room could say everything. This was a friendship that just grew more intertwined the older they got, out of the limelight, quiet and unshakable.

"Text me the hotel," Lyla said softly. "I'll see you soon."

The call ended, and Amanda set the phone down before walking to the window. The city outside shimmered beneath a gauze of dusk, all spires and movement and light. She didn't know if she was trying to keep pace with it or merely watching it pass.

She heard the soft click of the suite door opening behind her, but didn't turn right away. The city still held her gaze, shimmering and bold through the window's glass, as if daring her to try to keep pace.

Tristan's reflection arched across the glass, his movements casual and familiar. She felt the heat in her chest rise as he slipped his hands around her from behind.

"Hey," he said, dropping a light kiss to her shoulder. "You free for lunch?"

Amanda turned. "Now?"

He smiled like it was nothing. "Yep. They landed not too long ago. Everyone's going to be expecting lunch in a little while. And they said they'd like to meet us at the drinks bar."

"They?"

"Mmm," he nodded, wishing he could use his mouth for activities other than speaking as he held her close. "My parents," he reminded her.

"Oh... yeah," she blinked.

Tristan hesitated for just a beat too long. "Also, slight surprise. My sister's here too. Olivia. She flew in last minute.

Wants to see the launch, spend some time here before heading back to London."

Amanda stared at him, the word *sister* ringing louder than anything else he'd just said. Sister? He'd never mentioned a sibling, not once. Not even in passing. She'd asked, hadn't she? Or maybe he'd just been vague enough to make her assume. Now she wasn't sure which unsettled her more.

"You... have a sister?" Amanda finally stuttered, breathless, though more from the trace of his touch than the surprise itself.

Tristan lifted and dropped his shoulders in a shrug that looked more defensive than casual. "We don't exactly... talk. It's complicated. But I didn't know she was coming until now. She kind of surprised all of us."

"That *is* quite a surprise," Amanda said, trying to keep her tone light, but the words felt thin in her mouth. Her mind was already racing, cataloging what this might mean and what she was about to walk into.

"I know. Sorry. It's just lunch. And I think you'll love her. She's sharp, no filter, and overly observant. Think of it as a warmup."

Amanda raised an eyebrow. "A warmup for what? A tribunal?"

Tristan laughed, the tension easing from his eyes for a moment. "A warmup for the launch. After tomorrow, everything gets louder."

Amanda's pulse had picked up again, not from nerves, not *exactly*, but from the piling on of expectations. His parents. A sister. Press swirling. A handler waiting in the wings. A vengeful widow lurking. Governor Hansen inbound. And she hadn't even seen Julius and Esmé yet. She inhaled slowly, trying to center herself.

"What time are we meeting them?"

"Half an hour."

"Okay. Here we go, I guess," she feigned a smile. "Can't wait to meet your entire family on thirty minutes' notice during the most high-stakes week of your life," she added, saying her last words on an inhale, like she couldn't decide if she was joking or hyperventilating.

"You'll be perfect," he said, still smiling as he stepped closer and tugged her into him for a quick kiss.

Amanda let herself lean in for a second longer than she meant to, the warmth of his breath still clinging to her cheek when he pulled away.

"Perfect," she echoed. "Sure."

Tristan and Amanda entered the hotel restaurant with their arms linked. The space sat behind frosted glass panels at the end of a hushed corridor, elegant but not ostentatious, with soft lighting that spilled from alabaster sconces. It was designed with a discreetly chic taste, where everything from the weight of the napkins to the curated scent in the air whispered intention. Sunlight filtered through floor-to-ceiling windows, striking the white linen tablecloths with the kind of glow that would make even the most awkward introductions look cinematic.

Tristan's mother stood with perfect posture, dressed in a soft dove-gray blouse and pearls. His father wore a pressed navy jacket and held his phone like he was waiting for an important call. And then there was Olivia—tall, angular, and confidently perched on the edge of a chair like she'd been judging everyone who passed by.

Tristan reached for Amanda's hand and guided her gently forward. "Mom, Dad—this is Amanda Hopkins."

His mother offered a poised smile and extended her hand. "Evelyn Montgomery. It's lovely to meet you, Amanda. Tristan's told us a bit about you."

"Likewise," Amanda said, returning the handshake with equal grace.

His father barely glanced up from his phone but offered his hand with a distracted nod. "Harold," he said. "Welcome."

Amanda smiled politely, shook hands, and said all the right things, but Olivia's eyes swept over her with unsettling precision that wasn't just analytical. It was strategic. Like she was scanning for weak points, searching for a crack in a polished surface. She swallowed hard. Most of the time she was with Tristan, she didn't have to remember that she was technically a spy. She didn't have to worry about her name scrawled on the bottom line of a document somewhere she hadn't kept track of. But under Olivia's gaze, she felt as if she was exposed, already found out.

"Liv," Tristan said, his voice warm and practiced. "This is Amanda."

"Amanda Hopkins," Olivia repeated, tilting her head just enough to suggest amusement. "The pilot. I looked you up. Impressive flight record... and very few photos." She punctuated her words for emphasis.

Amanda smiled lightly, practicing a professional deflection. "It's pretty hard to get good lighting at thirty-five thousand feet."

That earned a faint smirk from Olivia, but she didn't even blink. "Still... curious."

She let the word hang, offering no clarification. Amanda held the silence just long enough to make it clear she wasn't going to chase it.

Lunch began smoothly enough: starter salads, champagne flutes, polite questions delivered with crisp, practiced voices. Amanda answered inquiries about her flying career with a polish that came from years of debriefings and press ops. She kept it light, human. Enough truth to seem completely sincere, just like she was trained.

"So," said Tristan's mother, delicately dabbing at the corner of her mouth with a linen napkin, "you two met through work?"

"Something like that," Amanda replied, voice even. Her eyes flicked towards Tristan. He looked far too relaxed, as if this was par for the course. That effortless charm of his was comforting in private, but it felt a little too performative now.

"Was it love at first flight?" Olivia asked, articulating each consonant, making her sound like a preschool teacher who was mocking the thought of *true love*. She sat eyeing them, swirling her champagne without drinking. Mrs. Montgomery gave her daughter a knowing look before picking up her own glass for a slow sip of disapproval.

Amanda let the silence stretch for a moment, then shrugged. "Depends on who you ask."

"She's underselling it," Tristan jumped in, lacing his fingers through hers beneath the table, hoping to diffuse the mounting tension everyone could feel. "It was a bit more cinematic than that. You know me," he added with a wink. That grin, the one that always disarmed, appeared on cue.

Amanda tilted her head and offered a graceful smile. "With less orchestral music, of course."

Polite laughter rippled around the table, but Amanda could still feel Olivia's attention pressing into her like a fingerprint left on glass.

"So, Amanda," Olivia said, her tone noticeably edged now, "what do you think about Elise?"

Amanda blinked. "I'm sorry?"

"Olivia," Mr. Montgomery blurted.

"Elise," she repeated, undeterred, resting her chin on her hand. "Tristan's ex-wife. I figured she must've come up. You know, while you guys were getting to know each other. Kind of hard to ignore, especially if you've Googled him at all."

The pause that followed wasn't overly long, but it carried enough weight that everyone knew a line had been crossed, and no one wanted to be the first to say so.

She looked at Tristan just in time to catch the faint tightening along his jaw, the smallest ripple in his calm exterior. A crack, if you knew where to look. He bit his lip, then opened his mouth as if he was going to step in. Amanda didn't give him the chance.

"She was part of a different chapter," she said, tone cooler than before. "We haven't spent much time focusing on our backstories, to be honest. It's only been a few months."

Tristan reached for his water, leaning toward Amanda just enough to let his voice fall out of earshot as he whispered. "And now you can see why my dear sister and I don't talk much."

Amanda gave a tight smile and pushed back her chair.

She stood slowly, eyes still on Olivia. "Excuse me. I think I'll take a moment to go to the restroom before the next round of character evaluations."

She'd barely taken two steps before someone blocked her path, politely, unintentionally, but undeniably. A man, a few years older than Tristan, had approached the table from the opposite direction. His expression was easy, confident, and unaware of the air Amanda had been desperate to reclaim.

"Apologies," he said, stepping aside just enough to let her pass, though the momentary pause gave everyone at the table a beat to notice him. "Didn't mean to interrupt."

Tristan looked up with a smile, standing to greet him. "Hey! Rafi. Perfect timing."

"Amanda," Tristan said as he stepped toward them, "this is Rafi Earlman. He's part of the tech team we worked with in Thailand. Rafi, this is Amanda Hopkins."

The man offered a warm, polite nod. His dark hair was buzzed close, a faint scar disappearing into one brow. He wore a crisp black shirt rolled to the elbows, revealing a discreet geometric tattoo just above his wrist.

"Pleasure. I didn't mean to interrupt your lunch."

"Not at all," Tristan said. "Join us, won't you?"

"Oh, I couldn't."

"I insist," Amanda said, widening her eyes with a visible plea, hoping that adding another member to their party would divert attention away from her.

"It's settled, then," Tristan smiled. "You're joining us," he said to the table, motioning for a chair to be pulled over. "Rafi's been running point on our system's integration protocols. Half the magic of this summit wouldn't be happening without his brain on the backend."

"Well, it definitely wouldn't have been running on time," Rafi added with an easy laugh before taking his seat. Then, as if sensing the spotlight lingering a bit too long, he deflected. "But let's be honest, the real genius is Tristan. I just help translate his chaos into something the rest of us can use. It's been an honor to be part of it."

He gave a nod to the table, and Tristan's parents acknowledged him with gracious, if slightly disinterested, smiles. Olivia didn't bother with the pretense. She just watched him with a glint of amusement, as if she were watching the reprise of a performance she'd seen too many times.

Tristan leaned into Amanda, voice low. "Smart guy. Quiet operator. And the one person I actually trust with the code." He was giving her more information. As if clueing her in on even more details of his work, filling in the gaps he left in their conversation from the night before,

Amanda nodded faintly, her eyes lingering on the space Rafi had just occupied. Something about his presence felt more deliberate than coincidental. She couldn't quite piece together why someone from the Bangkok tech team would be here, but she certainly clocked it.

The interruption had stalled her exit, but only momentarily.

She adjusted the strap of her bag on her shoulder and gave Tristan a small smile. "I'm going to sneak away for a bit, if that's okay. Just need a few quiet minutes before things kick off."

He looked like he might protest, but didn't. Instead, he squeezed her hand in quiet acknowledgment.

As the conversation resumed around them, Amanda offered a polite smile, leaving the table as her thoughts itched with fragments. Half-formed impressions and unspoken cues she hadn't had time to examine, but couldn't quite ignore.

And the summit hadn't even started.

CHAPTER EIGHT

Atlanta, Georgia, USA 6:30 a.m. local time:
Thirty-Two Hours Before the Summit

THE AIRPORT TERMINAL BUZZED around them, but Lyla stood still at the security checkpoint, her boarding pass folded tightly in one hand and her carry-on strap looped around the other. Kyle stood across from her, coffee in hand, sleep still clinging to the edges of his face.

"You're sure about this?" he asked in a gravelly morning voice.

"I felt sure about this days ago, weeks ago," Lyla said, clear-eyed. "But now? I'm certain." Lyla didn't need much sleep or coffee to have the energy of a Labrador.

Kyle grinned, nodding slowly, knowing his wife was never wrong. But still, he had to ask. "You really think something's wrong?"

"I don't know if it's wrong," she said. "But something's off. She's different. I could hear it in her voice, even when she tried to pretend that she's just super busy and super in love."

"She said she's in love with him?"

"God, no." Lyla laughed. *"I'm* saying she is."

"Yeah, that tracks," Kyle laughed. He looked down at the rim of his coffee cup, then back at her. "Do you think Tristan's hiding something?"

"No. I don't know… I don't think anything yet. But Amanda's holding her breath, and I know that version of her too well to ignore it."

Kyle's brow furrowed. "You want me to call him? See what's up. We haven't talked in a few weeks, but I just chalked it up to him being busy."

Lyla shook her head. "Yeah, it's a lot. Just let him prep. Let him be the genius tech mogul the world wants him to be tomorrow. I just want to be there for her. I'll let you know what I need from you once I get there, okay?"

"Okay," he agreed, knowing any protest of his would be futile. "I wish I could go with you. If we weren't in the middle of this construction…"

She leaned in and kissed him briefly. "I'll be okay, promise. I'll be there in less than twenty-four hours. I'll text when I land," she said, waving her hand while backing away, the hem of her coat catching on her heel as she turned with a wink that somehow managed to look both graceful and chaotic. Unmistakably Lyla.

Kyle returned the wave with a quiet smile, his love steady and unspoken, the kind of devotion that didn't need to follow her to be felt.

Tokyo, Japan: The Morning of The Summit

Amanda soaked in the morning, alone and unrushed, at a small breakfast table tucked into the back corner of the hotel's garden café. She held a cup of green tea growing lukewarm in her hand while the whirr of city traffic and bustling pedestrians faded into the rustle of leaves and the occasional clink of porcelain. Tristan had left early for summit prep with final rehearsals, sound checks, and press briefings. Amanda's day stretched ahead of her like an uncharted map.

Evelyn Montgomery entered the café with practiced ease, her eyes sweeping the terrace until they landed on Amanda. She moved with command disguised as elegance, dressed in a cream jacket cut to perfection and wide-legged trousers that shifted in broad strokes with each step. Her heels clicked softly against the flagstone path, a noticeable cadence that was more deliberate than loud. The permanent smile she wore was effortless and refined—warm at first glance, but completely unreadable beneath the surface.

"Good morning," she said. "I hope I'm not intruding. I thought we might enjoy a little time together. Just us girls?" She said it like a question she wasn't exactly asking.

Amanda brushed away any surprise, standing to greet her. She swept a few stray strands of hair behind her ear, suddenly aware of how little time she'd spent looking in the mirror before leaving her room. "Of course. Please. Have a seat," she gestured to the empty chair across from her.

Evelyn lowered herself into the seat, crossing her legs neatly beneath the table as a server appeared to pour her coffee. "I hope I'm not disrupting your peace," she smiled, stirring in a touch of cream. "I know how rare it can be to find a moment of silence before these kinds of weekends."

"Not at all," Amanda said. "I don't mind the company," she lied.

Evelyn smiled, knowingly. "I always think Tokyo feels a bit like a held breath. Everything is so polished and ordered on the surface. But underneath..." She lifted her coffee, letting the words trail off.

Amanda lifted her eyebrows. "Pressure?"

"Possibility," Evelyn countered, eyes twinkling above her mug. "But yes... pressure, too."

Amanda nodded, unsure what else to say. She wasn't used to making small talk with mothers, especially not the mothers of men she was actively trying *not* to fall in love with because, you know, espionage. She swallowed her tea with an audible gulp.

Evelyn's gaze drifted over the garden. "We didn't really get a chance to know each other yesterday, did we?"

The question was rhetorical, but Amanda answered anyway. "No, not really."

Evelyn's gaze continued across the café, taking in every detail before returning to Amanda with a soft, measured smile. It was easy to see where Tristan got his charm and power combo—polished and effortless on the outside, with gravity just beneath the gloss.

"So, you're a pilot," she said lightly. "And yet you strike me as remarkably... grounded."

"Yes," Amanda replied, unsure of how much to say. "It's been a while."

"Since meeting Tristan?"

Amanda nodded wordlessly.

"Mm," his mother didn't seem like she was content to be right about her assumptions. Her reactions felt more like curiosity than anything. "I wouldn't have pegged you for a woman who's willing to walk away from her career for a man," she maintained her sweet tone, but looked deeply at Amanda as if searching.

"I'm not, and I haven't," Amanda inhaled a quick breath. "Let's just say I'm on hiatus. The last few months have been a whirlwind. But I'll get back to it, I'm sure."

"So, you enjoy it?"

"Flying?" she said, through a breath, "Oh, there's nothing like it." Her face lit up with the thought of it, her smile profoundly genuine.

Evelyn'smouth curled upward, enjoying the first real moment she had sensed from Amanda. Evelyn Montgomery could easily be described as cold and aloof, but never unaware. Though her exterior was three feet thick, she could pierce the walls others put up with exactness that seemed clairvoyant. She had to maintain a front, keep her fortress secure. Most people didn't live like she did, and as the matriarch of the family with big dreams and new money, she had a lot to protect. Perhaps that's why she could appear gentle on the surface to strangers, harsh and surly with employees and manufacturers, and have a son who had never outgrown a little boy's need for tender affection.

"What is it that you love about it?" she asked.

Amanda took a moment to consider her words. "I like the control. The clarity of it. The space to think."

"And you don't need that now? The space to think?" Evelyn probed.

Amanda hesitated. "I'm not sure. It feels like, right now, the world is asking a different version of me to show up. One I'm still getting to know."

Evelyn didn't flinch. "That's not necessarily a bad thing."

"No," Amanda agreed. "Just... unexpected."

A pause lingered, not entirely uncomfortable, but watchful. The vibration of Amanda's phone on the table broke the moment. She picked it up, forgetting that she had placed it there, a habit she usually reserved for when she was alone. A pet peeve of hers was being at a table with friends and family, and everyone having their phones buzz all through the meal, mindlessly checking every notification.

"Sorry, I'll put it in my pocket..." Amanda started to say before the face recognition flashed on, revealing Katherine's text on her screen: *Are you somewhere quiet?*

Amanda's stomach dipped. "If you don't mind, I'll respond. My best friend decided to join the party, and she's flying today. It's her husband," Amanda lied.

She typed back quickly: *I'm with Tristan's mother for break-fast. Should be free after lunch.*

Katherine's response was immediate: *I'll send a car.*

Mrs. Montgomery stirred her coffee slowly, watching Amanda intently. "Everything alright, dear?"

"Yes," she said, too quickly, before softening her voice. "She's safely on her way."

"You look worried."

"Oh, no. Not about her. Just summit nerves, I think." The change in atmosphere was unmistakable, and Amanda knew better than to act like it wasn't clawing at her composure.

"I imagine this world of ours feels foreign," Evelyn said. "Summits. Security details. Billion-dollar ideas being whispered like bedtime stories."

Amanda gave a small, crooked smile. "It's a bit surreal."

"And Tristan?" Evelyn asked gently, setting her cup down. "Does he feel foreign, too?"

Amanda blinked, slightly caught off guard. "I'm not sure what you're asking."

"I've lived too long to waste time on indirect communication," Evelyn replied. "I'm not asking for secrets, Amanda. Just impressions. I'm still trying to figure out what kind of woman has his attention so quickly and completely."

Amanda let out a long breath as her eyes stared at her tea. "So am I."

That earned her a delicate laugh from Evelyn. "Fair enough."

Amanda glanced up. "He's... not what I expected, if that's what you're asking. And at the same time, he's exactly what he seems."

"Which is?"

"Passionate. Focused. Restless. A little too good at... everything, it appears."

Evelyn nodded slowly. "You just described his father, once upon a time."

That piqued Amanda's curiosity, but Evelyn didn't elaborate.

"But if you're asking why he chose me, or what qualities I have that made him decide to bring me into his life during such a crazy time, I have no answers for you. I... had no intention of getting involved. With him or anyone. But fate seemed to throw us together. And, the older I get, the more I believe in it."

Evelyn pursed her lips slightly before curling her mouth upward, never losing eye contact. Silence passed between them, broken only by the rustle of ivy against stone, before Evelyn continued. Her inquiries were more graceful than Olivia's, but aimed just as precisely.

"So, you said you're from Tennessee," she added, as if drawing a thread out slowly. "Have you ever crossed paths with Governor Hansen? He's making quite a stir arriving for the summit. And has quite the presence in American politics lately."

Amanda nodded, though her eyes gave away the strain it took to keep her face composed.

"We've met, yes," she said, lifting her teacup with steady hands. "A long time ago." Her voice was quieter, the words clipped but not cold.

She took a sip, letting the silence cushion her response. But in her mind, the past flickered like a dropped reel of film:

the warm Tennessee nights with Cooper Hansen, the hidden pregnancy, the hospital room where she never held her child. The scream of waves against the hull, the sharp crack of violence on the boat—a woman sprawled in blood and suddenly overboard, and Amanda dragged into silence by threats and money and men with too much power.

Whatever Evelyn had been fishing for, Amanda couldn't be sure she hadn't just handed it to her.

"Small world," Evelyn said, keeping her tone pleasant. "It's fascinating, really. American politics has taken on such... theatrical flair these days. Governor Hansen's name keeps surfacing, not just in Washington, but in places you wouldn't expect. Every stop we make, someone is asking who he is, what he stands for, and how he might fit into the larger global equation. It's curious, the kinds of people suddenly throwing their support behind him."

"It's not like we haven't seen that before," Amanda lifted her eyebrows dramatically.

"True," Evelyn agreed, then added with a measured tilt of her head, "I don't align with any particular party, but I do find the rise of certain figures fascinating. It's a remarkable time, politically. Leaders are being manufactured and revealed all at once." She let her gaze linger. "What do you think of him?"

Amanda felt the heat creep up her chest, the flush barely hidden beneath the thin fabric of her blouse.

"He... definitely puts Tennessee on the map," she said carefully, voice even, though her pulse ticked higher in her throat.

But she barely had time to recover before another figure emerged from the path's curve. Melody Drake approached without hesitation, her steps unhurried, and her calm smile perfectly timed. Amanda rose from her chair, relief washing over her like a sudden breeze. She greeted Melody as if it had been planned all along.

"Excuse me," she said lightly, turning to Evelyn. "This is a friend of mine, Melody Drake. Melody, this is Evelyn Montgomery, Tristan's mother."

Melody offered a polite nod, her gaze steady and warm. "Lovely to meet you."

Amanda reached for her purse, shifting the moment as quickly as she could. "I actually forgot. We're picking up our gala dresses together today. But thank you for joining me this morning. It was truly lovely spending time with you."

Evelyn tilted her head slightly, studying Amanda with an unreadable calm.

"Of course. I do hope you find something flattering," she said, her tone smooth but weighted. Then, with a smile just shy of warm, she added, "And thank you for your thoughts on Governor Hansen. I imagine Tennessee must be full of interesting stories."

Melody and Amanda walked in step along the path, the quiet rhythm of their footsteps filling the space between them. Amanda kept her gaze forward and her face composed, though her pulse still hadn't settled.

She didn't have to turn around to know Evelyn was still watching.

"She seems nice," Melody murmured, her tone easy, but with enough edge to leave room for interpretation.

Amanda let out a controlled breath. "Polished," she said. "The kind of woman who could butter toast and gut you in the same breath."

Melody laughed. "It's never easy meeting the parents." She reached out to give Amanda a comforting touch.

"That conversation was a performance. Every word, calculated. And the ones she didn't say?" Amanda shook her head, blowing out a sharp breath. "Louder than the rest."

She felt like Evelyn had scanned her like a dossier, pleasant and precise. Whatever conclusions she'd drawn were already filed away.

"It's natural for them to be suspicious of a new woman in their son's life," Melody continued to sound like a concerned and helpful friend.

"But that's the thing. According to Tristan, it's not like they are winning any parenting awards."

"People are complicated. And parents?" Melody all but scoffed. "When we're kids, we have no way of processing any information with a fully-formed mind. We're so limited. So the way we see the world, and all the decisions our parents make for us, is... completely skewed."

Melody spoke with a quiet fervor, as if trying to untangle her own parenting decisions in real time. She was still reckoning with the choices her sons never got to make—the homes they never chose, the roots they were never allowed to grow. She and Russell had raised them to be global citizens, moving them across borders with the promise of broadened horizons. And yet, she feared that what they might have wanted all along was something smaller. Something still. A life with less width, but arguably more depth.

"Yeah," Amanda said quietly, unsure what else to offer. If she turned that lens on herself—on what she'd lived, and what she'd lost—she wasn't sure she'd survive the view. "I just don't need them to be breathing down my neck, I guess. I've got too much to worry about already."

They let the rest fall away in silence, walking side by side through the hushed corridors of the hotel. The elevator ride passed without a word, the soft vibration of the quick-moving ride filling the space between them. When they reached Amanda's suite, she unlocked the door with a swipe and stepped aside to let Melody in first.

"Well, for what it's worth, thanks for saving me from further scrutiny this morning." Amanda quipped as the suite door clicked shut behind them.

Melody paused, "Who are you really working for, Amanda?"

Amanda looked at her, the question landing like a weight. "I guess I shouldn't be surprised that you're gonna cut to the chase."

"What do I have to lose?" Melody asked.

Amanda crossed the room to sit at the table and chairs positioned near the sprawling windows. A glass pitcher of water sat at the center, sweating into a small ring on the tray's surface beside two unused glasses.

"Yeah, well, I'm not sure. Because I don't know you, Melody. And I could ask you the same question. Who are *you* working for?"

"That's fair," Melody said, taking a seat across from her. "Ask me anything. But I can tell you this: I'm here completely solo. Russell's handler hasn't reached out. No one from the Agency has called. Nothing. When an agent goes down undercover, they don't leave a trail. They vanish. And the people who were supposed to have your back?" She shook her head. "They disappear too. So, you should know who you're dealing with... especially if you signed."

"My involvement isn't exactly like that," Amanda admitted.

"So, then tell me exactly what it's like."

"I wish I knew," she said softly. "Because from what I could tell, my paperwork was definitely not CIA."

She reached for the pitcher and poured herself a glass with a slightly unsteady hand. "That's what scares me the most," she added, setting the pitcher down with care. "I don't know which side is using me, or why."

Melody sat silent for a beat, then shook her head slowly. "What could they possibly have on someone like you?"

Amanda met her gaze but said nothing.

Melody exhaled. "You know, Russell volunteered. Back then, it felt like something noble, joining a network that promised purpose, protection, even a sense of tried-and-true patriotism. He believed in the cause, in the country. But that's not your story, is it?"

Amanda turned slightly, leaning her shoulder into the window frame. "If you want my help, Melody, you don't need to psychoanalyze me. Just help me figure out how to get us both out of this."

Melody didn't press further. Instead, she stood, stepping towards the mirror, and tucked a loose strand of hair behind her ear. "Well, that's something we both want. I just need to make sure you help me get on the *inside* first. And maybe a dress for Sunday night?"

Amanda scoffed, grateful for the shift in tone. "Sure."

"I'll also need credentials if I'm getting past security."

"I got you. My friend Lyla is coming in later, and I've already told the production team that I have guests, so you should be good. Bring a valid ID. They're scanning everyone, and if you want to attend the exhibits beforehand, I'll get you a badge."

"Perfect," Melody nodded, already halfway to the door. She paused with her hand on the handle and looked back. "Thank you."

Amanda lifted her chin toward Melody with a silent nod. It was all she had left in the moment.

CHAPTER NINE

Tokyo: One Day Before the Summit

THE CAR PULLED UP to the hotel entrance exactly on time, just as Amanda had come to expect. She slid into the back seat without hesitation.

Katherine sat in the back seat with a leather portfolio resting on her lap, her posture crisp and expectant.

"These are the names," she said, flipping the folder open without preamble, "Confirmed attendees with the most relevance. Some carry diplomatic weight. Others, financial. And at least three operate in the kinds of shadow networks we both know exist, but never appear on paper."

Amanda glanced down as the folder was handed over, her fingers brushing the edge before opening it. Neatly typed names filled the page, each one more loaded than the last. She didn't need the dossiers to know how much power was going to be packed into the summit halls. She only recognized a few of the surnames. The kind that rarely showed up unless something world-altering was about to happen.

Through the tinted glass of the car window, Tokyo moved in dense, deliberate layers. Their vehicle, along with innumerable others, flowed like a stream, looping, winding, and packed to the edges without spilling over. Motorbikes slipped between lanes with silent precision. It wasn't like New York or London with shouting drivers or honking horns. Just the low, constant rhythm of movement: the soft pulse of tires on asphalt, the flick of signal lights, the faint electronic chirp of pedestrian crossings echoing at intervals like a metronome. And beneath it all, the almost hypnotic rustle of bodies in motion—thousands moving as one, like silk sliding over pavement. In places like the Shibuya crossing, the city didn't stop; it merely shifted, like a living organism resetting its flow.

Even at its busiest, the city didn't clamor. It inhaled. A thousand things happening at once, grooving to a melody choreographed in perfect synchronicity. Deliveries were unloaded, suited men crawled into taxis, schoolchildren clutched backpacks as they filed onto trains, and yet it all passed with an uncanny urban composure. Tokyo didn't scream its chaos; it whispered it.

"Do study the seating," Katherine said, turning the page with calm deliberation. "Note the clusters, who huddles, who scatters. Watch who arrives late, who slips out early. And most of all, pay attention to those watching you when they think you haven't noticed. They're often the most important."

Amanda closed the folder, letting it rest on her lap, her eyes now fixed on the steady sputter of the city.

"Is there anyone I should stay close to?"

Katherine turned, folding her hands neatly over the folio. Her voice dropped low and measured. "No one. Not yet. Not until we're certain who's clean."

"And you think I can accomplish that over the next few days?"

"I think you're on the path to getting us closer to what we need," Katherine confirmed.

"Then I guess this is the wrong time for me to object again, huh?"

"It's always the wrong time for that, dear," Katherine grinned.

"Oh, I need clearance for Melody. I told her I'd get her in, so... I guess you can take care of that?" Amanda asked with a flicker of guilt in her eyes, buried beneath a grin that said: *I already told her yes, but you'll help me, right?*"

"I'll handle things for Melody, but don't make any promises to her you can't keep."

"I haven't... but she did help me secure the prototype... without even knowing what she was doing."

"Keep it that way," Katherine spouted.

"I will. I just can't seem to leave her hanging, you know? If I were her..."

"You're not. And she's not your responsibility. I will do what I can to pull some strings," Katherine said.

A crease formed between Amanda's brows. "You will?"

"There's a quiet distinction in how we deal with our dead, Amanda. The ones who fall publicly—uniformed, traceable, commendable—they're mourned properly. Their stories are curated, their legacies tidied up and handed back to their families with medals and folded flags."

She paused, the weight of the unsaid lingering just long enough to matter.

"But those embedded too deeply off the books, and under unofficial cover, are erased. Not for cruelty. For containment. When their deaths threaten operational integrity or risk exposure to others still in the field, silence becomes policy.

"Like Russell threatening Julius' cover?" Amanda asked.

Katherine only nodded. "That's why no one's come for Melody. The dutiful wife of a family man with the perfect cover. She wasn't expendable until she was."

Amanda didn't reply.

Katherine's gaze returned to her, steady and without flourish. "She isn't mine to protect. Not officially. But I've no intention of watching her be discarded. If helping her gain entry to the summit gives her visibility and makes it more politically convenient to acknowledge her, or safer for someone to offer quiet assistance, then I'll see that it happens."

"Thank you."

"But don't be naïve enough to believe she'll get the answers she's seeking. We rarely do in this business."

Amanda studied her face intently. "Way to sell it to me," she said.

"I am not remotely attempting to sell you on this life, Amanda."

"No, but you sure do play tug of war with me."

"It's the only way I know how to be," she admitted. "I've been in this too long to change my ways."

"I've wrapped my head around it all, Katherine, I have. But really, how long have you been balancing MI6 and Hansen and the whole vigilante-spy-charade without it collapsing? I think that's what scares me most. Tristan's mom asked me about Hansen. And I froze."

"Don't worry about Evelyn Montgomery. I'll handle her. You just stay concentrated on observing and remembering these names and roles."

"I won't forget," Amanda promised.

"But don't mistake proximity for protection," Katherine added, her tone clipped but calm. "Especially not with Tristan. The sharks are circling."

Amanda's jaw tightened, her silence doing little to hide the sharp intake of breath behind it.

"You've done well, Amanda," Katherine reassured. "Better than many in your position. But tomorrow, you'll be the anomaly—the one variable no one accounted for. They'll smile. They'll charm. They'll make space for you at their tables. And all the while, they'll be calculating how to leverage you and your relationship with Tristan. But you're the one with the leverage. Remember that."

Amanda shifted her gaze back to the window, letting her eyes follow the rhythm of passing storefronts and narrowing alleyways. For the first time, she registered the repetition—the curved geometry of the same stone facades, the flicker of a red awning she'd passed once before, maybe twice. The city had folded in on itself without her noticing, each turn quiet, intentional, almost lulling. This hadn't been a route; it had been a circuit. Not designed to deliver her somewhere new, but to give her time. Time to listen, to absorb, to be observed.

As the car began to slow, the shape of the hotel emerged with its sleek glass, warm lights, and discreet elegance. They had returned to the exact spot where the ride began.

Amanda sat back slightly, letting the folder rest on her lap as the engine idled at the curb. "You could've at least let me run my errand and get my dress," she said, casting a sideways glance at Katherine, her voice edged with mock reproach.

Katherine simply closed the portfolio and smoothed the cover with one hand, as if tying a bow on the conversation. "It's already in your room," she replied evenly. "Steamed. Hung. The tailor made one final adjustment to the hem and sent it up this afternoon."

Amanda's brows lifted. She let out a slow breath, equal parts impressed and unsettled. "I should've known."

Katherine's lips curved faintly, the barest expression of approval, or possibly amusement. One could never tell. "Best to assume, going forward, that you're rarely the only one preparing."

Amanda drew in a quiet breath, adjusting the folder in her hands. "Then I'd better get to my homework," she said, reaching for the door.

She stepped out without waiting for a response, the city settling into evening as the car pulled away.

She adjusted the folder beneath her arm, already plotting her next move, when she caught a flash of blond curls and the typical, recognizable, hand-on-the-hip stance of her best friend just inside the hotel entrance. Lyla stood near the reception desk, one hand over the handle of a compact carry-on, wearing a linen blazer over a T-shirt that read: *Jet Lag Looks Good on Me.*

She lit up the second she spotted Amanda.

"Oh, thank God. I was starting to think I'd hallucinated you in Tokyo." Her voice sliced through the lobby's hush like only

Lyla's could—cheeky, warm, and just loud enough to turn a head or two.

Amanda's lips curved, the weight of her day momentarily lifting. "You made it."

"Barely," Lyla said, stepping forward for a quick but fiercely affectionate hug. "The train from the airport was like riding inside a vending machine. It was clean, efficient, but offered no emotional support."

Amanda laughed quietly into her shoulder. "I'm so glad you're here."

Lyla leaned back, giving her a once-over. "You look like you've been debriefed, reprogrammed, and spat back out. Everything okay?"

Amanda hesitated for a beat too long. "It's... a lot."

"I figured," Lyla said gently, reaching for her suitcase. "But we're not going there tonight, right? I've been awake for what I'm pretty sure is eight and a half days, and I need to take a long, committed nap."

Amanda let out a small laugh, one that softened the edges of her posture. "I promise, we'll catch up in the morning. Things really kick off then anyway."

They crossed the lobby side by side, their steps falling into an easy rhythm as they boarded the elevator.

"Perfect," Lyla said, leaning against the wall. "Wake me for coffee and chaos."

Amanda allowed herself to lean into her bestie as the numbers lit up, floor by floor.

"Deal," she agreed.

Long after the lights of Tokyo had quieted and the city's pulse had dipped into its nighttime vibration, Amanda lay awake in the dark, the silk of the sheets cool against her skin. She heard the door open gently, then close, followed by the soft rustle of discarded clothing and the subtle clink of a watch dropped onto the nightstand.

Tristan slid into bed beside her, his skin warm from wherever he'd come from, his breath faintly tinged with wine.

"I didn't mean to wake you," he murmured, settling against her.

"You didn't," she said.

"Good. I'm glad you're awake," he said. He let a long breath slip out, slow and steady, as if it might soften the vulnerability of putting his life's work under the world's gaze. "Tomorrow's the big day," he said with a hint of excitement rather than nerves.

Amanda turned to face him, her eyes desperate to trace the outline of his sharp features in the dark.

"I saw the stage design again tonight," he continued, his voice lighter than it had been in days. "It's... unreal. They're layering projection mapping with augmented visuals, timing it all with lighting cues so sharp it feels like we're stepping into the future. The whole thing's got this cinematic drama. Like we're building a world, not just unveiling one. I swear it's going to look like something out of a sci-fi film."

She let him talk. He needed to release the flood of excitement into his words unfiltered, crashing over everything in its path. And she wanted him to have it—this brief return to an almost childlike wonder.

But as the rush tapered off, his voice quieted. "I've been thinking about what you said," he murmured. "About bad actors. People with agendas."

Amanda stayed still, listening.

"I wish I could say it hadn't crossed my mind before. But it has. I just kept brushing it aside, convincing myself I was being paranoid. That if I focused on the mission, everything else would align. But your words... they didn't introduce doubt. They clarified it."

He drew a breath. "Even Julius," he said at last. "He's never been exactly warm, but lately... I can't tell if he's safeguarding the Grid, or setting himself up to control it."

Amanda reached out, tracing the back of his hand with the edge of her fingertip, letting the quiet stretch between them.

Amanda blinked slowly, her fingers still tracing his. The flicker of the city lights that peeked through the corners of the drawn curtains caught the edge of his expression. It was honest, open, and raw in a way she had rarely seen. Her throat tightened, but she didn't speak. She slipped her hand into his, letting their fingers intertwine naturally, but her mind was spinning. Her thoughts darted between past and present, between what she knew and what she feared.

He pressed his forehead to hers. "I don't want to be used, Amanda. I don't want to wake up one day and realize I handed them everything they needed to control the world."

Amanda closed her eyes, unsure whether the ache in her chest was for him or for herself.

"Then don't," she whispered.

Tristan shifted closer, his forehead still resting against hers, but now his hand slid to the curve of her waist, warm and deliberate. "Just tell me I'm not alone in this," he murmured.

Amanda didn't answer with words. She leaned in, brushing her lips against his—a question, a confirmation, maybe both. He kissed her back like a man who needed the world to fall away, if only for a little while.

The weight of what surrounded them didn't disappear. It hovered just beyond reach, a quiet reminder. But for now, it receded—eclipsed by breath, by touch, by a stillness that belonged only to them. A moment suspended between everything they feared and everything they hoped.

His hands moved over her slowly, reverently, as though she were the only safe thing left in the world. And for a few fleeting hours, Amanda let herself believe it.

Whatever storm waited on the other side of dawn, they were still here. Still together. Still burning quietly in the dark. Still daring to hope that, even surrounded by power and danger, the illusion of their relationship might hold.

Chapter Ten

THE TOKYO INTERNATIONAL FORUM towered before Amanda, a monument to the future, cast in glass and steel. The surfaces caught the pale morning light, refracting it across the plaza like a prism in slow motion. Its curved hull, sleek as a ship slicing through time, loomed above the city's pulse, as if daring the world to look away. No one could. Not today.

A crowd had already gathered—hundreds of people were pressing against the velvet-roped corridor. It was a living tide of journalists, delegates, tech enthusiasts, and political onlookers with phones lifted high, their lenses gleaming like watchful eyes, unblinking, hungry, and always recording. Flashbulbs began to pop in rapid succession while the murmur of global languages formed a strange kind of orchestra: sharp-edged Mandarin, rolling French, incisive English, and brusque German all braided together, underscored by the static of anticipation.

The car door opened with a hiss of hydraulic release, drawing a fresh ripple through the crowd. Amanda stepped out alone—deliberate, unaccompanied, exactly as planned, with no entourage and no hand to steady her. Just the weight of every watching eye as she inched into the light.

The press line continued its chorus of questions, though a subtle pause followed the soft click of the closing car door. Amanda lifted her sunglasses with the ease of someone who knew she was being watched and had already decided how much she would allow to be seen.

Cameras turned as the crowd seemed to lean, ever so slightly, in her direction. A photographer called her name tentatively, like testing a half-remembered story. She hadn't been introduced. But already, theories were threading through the crowd—some attaching her to Tristan, others reaching further, trying to place her as the mistress who broke up Tristan's marriage.

Her name began to rise in volume, initially as a question, then as a bold accusation.

"Miss Hopkins! Amanda! Are you speaking today? Are you involved with the Ocular Grid? What's your relationship to Montgomery?"

She ignored every syllable while flashbulbs flared. The line of cameras twitched like a nervous animal. She could feel the reporters angling for eye contact, hands itching toward microphones, each hoping she would pause just for a moment and offer a headline. But Amanda moved forward with the grace of a woman who had navigated private airfields at midnight, foreign embassies under scrutiny, and high-rise boardrooms where power shifted with the pour of a drink. She had flown presidents. She had ferried billionaires to private islands and whispered deals inked over aged scotch. The kind of passengers who never carried passports, only power. And this morning, she walked the crimson runner of global scrutiny without even flinching.

Still, even as her stride remained steady, a slight tremble stirred within her, not from fear, but from awareness. This was monumental, and it was global. This wasn't just a tech summit or a product launch.

It felt like a coronation—a new world taking its first breath beneath halogen lights, veiled in spectacle and ambition. And the world had come to witness it.

The moment Amanda stepped through the sliding glass doors, the noise of the outside world muted into a dull throb. Inside, the Tokyo International Forum was a wash of polished marble, soaring steel, and filtered sunlight that streamed through the multi-story atrium. Conference signage in multiple languages was suspended from sleek chrome beams, directing the influx of international guests toward registration desks and private elevators. Uniformed staff moved with practiced ease.

A voice came from just ahead of her, "Amanda." Melody Drake appeared from behind a column near the reception station, her dark blazer swapped for a midnight jumpsuit and low heels, a lanyard tucked discreetly into a pocket. Her hair was loosely curled, and there was the faintest smudge of eyeliner at the corner of one eye. Amanda could tell she'd been up since dawn.

"Hey." Amanda offered a small, crooked smile. "You good?"

Melody's brow lifted. "Yeah, I'm new to the world of espionage, so I'm not particularly great at the whole presentation thing. I don't think it was something Russell was very skilled in either," she said with a side grin.

"Well, you do clean up nicely," Amanda comforted, taking a tissue from her bag and dabbing it softly on Melody's under eye.

"I could say the same, though your version of 'nice' probably involved luxury bath salts and a panic-proof wardrobe."

Amanda tilted her head, accepting the jab. "Something like that."

"It's alright. We'll make a good little clandestine team, won't we?" Their whispered voices drew no attention or suspicion among the crowds. Melody took the tissue from Amanda's hand with a grin. They fell into a stroll, their pace relaxed, walking past glass panels etched with geometric kanji and into a corridor pulsing with staffers checking schedules, tech experts testing live feeds, and diplomats sipping espresso from tiny white cups.

"Looks like they've got eyes everywhere," Melody muttered, scanning the walls. "Drones–look at those mirrors; there have to be cameras behind each one. Ten people are probably watching us walk right now."

Amanda didn't doubt it. "Yeah, get used to it."

"I guess we have to. But are you getting used to walking into international press conferences like a Bond girl with a classified file under her arm?"

Amanda smirked. "No file. Just good posture," she quipped, enjoying the banter she and Melody had established in a short time. There was an instant camaraderie to their acquaintance that kept each woman both intrigued and somehow trusting.

Melody laughed, giving Amanda a little side eye.

They reached the velvet-lined checkpoint where VIP badges were swiped and biometric scans discreetly verified identities. A well-dressed staffer waved them through to the next level—an elevated platform overlooking the main exhibition floor. From there, the scale of the opening event came into full view: wide, tiered seating; a central stage lit in cool, dramatic tones; translation headsets hanging on every chair; banners fluttering softly from the rafters like flags from a new global alliance.

Amanda's gaze wandered. In the front row of the VIP section, seated like monarchs observing their kingdom, were names not printed on any program.

Clarisse Filby sat with her signature flair, a tailored white blazer draped over her shoulders like a cape—clothing that balanced sophistication with unmistakable control. Her platinum-blonde bob curved sharply beneath sculpted cheekbones, and her mouth held the kind of smile that warned it wasn't there for comfort. Her husband, Anton, adjusted the cuff of his jacket with a flick of his wrist. His expression looked unreadable behind dark-rimmed glasses, his salt-and-pepper hair combed back neatly. They sat in uncharacteristically still attention, not just watching the stage; they assessed it, as if determining its return on investment.

Tristan's family was already seated a few seats down, chattering to each other while awaiting the opening ceremony with reserved anticipation. His mother adjusted the collar of her silk blouse with habitual precision, while his father glanced frequently at his watch, a faint crease between his brows betraying his otherwise composed demeanor. His sister, Olivia, leaned in and whispered something, her expression flickering back and forth from the stage to her parents, though Amanda couldn't tell if this was out of excitement or anxiety. Two seats down, Lucien Beaumont lounged with the relaxed elegance of a peacock who'd never had to compete for attention. His gaze swept the room with idle amusement, but Amanda knew better than to think he wasn't cataloguing everything. When their eyes met briefly, his lips lifted, not in a smile, but in a knowing twitch, like he was in on a secret. She glanced at Melody before looking back at Lucien with a nod of acknowledgement.

"I don't think they have assigned seating in that section," Melody whispered.

"Probably not," Amanda scoffed.

They had a perfect view of the main floor from where they stood, and Amanda spotted Julius standing apart from the others, his face turned toward the main stage. On the front row below, center stage, Esmé draped herself across a seat like she'd designed it herself, while Julius remained attentive to the stage displays, casually chatting with what Amanda assumed was a member of the production team. But she felt a subtle shift in the air when Julius looked up.

There was a nearly imperceptible shift in the atmosphere, like pressure recalibrating in a sealed cabin. His gaze met hers across the crowd, calm, unblinking, as if she were the only fixed point in a room full of movement. Their eyes held for the length of a breath, neither offering polite recognition. It was not a greeting, not even a gesture, just a quiet suspension between them, long enough for anyone watching to sense that something had momentarily stilled. The moment dissolved as quickly as it came, the crowd folding back in, and the silence between them replaced by motion and murmur.

Melody's voice broke the spell. "Do you want to sit? Or just stand here and pretend that we're only half-involved in this thing with our special badges?"

"I don't know yet," Amanda said, her laugh barely more than a breath. Melody's composure was steadying. She was cool and unshaken, and Amanda let herself lean into it.

Her gaze drifted again over the polished sea of suits and scripted smiles, the shimmer of soft lighting, and the quiet gleam of surveillance. The VIP faces that she had barely known a few weeks ago now felt tethered to her by the sharp, invisible thread of shared trauma.

"But, my gosh," she murmured, "tragedy doesn't look good under this lighting."

"No," Melody said, elongating the vowel, her tone almost wistful. "But vengeance does."

Amanda turned to her slowly, her eyes widening with quiet disbelief.

Melody's lips curled at the edge as she offered the faintest nod. "It's a joke," she whispered, gesturing to the seats closest to them, discreet and slightly distant, perfect for watching without being watched.

As they settled into their seats, the lights began to dim with the slow, deliberate fade of a curtain being drawn. Conversations thinned to whispers, then stilled entirely. In the hush, a single spotlight flared to life, then dissolved, replaced by a wash of shifting color across the stage floor: first, deep indigo, then blue, then gold that scattered and fluttered through the air like glitter. The applause was instant.

A booming voice, disembodied, carefully rose from the overhead speakers.

"Welcome to the Future World Summit. Where innovation meets intention. And every idea is built to scale."

As the voice spoke, the screens came alive—not just behind the stage, but along the walls, wrapping the audience in a panoramic field of light and image. Satellite views of Earth rotated in slow motion, followed by soft-glow overlays of circuitry and code, stock exchanges blooming with data, cities flickering to life across continents as dawn crept from east to west.

"Today, we begin not with promises, but with possibility."

A soft pulse of music underscored each spoken word like a movie soundtrack, engineered to elevate every emotion, coming to a crescendo before the next phrase thundered through the speakers.

"Ladies and gentlemen. Delegates. Dignitaries. Innovators. Dreamers. History is not made in hindsight. It is forged in the audacity of now."

A brief stillness followed, suspended like a breath. Then the room responded with a rising swell of applause that filled the entire auditorium with refined enthusiasm.

Cheers naturally abated as the bright visuals faded into black. Then a single spotlight returned—this time focused on the center of the stage, where a figure emerged from the wings, moving with the ease of someone who was thoroughly practiced in presence, their temperament perfectly calibrated to the room. At the blurred threshold of the spotlight's edge, a distinguished tailored cuff came into view first, arms lightly swaying, as Amanda watched a familiar silhouette step into the full beam of light. She held her breath.

Julius placed both hands on either side of a podium that emerged from the stage floor and looked out, not at anyone in particular, but through the room itself.

For a moment, Julius said nothing. He simply looked out over the sea of faces, as if daring anyone to stop him. The rows of delegates, diplomats, journalists, and financiers were all waiting to be told what was next. But this man didn't act like an announcer or an emcee. Before he even opened his mouth, Julius had them begging for more.

"Many of you don't know me," Julius finally began. "And that has been by design," he said, his composure unshaken, as if the stage and scrutiny had always belonged to him.

Amanda hadn't known him long, but it confounded her how every interaction with Julius Babb seemed the same. As if he were only ever slightly affected by life, no matter the circumstance.

"For decades, I've kept myself and my family away from the spotlight. It wasn't out of arrogance or secrecy, though some of you have your own theories. It was out of safety. And sanity. And, in time, it became a strategy." His voice was smooth and grounded, cutting through the crowd with ease.

"But you can't build anything that lasts if you're constantly trying to outpace the noise."

Amanda's stomach tightened as pens paused around her and heads tilted in unison, the collective focus steady. She could sense a ripple of curiosity passing from row to row, swelling like an evening tide across a quiet shore.

"I've been called a recluse. A hoax." He smiled faintly with a dramatic pause. "A name on a trust document. Someone who didn't exist."

He paused again.

"Well. You're all looking at me now."

A few journalists in the press pit began whispering urgently, fingers moving across keyboards. Someone leaned toward another and muttered, "That's Julius Babb. That's him. He's the guy who's hardly ever been photographed."

He let the reaction swell for a beat before continuing.

"Today, I'm here not as a myth, not as a rumor, not even as a billionaire—though I'm all of those things, depending on who you believe." The crowd offered a short laugh, everyone now releasing their stifled breaths, warming to the man they'd anticipated seeing someday.

"I'm here," Julius continued, "because the world is at a tipping point. And we don't get to drift through it. We choose what's next. We choose whether to surrender to instability, to fractured systems, to digital chaos and economic entropy, or whether we create something better. Something integrated. Something coherent."

Amanda could feel the room syncing to a new rhythm. The focused, curious energy—energy-the *who's-that-guy* edge—had smoothed into something more deliberate. People were no longer just watching. They were investing. The collective pulse had shifted from interest to belief.

"I've spent years funding ideas I trusted that might save pieces of the world. But with Envisage—this is the first time I've stood behind something that might save *all* of it."

He stopped momentarily, letting the silence stretch in the space he'd carefully carved open.

"That's why I've come forward. Why I'm placing my name, and every resource, every network, every ounce of leverage I have behind this company and its vision."

He glanced toward the wings, the corner of his mouth lifting slightly.

"And it starts today."

Julius continued, his voice warm and expansive, like the announcer before him, only without major digital enhancement. He didn't need the embellishment to capture the hushed attention of the audience.

"I invite you to spend today exploring. See what's been built. What's been risked. Walk through the exhibits. Speak with our teams. And tonight—" his voice curved upward with theatrical poise, "you'll see the man who made it all possible. A man whose dreams of the future outpaced even our imaginations." Julius stretched out his arm toward one side of the stage, looking like a ringmaster beckoning his next act.

A chirr rumbled across the rows like wind through dry grass. A few people stood to look, craning their necks for a better view. Phones began to lift, and Amanda caught a flicker of motion from Melody beside her, fingers tightening on the edge of her armrest. She placed her palm on her new friend's knee.

Julius paused again, just long enough to draw breath, to tilt the moment toward reverence without overplaying it. It was the kind of stage moment crafted not for applause, but for surrender—the gap between a prophet's promise and the moment his followers, without quite realizing it, give in.

"Mr. Tristan Montgomery," Julius bellowed.

Applause broke like a wave, almost breathlessly measured at first, then rising into a sustained groundswell of noise. The crowd didn't exactly roar with excitement like they would at a sports stadium, but the onlookers rallied, their support for this idealistic promise inevitable.

As the applause was still rising, Amanda's thoughts intensified. She clapped her hands together, slow and off beat from the rest of the exuberant crowd. Tristan entered the stage, coming to a stop, meeting Julius in a diplomatic handshake. When Julius raised Tristan's hand into the air like a champion, another swell of cheers lifted, but a soft shift in the row behind her drew Amanda's attention.

"Did I miss the part where the world gets saved?" Lyla asked, breathy and dry, her voice just behind Amanda's shoulder.

She turned towards her best friend, easing into an empty seat with the slow, careful movements of someone whose body still thought it was in the West.

"You made it," Amanda murmured.

"Barely. But I followed the sound of polite clapping and corporate ambition."

Amanda stifled a laugh, grateful for the momentary grounding.

Her heart gave a quick, surprised flutter at the sight of Lyla slipping so effortlessly into this surreal world. "Melody, this is

Lyla," she said over her shoulder, her voice carrying the quiet relief of someone suddenly reminded she wasn't entirely alone.

Lyla gave a little wave, "Good to meet you," she whispered, her eyes drifting toward the stage. "Who's that guy with cult-leader energy?"

Melody gave a short, surprised laugh, but Amanda was never surprised at Lyla picking up on anyone's energy.

"That's the quiet architect," Melody said. "Julius Babb."

Lyla blinked. "*The* mysterious Mr. Babb? Kyle's always acted like he's some kind of fake Charlie's Angels speakerphone type."

"That's him in the flesh," she said, her eyes meeting Lyla's with a look somewhere between awe and disbelief.

"Well, well. Welcome devotees," Lyla exhaled and sank back in her chair. "Fantastic. I can't wait to see what kind of overpriced hors d'oeuvres this kind of drama gets us later."

Melody knew she was going to like Lyla, but eyed Amanda as if to ask how much her best friend knew.

"Well, let's head to the exhibits," Amanda said, trying to convey a wordless, *not now, please don't say anything* through her sharp eyes.

The crowd dispersed throughout the building, wandering in and out of large immersive displays, light flaring and fading beneath the crowd's footsteps, reacting in real time to motion and movement, as if the building itself were awake and responding.

Walls pulsed with motion: holograms unfurled like petals, sensing motion, whispering tech specs and global projections in tones that felt more like seduction than information, drawing the women deeper into the curated dreamscape in a dozen languages. Around every corner, delegates and influencers stood inside glowing demo spheres where climate models bloomed overhead, or walked through simulated cityscapes that promised security without friction, and convenience without questions. It was part museum, part theater, part lucid dream.

Melody moved delicately, but continued tracking exits while pretending to browse, eyes flicking from badge to badge, noting who she may need to remember. Even she wasn't sure who or what she was looking for here.

Lyla, wide-eyed and sleep-deprived, stopped every few feet with the expression of someone touring a theme park.

"Did that drone just wink at me?" she asked, pointing to a polished chrome orb that hovered near a display on data-integrated neighborhoods. "This is crazy."

Chapter Eleven

Tokyo: First Day of Summit, The Presentation

THE HOUSE LIGHTS DIMMED as people took their seats, and a hush fell over the auditorium in a stillness that held an electrifying charge.

"Ladies and gentlemen. Delegates. Dignitaries. Innovators and dreamers," the now familiar voice repeated. "Please welcome the visionary, architect, and the mind behind the technology hailed by *TechSphere* and *Global Wired* as humanity's next great leap—Tristan Montgomery!" the invisible commentator boomed.

Applause erupted like a sonic cascade from surround-sound speakers, a standing ovation for a man not yet on stage.

Hours had passed in a blur of motion and noise, as if the entire day had been condensed into fast-forward. Startups jockeyed for attention, pulling passersby into curated experiences and photo ops like carnival barkers in designer sneakers. But beneath the shimmer and noise, everyone knew why they were here. The real draw wasn't the gadgets, the networking lounges, or the smart coffee carts. It was Tristan Montgomery.

His name ricocheted through every corridor. His face had flickered across promo screens all day.

Everyone had come for the same thing: the unveiling. The pitch. The price. In twenty-four hours, the bidding would begin, but today was about seduction and influence. About setting the stage for the kind of announcement that could shift the axis of the entire tech industry.

A collective breath pulsed upward, like a soft echo before an avalanche. Then, without any more commentary, spotlights swung, catching the geometric ceiling in a prism of white and cobalt, while the massive stage screen came to life with a slow, deliberate pulse.

Amanda stood at the edge of the platform, in the shadow, watching as he stepped into the light. She had agreed to join him backstage this time. He knew they wouldn't see much of each other throughout the day, and when he dreamt of this moment, she was the one waiting for him in the wings. Not his family, or the men wooing him into their networks. He wanted *her*. She watched him, heart tight in her chest, reading every detail of his body language as if it held the truth behind his performance.

Tristan didn't wave as he walked into the limelight. He didn't grin broadly or bask in the adoration. He paused, center stage, as if absorbing it—every camera, every heartbeat—before speaking.

"I didn't come here to sell you a product," he began, the lights halting around him. "I came to offer you a mirror. A mirror to the future you say you want. A future of efficiency. Of cooperation. Of sustainability." His punctuated sentences were a drum beat, beckoning the crowd to join in rhythm. "We dream of a world no longer divided by misinformation, by scarcity, or by digital warfare. So, I came to ask you something. What is that worth to you?"

The screen behind him flickered to life, first with images of melting glaciers, drought maps, and destabilized currency markets. Then came rendering with simple slogans painted across the images: *A Vision of Tomorrow.* Cities running on clean networks. Real-time decision-making fed by balanced data. Governments proactively interconnected instead of behind the curve. Resources intelligently allocated. Waste eliminated before it began.

"This is not a device," he said. "It's a new infrastructure. A global nervous system, built not to control humanity, but to empower it. To protect the things we say we value—democracy, truth, nature. The Ocular Grid is not a tool. It is the guarantee for tomorrow."

The crowd leaned forward, caught in a collective inhale that seemed to suspend time.

Amanda felt her pulse slow, matching the hypnotic downbeat of his cadence. Whatever doubts she'd harbored about his ego or motivations, even she was dazzled by him tonight. Tristan's commanding presence filled the space not with force, but inevitability. She, like everyone else in the building, wanted to believe him.

The screens around the room lit up again, a subtle melody playing behind a rendering of the Grid's full functionality. The imagery moved like a breathless simulation: foot traffic mapped in real time, supply chains rerouted with a swipe, crowd behavior visualized as swirling patterns of light. Digital faces flickered with biometric scans that bloomed momentarily, then dissolved into streams of code. Every object, every movement, was tracked, tagged, and rendered part of a seamless, pulsing system.

Tristan stood, gesturing toward the projection behind him.

"Now imagine this applied in real-time during a natural disaster," he said. "The Ocular Grid identifies structural weaknesses before collapse, and reroutes emergency responders through passable streets, tracking missing persons by biometric signature—even if their phones are dead."

The next image floated seamlessly across the screens with a high-rise evacuation sequence. Arrows glowed through digital corridors, illuminating in blinking points above figures in motion.

"It doesn't just observe," he added. "It predicts. Based on behavior, voice tone, movement, and pattern. Not to replace human intuition—but to augment it."

Attendees sharpened their attention as Tristan walked toward the edge of the stage. "Want to know if your city's next protest will stay peaceful or escalate into violence? The Ocular Grid sees it forming in the crowd before the first bottle is thrown."

A collective breath spread throughout the room. "No, it doesn't read minds. But it reads patterns. Movement, heat, noise, heart rate, and microexpressions. The data humans give off without thinking. And it picks up Bluetooth, 5G, WiFi, infrared, and LiDAR. Anything we can't hear, it hears."

He smiled. "Let me show you."

A live feed flickered on. The camera zoomed in on a seated journalist. Her name, temperature, recent location pings, even her coffee order scrolled briefly beside her image, then disappeared.

"And don't worry," Tristan continued as she flipped her palms upwards. "She's an informed participant. That's what we envision for the future. Informed participation from citizens. This is one of a hundred capabilities. And yes," he added, "every bidder that's registered for tomorrow's auction has been given access to test footage and sandbox simulations. This isn't vaporware. It's already operational. And tomorrow, the Ocular Grid will be made available to global stakeholders through an open auction."

His words landed again like a thunderclap. "We will not do this in secret. Not behind closed doors, or in hushed corners. But with transparency, oversight, and participation. Because the influence of this system must take root in its inception exactly as it intends to operate during its function, completely out in the open."

Bright words illuminated every screen with the starting bid: one billion U.S. dollars.

A ripple of gasps ran through the room, but Tristan let it settle before delivering the final line.

"In twenty-four hours, the future chooses its architects."

The lights cut to black. Then, an eruption of applause and chatter swirled all around them. A scramble of journalists elbowed their way to transmit headlines. Amanda stood motionless, watching. He stepped down from the stage into the wings, his face aglow with the certainty of a man who had just orchestrated a turning point.

She stayed frozen in place, her arms loosely crossed, eyes fixed on the massive stage that moments ago had been dressed like the altar of a new world religion.

And it *was* a religion, wasn't it? Didn't Lyla use the word "messiah?" Amanda shook her head, grasping her hair in her hands and tugging slightly. She had gotten into the habit of massaging her scalp as a calming tactic when she was younger. Now, her fingers instinctively sought the roots of her hair, anchoring her with the familiar sting—a grounding ritual she barely noticed anymore, as if pain had become her tether to reality.

She breathed in slowly.

"That was amazing, wasn't it?" Tristan wrapped an arm around her waist, pulling her in for a kiss that still buzzed with adrenaline.

"Incredible," she said, genuinely as terrified as she was impressed.

"Thank you," his breath hot against her ear, and his face pressed close for one suspended second before the production manager appeared, headset-first, and whisked him away toward his next carefully staged moment.

Amanda wasn't sure what she'd just witnessed. The world Tristan presented was built on promises of equity, ecology, and empowerment. On data as salvation and innovation as a moral compass. A global nervous system. He'd proffered it like scripture.

She remembered him in the dark, telling her he wanted to be the kind of man who uses influence for good, but could it be? An open auction that was transparent and inclusive? Amanda knew enough about global tech conglomerates and shell bidders to know exactly how opaque "open" could become.

But could power ever share? Everything in her screamed *no*. Especially when she had seen so many men dodging questions about ethics and avoiding conversations about control.

She could only hope that the players now, the bidders whose names she had memorized and companies she'd studied, were either integrous or stoppable.

Amanda glanced toward the glowing edge of the curtain, where the masses still thundered their applause, desperate to believe they had just witnessed the unveiling of a benevolent genius.

Tristan now pulled into another conversation. She turned from the backstage corridor and slipped through a service hallway marked for event staff, her heels clicking softly against the industrial concrete. The roar of the presentation's aftermath faded with each step. Amanda welcomed the change in volume—the transition from curated spectacle to utilitarian quiet.

She didn't look for Melody or Lyla. She craved Katherine's perspective. Not just for answers, but for grounding. But as she stepped into the backstage corridors and into the quiet hallways away from the curated chaos of the summit floor, a familiar voice caught her mid-stride.

"Amanda?"

She pivoted instinctively, and regretted it just as fast. The attendants must have ushered the VIP guests away from the rest of the crowd and into the back hallways. Esmé, clad in a form-fitting lavender cocktail dress and diamond-drop earrings that glittered beneath the overhead lights, approached with the breezy confidence of someone who had just witnessed the Second Coming and was personally invited to the after-party.

"I wasn't sure it was you at first," she said, her eyes warm, and her grin impossibly bright. "Was he not spectacular?"

Amanda hesitated. She felt like she should have rehearsed reactions, tried anything to prepare herself for the overwhelm this would bring. "It was... something else, wasn't it?"

"Something else?" Esmé's eyes widened. "Amanda, it was historic!" she exclaimed. "I mean—what he's building, what Julius is funding—it's the most ambitious tech effort since... I don't know, the first moon landing?" she laughed. "It's so much bigger than we thought. I had no idea what the scope of the Ocular Grid was before. Did you?"

Amanda gave a careful shake of her head, buying time.

"I always knew Tristan was a visionary," Esmé continued, her voice like a ribbon being drawn through the air. "But this? It's beyond him now. It's planetary."

Planetary? Amanda thought. She swallowed the word like a splinter, sharp and dissonant in her throat.

"And what do you think of that starting *price?*" Esmé said the word breathlessly as if Julian's wealth couldn't hold a candle to what Tristan was about to experience.

Everything about this night scraped against Amanda's instincts, setting off an internal recoil she tried to mask with a steady breath.

"I think it's smart," she replied flatly. "Start with a big number, paint the overall picture, and let the world fill in the rest."

Esmé tilted her head. "You sound a little skeptical," she said, allowing the first sign of real disappointment in Amanda's reaction to move from the back of her mind and into her voice.

Amanda kept her grin tight. "Sorry, Tristan was great. I guess I've just been in too many rooms where the biggest promises were made by the least accountable people. But, we have good men we can trust who are leading the way in this case, right?" She almost wanted to see if she could get the slightest hint of doubt from Esmé, or at least plant a seed, wondering if she, too, ever asked questions. "So, you know, that's a good thing."

A flicker of curiosity appeared in Esmé's eyes, but she dismissed it almost as quickly as it appeared. "Well, not just good," she emphasized. "I thought it was simply magnificent," Esmé said, adjusting the strap of her designer clutch. If Amanda wasn't going to gush about Tristan, Esmé was going to switch the focus. "And Julius looked so composed. Don't you think? That's real leadership, if you ask me, lending his full support now. At a time like this."

Amanda felt a burst of heat rise behind her collarbone. Composed, yes, Julius was. Like a chess master watching a pawn advance into checkmate. Her trust of Julius had never been full, but after seeing him on stage, the words she would have used would not be "composed" and "leadership", but more like opportunistic and manipulative. But it shouldn't have surprised her. She had been just as much a pawn as anyone.

She forced herself to breathe evenly, deflecting any further response. "Yeah," she said simply. "If you'll excuse me, I was actually on my way to find someone."

"Of course," Esmé said, with an elegant nod. "I'll see you at the afterparty. And let's catch up after the auction tomorrow? I have a feeling we're going to be part of something very, *very* big."

Amanda turned away before she said something she couldn't take back. But when she did, another warm voice floated toward her.

"There you are, darling. We've been looking everywhere."

Evelyn Montgomery approached first, wearing a pristine ivory coatdress that looked as if it had never known a wrinkle. Tristan's dad, Harold, followed, and trailing behind them a few steps was Olivia, grinning automatically, the social reflex kicking in before she could intentionally stop it.

"I didn't realize you'd be backstage," Amanda said lightly.

"We were told to come this way. Tristan should be back here in a few minutes before we can all go to the lounge for cocktails," Evelyn explained.

Amanda blinked, carefully neutral. "Oh, okay. No one told me where to go," she chuckled. She couldn't tell them that she was trying to dodge everyone and had been lucky enough to avoid people.

"Just stay with us, dear," Evelyn insisted, extending her perfectly manicured hand.

Amanda felt her chest tighten, her practiced grin beginning to strain. "Oh, I was looking for my friends," she started before Olivia interrupted.

"Well, everyone's already looking for you. You've made quite the impression," she chimed in, her voice smooth, eyes skating across Amanda's face like she was cataloging her. "The media's been asking who you are. They all want to know what role you play."

Amanda turned away slightly, just enough to reset. She anchored herself with the smallest exhale, pretending she wasn't counting steps to the quietest corner of the room.

"I play a lot of roles," she said, turning back toward them, a lightness in her tone that defied her thoughts. "None of them are very public, though."

Evelyn laughed as though it were charming. "Well, now is not the time to be too modest. You'll be *very* visible tomorrow."

Amanda's mouth twitched involuntarily, and her head turned sharply.

"Oh, don't let the nerves get to you, dear," Evelyn said, stepping closer, lowering her voice just enough to make the next sentence sound intimate. "It's important, darling, that you understand how much weight perception carries right now."

Amanda met Evelyn's gaze with a cool nod of reassurance.

"I understand perfectly." She, of all people, knew the performance required of her.

Evelyn touched her lightly on the arm, a subtle nudge toward the elevator. "Let's just go join the others downstairs. He will be there soon enough. They've opened the premium terrace bar. And you know how much Harold loves a good scotch after a spectacle."

Amanda nodded, falling into step with the family, though she knew nothing of Harold's scotch habits, and everything in her resisted.

As the elevator ascended, she felt the air in the glass lift grow thinner, like oxygen was being siphoned out and replaced with carefully perfumed expectation. Evelyn continued chatting about evening logistics—VIP cocktails, a private dinner, more cameras. Harold nodded along, mostly silent, save a few grunts and moans that indicated his full compliance with everything planned for him and not by him. Olivia had her phone out, constantly texting and scrolling, thumbs on autopilot.

Amanda was grateful to the drone of Evelyn's voice that required no response to her observations or commentary. Her phone buzzed in her palm, and she saw a text not from Katherine but from Lyla. As she read the message, her heart opened like a window letting in the fresh spring air.

Sorry! Missed the grand sermon but caught the last few minutes on a screen in the lobby. Went to change and ended up taking a nap. Damn jet lag. Double espresso'd. Where are you, and how do I crash this party?

Amanda experienced the first real sense of ease she'd felt since being escorted backstage to watch Tristan.. She held her phone discreetly at her side, thumbs gliding as Evelyn commented on the light show at one of the exhibits she'd attended.

Amanda replied: *You're the best. Meet me at the entrance of the northeast terrace bar. Third floor, next to the mirrored atrium. Ignore the security guy with the dramatic eyebrows. Your badge will get you access.*

Lyla's reply came instantly with a peace-sign-duck-face selfie attached. *On my way. Am I underdressed or overdressed for the apocalypse?*

You're perfect, Amanda typed with a smiley emoji. *Bring your sparkle and a healthy dose of skepticism. You're walking into the future, baby!* She added a clenched-teeth emoji. *And the lighting is very flattering.*

Lyla's reply was a single emoji: the disco ball.

The Montgomerys and Amanda walked out of the elevator after stopping at two different floors to pick up more people. Amanda was grateful for the distraction of others that allowed her to avoid further discussion. Evelyn, by contrast, was always ready to pick up a conversation with an important person as if they'd known each other for a lifetime. It was like she was constantly networking with anyone she felt worthy of her time. Amanda tucked the phone into her clutch as Evelyn turned toward her again in the hallway, smiling with a smooth, socialite grin that always felt one layer too polished.

"I think it's right this way."

"Oh, I'll meet you all inside," Amanda said lightly. "I need a moment to freshen up."

Evelyn arched a brow but didn't protest. Harold barely noticed, and Olivia glanced up just long enough to offer a vague nod.

She stepped aside, weaving through a corridor of tall glass partitions and reflective surfaces, her pulse finally slowing. If she couldn't have Katherine's insight right now, at least her best friend could talk her down. But could she? Given how little Lyla knew about what was really going on? She'd been hiding so much from Lyla, and she wasn't sure she could do it anymore. Everyone has a breaking point, and the horrible thing about that is we rarely know when ours is about to come.

Amanda spotted Lyla wearing a dark green dress cinched smartly at the waist, her hair swept up like she'd just woken from a perfect nap and wandered into a film premiere.

"Hey!" Lyla said in her quintessentially effortless way. Her voice felt like a liferaft in an unforgiving storm.

Amanda looked at her with a half-grin, falling into her best friend's arms with a quiet exhale. It wasn't a sob or breakdown, just a release. A slow leak from her internal pressure chamber.

Lyla pulled back, studying her face with immediate suspicion, brows tightening as Amanda shifted her weight, eyes flicking briefly toward the city beyond the windows, like she might rather be anywhere else but here. "Whoa, what's wrong?"

"Nothing."

Lyla's eyes narrowed. "Bullshit."

Amanda gave a soft huff of protest that turned into a laugh. "You're like that Poker Face woman," she said.

"I know. I've told you. You can't lie to me." Lyla tilted her head, eyes narrowing as she studied Amanda's face. She reached out, brushing a stray hair from Amanda's shoulder, then tapped a palm on her shoulder. Her voice dropped, teasing but unshakably sure.

"You look like you've been holding your breath since noon."

Amanda tried to laugh it off; she wanted to deflect, but Lyla didn't let her.

"Don't try that polished pilot face with me," she said, leaning in with a smirk. "I invented your polished pilot face."

Amanda exhaled, though it caught abruptly on the tightness in her chest, a reminder of everything she hadn't said. "The whole thing was... interesting."

"Yeah, it looked intense. But this isn't about the summit, is it?" She tilted her head again. "Is it more about him?"

Amanda didn't answer, and that was answer enough.

Lyla stepped closer, her voice un-sarcastically low and calm. "Look, I know I introduced you two, but just because I played cosmic matchmaker doesn't mean you owe me some fairy tale ending. It's not like I expect you to marry the guy."

Amanda grinned faintly. "I know." She nudged her shoulder against Lyla's. "I'm seriously glad you're here, you know."

Lyla smiled. "You always are. You just sometimes forget until I show up."

"Yep," Amanda leaned in, letting her forehead rest briefly against Lyla's. She didn't have words for it, but God, was she glad she wasn't alone.

Chapter Twelve

Tokyo: First Day of Summit, Cocktail Hour

THE LOUNGE SHIMMERED WITH candlelight and quiet wealth, with a jazz trio playing softly in the corner, unobtrusive, blending into the current of conversations and clinking glasses. Every guest looked curated with their pressed suits, timeless gowns, and shoes that had never met dust.

Lyla and Amanda settled onto a velvet settee tucked along the back wall, half-shadowed and comfortably removed. They chatted with each other and occasionally with others who approached, as they people-watched and discussed their mutual love of exquisite fashion. Amanda, relieved that she had been fairly successful in avoiding further long conversations with Tristan's family, noticed a palpable shift in the atmosphere—Tristan had arrived. His appearances were always planned but never announced, and his presence sent a quiet rimple through the room. And this time, he wasn't alone.

When Amanda saw who walked in beside him, she swallowed down the sharp coil of dread rising in her chest. The last thing she wanted to see was Governor Jim Hansen walking side-by-side with the man of the hour. She knew he had arrived in Tokyo, but he hadn't been in the VIP section for the opening of the summit, and she hadn't run into him all day. Perhaps *he* had been the one in the wings with Tristan during the opening ceremony. The thought made her stomach turn.

"What the hell?" Lyla gasped. "Does Tristan know the Governor?"

"Julius knows the Governor, so... yeah. Tristan knows him too," Amanda murmured, barely above a whisper.

"Good God," Lyla said, shaking her head. "I mean, I knew he was coming, but *this* entrance? What, are these two suddenly BFFs?"

Lyla found it surreal to be in an intimate setting with a man who used to scold her for dripping water from the pool onto his precious marble floors. Lyla hadn't seen him in years, and the last time she had interacted with any member of the Hansen family was the day she told Cooper off for not having the balls to stand up to his father.

Amanda only nodded.

"Don't worry, I'll play defense. I've got you," Lyla said. "Bet I'm the last person that man expects to see." She grinned. "Can't wait to call him *Jimmy.*"

Amanda smiled, leaning into her best friend with a touch that said, "Thanks, and I love you," without having to utter a syllable.

Tristan and Governor Hansen moved through the room with practiced elegance, silver hair catching the light. He made no noise, yet his arrival bent the focus of the space, straightening postures, and redirecting conversations. Lucien Beaumont and Azizi Malonga turned from the bar to greet him, while Evelyn Montgomery approached the men with her usual shimmer of pearls and champagne. The swarm of hellos between diplomats and dignitaries made most of the crowd oblivious to Amanda and Lyla on the fringes.

Lyla leaned in, her voice low and awestruck. "Dude. What is happening?"

Amanda shrugged, offering no explanation, her gaze already sweeping the room. Just beyond a marble column, she noticed Melody and gave a subtle wave, motioning her over with the kind of quiet urgency that didn't draw attention.

As Melody approached, the terrace doors beside them opened with a hush of cool air. Julius stepped inside, making all three women shift.

"Miss Drake," he said smoothly, settling his eyes on Melody first. "I want to offer my personal condolences. Russell was a friend to many of us. A loss like that... it reverberates in a way that's hard to explain."

Melody's spine straightened. "Thank you. It has."

Lyla's eyes narrowed slightly.

Spotting her partner in the corner, Esmé approached to join them. "Oh, hello. I don't think we've officially met," she said, extending a hand to Melody. "Esmé," her grip was soft. "I knew your husband, but I haven't had the pleasure of knowing you, sadly. My deepest condolences."

Melody took her hand. "Thank you," was all she could manage to say.

Amanda bristled slightly at the tension behind Melody's words. Her smile that held too long, the flicker in her eyes that aimed the pain from her heart like little daggers seeking to pierce anyone who refused to see how much she was suffering.

"Good to see you again, Amanda. You must be so proud today," Julius said, redirecting his attention.

"Of course," she nodded quickly, "And you! It was quite a surprise to see you on the mainstage. What a performance."

The tiniest flash of resentment at the word "performance" swept Julius' face, but his tone was tranquil. "Thank you," he said simply.

The couple said no more before drifting off into the crowd for more mingling as Lyla took a dramatic, slow turn toward the two of them. "Okay. You guys gotta spill."

Melody didn't hesitate—she was still trembling slightly. "That trip to Tenerife... it took my husband from me." Her voice was calm, but tight with controlled rage. She was a bit loose-lipped with Amanda, but she knew she had to be measured to some degree, so she kept it simple. "I won't stop until I know the truth about what happened."

Amanda's stomach twisted. Lyla caught the flash of a passing storm darkening Amanda's face with a twinge of guilt.

"Amanda?"

"Not here," she said quietly.

Tristan had yet to make his way over to their quiet corner, still busy with VIPs waiting for their turn to chat with the main attraction, so Amanda took Lyla's hand and led her outside, leaving Melody behind. The terrace was quiet and lantern-lit, with the city glittering in the distance. Amanda leaned on the railing, her back to the sparkling city.

Lyla didn't pause for a moment. "Start talking."

Amanda let a long inhale flood her lungs. "Look, I know you've known Tristan for a few years, but I don't think you know his friends. And I don't know how they operate, exactly, but I'm in over my head. I've been manipulated into spying, and the operation is tied to Governor Hansen."

Lyla blinked. "What? Spying? Are you joking?"

Amanda shook her head sheepishly.

"Seriously?" Lyla took a long pause. "Like *our* Hansen? Governor James Hansen of Tennessee?"

Amanda nodded. "Yes, stop repeating it. You know they have leverage on me. Enough to keep me on the hook."

Lyla softened. "Leverage? That's not exactly what I'd call it. I know you have... history..."

Amanda looked away. "Yeah, well, you don't exactly know all of it."

Lyla reached for her hand, not demanding, but just assuring. "What do you mean?"

Amanda's throat closed. Lyla's touch anchored her, like a hand catching the edge of her heart before the fall went too far. If anyone could hold space for the truth, it was her.

"I wish I could tell you every last detail, but the fact is, I'm not even sure I know what I'm involved in. You saw what happened today. It's smoke and mirrors and lights and lasers. But the whole globe is enamoured, and these men are powerful."

"You're scaring me," Lyla whispered, stepping closer to Amanda, enveloping her in an embrace. They suddenly heard the terrace doors swing open, laughter billowing outside.

"There you are," Tristan said, relief breaking across his face. "I've been looking everywhere."

Lyla glanced between them, then back at Amanda. She gave a quiet nod and a to-be-continued look.

"I'm gonna go use the loo—isn't that what they call it here?" she winked, hopeful that her silly humor would deflect any suspicion.

Amanda rolled her eyes, and Tristan snorted, "Yeah, it's down the hall."

"Hey, everything okay?" he let his fingers trickle down her arm from shoulder to elbow.

Amanda straightened, smoothing the front of her dress like it could iron out her nerves. "Of course," she said a little too brightly. "Lyla and I were just catching a little fresh air."

He studied her for a moment. She did her best to give him a sincere smile, ethereal and slightly illuminated by the evening light. She wasn't trying to convince herself of anything, but she did hope it would be enough to deflect any type of suspicion or concern that may have been rising.

Tristan lowered his voice. "I meant what I said about being cautious last night. This whole summit is just the pageantry. The press. The politics. But the tech? The future we're building? That part, I will never take lightly."

Amanda nodded, her pulse loudening in her ears. She didn't know if she believed him or just wanted to. She couldn't help but wonder if there was truth behind the idea that power corrupts and absolute power corrupts absolutely. Could he still "never take it lightly" once billions of dollars seemed like an arbitrary number? Could he truly fathom that kind of lifestyle? Could she?

Tristan touched her wrist gently, snapping her out of her thoughts and into her body again. "And you... You help me remember what matters," he said, leaning into her fully.

She looked at his forthright grin and was almost startled by the honesty she saw in his eyes.

He pulled her close, his gaze drifting unhurriedly over her face. "And I can't stop thinking about how you'll look tomorrow in that gown."

Amanda's mind flashed back to their evening—Tristan, stripped of polish, whispering doubts, fears, hopes, and dreams into the dark. She wanted desperately to believe that was the real man, the one whose hands made her forget the world had ever felt cold.

She let the thought hold for only a moment. *How could she expect him to be who he seemed when she wasn't?*

He touched her like he had all the time in the world, fingers trailing down her back, settling at her waist, making her breath catch with every movement.

"You always look good," he pressed into her fully, voice low, "but when you dress to kill? You might ruin me."

She kissed him—not deeply, but not safely either. Just enough to feel the shape of his mouth, to remind herself how easily she could forget everything else, if only she could afford to.

"No need to get ahead of ourselves," she said, placing her palms on his chest, her voice calm, but not exactly steady.

As she pulled back, his fingers lingered at her waist like an afterthought. Her body tilted toward him before her mind had the strength to pull it away. She turned slowly, composed, the taste of him still on her lips. But behind the practiced ease of a smile, her pulse kept racing.

Tristan let a sharp breath escape through his nostrils. "You are an enigma," he remarked, his hand still tracing her skin, coming to a stop with the grip of her hand.

She looked down, naturally interlacing her fingers with his. "High praise," she winked.

If ever there was something she longed for a man to understand about her, it was her complexity. Her ability to go from one thing to another and not be considered erratic or a problem to be fixed. The ability to change on a dime and have it seem almost expected, natural, received, and even appreciated.

He didn't say another word, just brushed his nose against her cheek, his breath still warm near her temple, when the terrace doors burst open behind them.

"Ah! *Les amoureux!*" Clarisse's voice rang out like a champagne cork, her arms stretched wide in theatrical delight. The sound of clinking glasses and jazz-laced laughter spilled into the night air with her, the party surging behind the doors like a tide.

Amanda stepped back instinctively, but Tristan didn't release her hand.

Clarisse glided forward in a shimmer of silk, her silver bracelets clinking together like wind chimes. "There you are, my loves, tucked away like a secret! What a crime to keep the two most beautiful people at this summit hidden out here. *Come, come!* You mustn't disappear—not tonight."

Her eyes twinkled, but her tone held just enough demand to remind them both who had walked in. They looked at each other with a knowing *gotta-love-Clarisse* smile.

"We are celebrating, are we not?" she added, taking Tristan's free hand in both of hers and kissing the air near his cheeks. "Your brilliance on that stage deserves more than starlight and stolen kisses."

Clarisse turned to Amanda, her smile softer. "And you, *ma belle,* you keep him grounded. It shows." She gave a conspiratorial wink. "I think you've done him more good than any of us ever have."

Amanda felt the blood rush to her cheeks as she smiled politely, feeling a sudden shiver run down her spine.

Clarisse lightly clapped her hands twice, summoning them. "No more hiding. Tonight is for joy. For healing. We've all earned a little light after the darkness, have we not?" Her voice dropped, not sad or mournful, but reverent. "Russell and Vivian would've wanted us to move forward, no? And what better way than with music and champagne?"

She stepped back toward the open doors, her silhouette framed by the glow inside. "Come. The night is young, and Tokyo waits for no one."

Then, as if she hadn't just stirred ghosts with her velvet tongue, she turned and rejoined the party, waving for them to follow behind her.

Inside, Lyla hovered near the bar, a pink Cosmopolitan in one hand, her phone in the other. She was trying to decide how to continue the conversation with Amanda. She couldn't make sense of it, not really. She'd meant what she said—she didn't expect Amanda to stay with Tristan, but her gut kept whispering: *this is bigger than anything I was prepared for.*

Tristan and Amanda moved through the room, cutting a quiet path, like wind threading through still branches. It was as if they both had elegance training—magnetic, and impossible not to notice. Wherever they paused, conversations swelled around them, hands extended, and glasses were raised in their honor. He was every inch the celebrated visionary, his charm precise and practiced; she, his effortless counterpart, was poised, offering warm smiles that gave nothing away. They didn't cling to each other, but their closeness was unmistakable, like two halves of a story that everyone wanted a part in. In a room designed to celebrate them, they gave the illusion of ease and certainty.

Lyla observed without inserting herself, content to hover just outside the swirl of conversation. Tristan's mother was laughing with a foreign diplomat, her voice wafting through the air with the crisp pitch of a radio signal. Julius and Esmé had disappeared in the comings and goings of other guests.

She clocked the Governor standing near an ice sculpture, accepting greetings with the ease of a politician: disarming smiles, practiced nods. When his gaze swept the room and landed on Lyla, he faltered.

She met his stare and didn't look away. Slowly, deliberately, she lifted her arm from the edge of the bar, raised her glass in a casual salute, and took a sip, grinning as if she'd been waiting for this exact moment.

With a spark of Lyla hutzpah and just enough liquid courage to make it fun, she peeled herself away from the bar. She wasn't rushed or hesitant, just deliberate enough to make him wonder if she was coming to say hello or deliver a reckoning.

"Governor," she tipped her class again towards him.

"Lyla McCafferty," his voice sang, without missing a beat.

"It's Lyla Grant these days," she corrected him, with only a hint of propriety.

"I wouldn't have pegged you for a woman who'd take a man's name," the governor said, smiling.

"I don't think you've ever had me pegged, Jimmy," she returned, smile intact. Then, with a nod, she turned and slipped back into the crowd, leaving him with his assumptions and not a word more.

At least he knows Amanda isn't alone, Lyla thought.

She moved through the room with her usual charm, effortless and magnetic, making friends of anyone who paused long enough to chat. Eventually, she spotted Melody near the same cluster of low couches tucked into the corner and made her way over.

"Tired of the schmooze-fest?" Lyla asked, sinking into the seat beside her.

"Just observing," Melody replied, her gaze still scanning the room.

Lyla turned toward her, without a hint of playfulness. "Hey... I'm really sorry about your husband."

"Thanks." Melody nodded, her tone even. She'd been weaving through the crowd all evening, present, but always retreating back to the edges, watching, collecting pieces of something only she could see.

"Do you really think these people had something to do with it?" Lyla asked, lowering her voice.

Melody gave her a look—flat, unreadable, but totally loaded. Lyla exhaled. "Right. Got it."

"I don't know what I'm looking for," Melody admitted after a pause, "but I'll know when I see it."

"I'm sure you will," Lyla said, nodding. "And I'll keep my eyes and ears peeled too."

She looked at her with a faint smile. "Well, if we solve this in the next few days, we should probably go into business."

"Hey, I'm not going anywhere. Not for a second," Lyla said with a fiercely empathetic kindness.

For a brief moment, Melody felt something sharp twist inside her—a pang of jealousy, quiet and cutting. The kind that comes from realizing someone else has what you lost. A person who crosses oceans for you. One who comes to the rescue. A person who stays.

She reached across the cushion, her hand closing gently over Lyla's.

"Good," she whispered. It was all she needed to say.

Chapter Thirteen

Tokyo: Second Day of Summit, The Auction

"They love him." Amanda's voice was quiet and low, almost detached, as she turned to Melody and Lyla without taking her eyes off the front of the room. She had texted Katherine three times with no reply. Her mind was begging for intel, and yet her heart kept convincing her to trust the unfolding of the maddening world she had entered.

Flashbulbs sparked like fireworks as people entered for a pre-auction press conference. The morning event had drawn global media—economics correspondents from London, tech journalists from Dubai, even a few military analysts and government officials slipping in under vague titles or disguised as podcasters, likely hoping to avoid public acknowledgment of their presence.

Amanda stood at the back of the room, arms folded loosely across her waist, the tailored sleeves of her blazer concealing any tension winding through her body. Her hair was down, smoothed and composed, unlike the nerves skittering beneath her skin.

Melody nodded. "Every camera, every headline—they're already sold, and he hasn't even said a word."

"Should we sit?" Lyla shrugged, feeling a growing sense of responsibility for her best friend's current situation.

At the front, a long white table bore the Envisage logo, embossed in gold. Tristan entered, taking a seat center stage in a steel-gray suit, crisp and camera-ready, his expression a practiced blend of charm and authority. To his right sat the company CFO, Andre de Villiers, a South African-born numbers genius with a reputation for surgical clarity. To his left sat the public relations director, who took her seat in a crisp white suit—Renée Cho, a woman who smiled at the cameras like someone who understood exactly what her silence was worth.

On the left, Julius stood off-mic and offstage, his eyes following the flow of the room like a man calculating the net worth of everyone present.

The moderator lifted a card, signaling the start, as the room fell into a vibrant hush, and the first hand was raised.

Renée gave the smallest nod, barely perceptible, but it was all the indication the press needed.

"Many are saying this will be the most aggressive private tech auction in recent history," a reporter from the *Financial Times* said. "Some are speculating that the sale of your tech will exceed double or triple the opening bid of a billion dollars. Can you speak to that?"

Renée smiled smoothly. "We don't comment on speculation." She turned to Tristan. "But I'll let Mr. Montgomery add his perspective."

Tristan leaned forward, folding his hands loosely in front of him. "What I *can* say," he began, "is that today isn't just about valuation. It's about vision. This auction is the culmination of years of innovation, and the global interest we've seen is... well, let's just say, *historic* doesn't feel like hyperbole."

De Villiers nodded, speaking up in his recognizably precise tone. "We're not looking for the highest bidder—we're looking for the right steward. The numbers will be extraordinary, yes. But more important than the price tag is the alignment of values and infrastructure. This isn't just a device—it's a cornerstone of what's coming."

Another reporter jumped in. "But there's concern over sovereign bidding. Some worry about which countries will be granted access or influence over the Ocular Grid. Will Envisage limit eligibility? And will you release the location of all sites to the buyer? We understand that the Grid's reach is limited to five hundred miles, and there are multiple sites around the globe. Are they all in working order?"

Renée leaned forward again, her smile firm. "That's a matter for the advisory committee and legal teams, but I assure you—national security is top of mind. Every bidder has been vetted through a multilayer process of compliance and ethical review."

Amanda scanned the room, taking in the faces of names she'd studied. Esmé sat near the front, chin lifted, legs crossed, and ankles tucked elegantly beneath her chair. A man in a sharp military uniform sat one seat over. She couldn't place the insignia, but her gut told her he was a representative of a Middle Eastern country. On the other side, Azizi Malonga leaned back in his chair, not taking notes, not glancing at the panel, but watching the watchers.

She didn't hear the next question. Her gaze was still fixed forward, but her mind was already sprinting ahead—leaping borders, crossing oceans. North Korea.

She didn't need a classified briefing to understand what it would mean for a regime like that to gain access to predictive surveillance with a five-hundred-mile radius. Missile activity, troop movements, civilian tracking—all of it could be orchestrated in silence, in secret, with no one the wiser until it was too late.

And where the hell was Katherine? She hadn't responded once. Amanda exhaled through her nose, too shallow to settle her nerves.

She turned her attention back to the front of the room while Tristan resumed the narrative, pulling the focus of every eye with masterful ease.

"Let me be clear," he said. "Envisage isn't selling out—we're opening a door. We believe the Ocular Grid will redefine not just connectivity, but clarity. Surveillance that protects, but doesn't control. Transparency without tyranny. We have the technology to aid countries, not control them. But it is of utmost importance to us that those involved have a commitment to ethics and morality that are in alignment with Envisage's mission."

A hand shot up near the middle. "What about implementation? This version—is it fully functional? If today's auction is for partial access or rights, how does the rollout work?"

This answer came from the CFO again. "Yes," De Vallies began, "it's fully operational. What's being auctioned is the first complete working model of the Ocular Grid. Access will be granted through a phased licensing structure with regional implementation tied to compliance and infrastructure readiness. Strategic partnerships will be locked in at closing, and activation begins immediately."

The lights caught another wave of flashes, cameras clicking in a rhythm so fast it barely registered as anything other than a stream of light. Amanda checked her watch for the time. It was 11:45. In fifteen minutes, the whole thing would shift from performance to purchase.

She swallowed hard, the metallic tang of guilt rising fast and uninvited. What if someone traced the prototype back to her? What if this auction turned volatile, and she was the one holding the only piece that couldn't be replaced? The thought twisted her stomach, sharpening her awareness of every gaze in the room—even the ones not yet aimed her way.

"I'm gonna go to the bathroom," Amanda whispered in Lyla's ear. She didn't glance back as she slipped out of the auction room alone. The press conference would be ending in minutes, and she wanted to see if she could get a glimpse of the auction hall before it all began.

Across the corridor, the lighting dimmed and shifted as she entered the mezzanine. She scanned her badge at the entrance to the quiet stretch of hallway that opened onto a private overlook above the gallery-level auditorium. Below, rows of seats were already filling with motion: aides checking messages, advisors murmuring in low tones, military liaisons in pressed uniforms scanning the space as if calculating threats. These were not the ones who would raise hands or press buttons.

The real bidders would sit separately, in a semicircle of enclosed booths closer to the stage, partitioned, elevated, and mostly anonymous. A few nameplates read like headlines. The rest were placeholders in code, disguised as corporate logos, but Amanda had done her homework. Katherine had warned her about what to look for.

"They'll show up in pairs," Katherine had said. "Look for double-country interests. A Russian bidder won't bid as a

Russian. He'll come in through a Southeast Asian hedge fund or a Belarusian shell. Track the proximity. Who's seated near whom. Who exchanges notes."

Amanda scanned the booths, trying to keep her focus. She read each name carefully. Carpathian Group, Vallant Technologies, Zurich, Port Ascend Investment—a cover for Gulf State intelligence, if Katherine was right. Then she saw what she had been looking for:

Cerberus Index Holdings, registered in Cyprus. "Watch for this," Katherine had told her. "They're a false flag. A Western front with Eastern loyalty."

Amanda hurried to the hallway again, hoping to nonchalantly find Lyla and Melody and make their way into the auction hall, but she practically ran into them as she stepped out.

"Hey. What's going on?" Lyla asked quietly.

"Oh, nothing, just thought I'd peek in before it started. Did they wrap things up?"

"Yeah, just as you left. They told us to all come this way."

"Okay, cool. I guess we can go into the lower level, our seats will be down there," she said.

They joined a small crowd of people, a stark contrast to the fifteen hundred or more that had been at the demonstrations a day before. Only bidders, press, and approved guests would be allowed at the live auction. All other entrances had been closed as the group entered one by one through a door to the main hall.

As the women shifted among the people, suddenly Azizi Malonga stepped beside Amanda, separating her from Lyla and Melody. Another man was accompanying him closely, eyes never fixed on one thing for very long, sticking to him like a bodyguard. Amanda assumed that's exactly what he was. Malonga was a man in need of protection—born into a world of contradictions, he had both privilege and struggle. The son of a respected diplomat and a brilliant economist, he was educated in Europe but raised with a deep sense of responsibility for the continent that shaped him. From an early age, Malonga understood the delicate balance of African leadership, navigating foreign influence, internal rivalries, and the ever-present question of sovereignty in a world where economic dependency was often disguised as aid.

"Miss Hopkins," he nodded politely.

"Hello," she extended her hand, and he took it into his—not shaking it, but holding it lightly between his own, as if measuring its weight. Then, with the ghost of a smile, he bowed his head slightly.

"It's a pleasure to meet you, Mr. Malonga," Amanda said as they continued moving with the crowd. "I've heard a lot about you," she smiled.

"And I have heard less about you than I wish," Malonga smiled widely.

"Perhaps we can get to know each other over the next couple of days, then," Amanda said. She was artfully skilled at dealing with diplomats, and there was something about Malonga that didn't shake her to the core like many of the other players. She didn't have to fight her nerves, pretend to suppress any rising tension, or combat the urge to vomit like she sometimes had to do. Arguably the most powerful and talked about man there besides Tristan and Julius, and Amanda felt calm as a cucumber next to him. She didn't pay it too much attention at first, but she did file it away.

"Perhaps we shall," he replied with another warm nod.

Amanda stepped aside, watching as he entered alone, the man with him turning around to survey the exterior quickly before following behind him. She had asked Katherine if Malonga had the capital to compete at the auction, but no intel was provided, and now that she'd seen him up close, she couldn't shake the mix of curiosity and confusion that swirled in her gut. Something was compelling about his stillness, about the way he occupied space, as if he knew far more than anyone else in the room and was just waiting for the perfect moment to prove it. And she, like everyone else, seemed to be waiting with bated breath to find out.

She turned to see Melody again, only steps behind her.

"Who was that?" she asked.

"His name is Azizi Malonga. Everyone's talking about him. Apparently, he's been trying to compile the funds to bid today, and with so many people speculating about who he's in bed with, he's the one to watch."

"I thought the Russians were the ones to watch out for."

"Well, we are American, so isn't that always the case?" Amanda responded.

"Ah, our common enemy for generations to come," Melody added, like she was narrating a documentary.

"Where's Lyla?"

"Bathroom," Melody clipped her head upwards with a shrug.

Amanda began to scan for Russian indicators, but there were no overt signs. And if there were no Russian presence, it would definitely be considered suspicious. That was how Katherine framed it: "If they're not here, they're already inside."

The women made their way up to the viewing corridor and watched the bidders move into place as Tristan stepped onto the stage to greet the auctioneer.

Katherine had told her: "The first bid will be theater, but the second? The second will tell you everything."

Amanda turned and nearly collided with Lyla.

"Whoa," Lyla said, steadying her with a hand on her elbow. "Had to pee. Did they start auctioning off the world already?"

"Not yet," Amanda scoffed.

Lyla grinned and waved her badge like she was holding a golden ticket. "Good. Because I have questions. Like, where do I pick up my paddle? I'm thinking of putting a casual two bill, give or take, on the table just to mess with people."

Amanda let out a soft laugh. "You'd definitely cause an international incident."

Lyla raised a brow. "You say that like it's a *bad* thing."

Screens had been installed above the tiered seating, catching onlookers' attention, displaying the Envisage insignia and a countdown timer ticking down the final three minutes. An usher gestured them toward a section reserved for Envisage guests and high-level staff.

Lyla wore her usual calm, a quiet witness to the gravity in the room, even if she didn't let it rattle her. Her calm wasn't the absence of fear, just her refusal to feed it. She leaned in close to Melody as they walked.

"So, do we clap? Cheer? Or is this more of a 'poker face and slow nod' kind of situation?"

"Definitely the latter," Melody murmured.

They took their seats and looked around, Lyla looking more wide-eyed than anyone. "Wow. Everyone here looks like they own at least two offshore banks and one endangered animal.

Are you sure we're allowed in here without a secret handshake?"

She had lowered her voice to a whisper after getting no response from either woman other than a stern look.

On stage, Tristan took his seat behind the ceremonial desk, flanked by legal advisors and the auctioneer. Julius sat at the end of the stage with Renée Cho and Andre de Villiers.

The lights dimmed slightly, and the auctioneer stepped forward. "Ladies and gentlemen," she began, voice smooth and captivating, "on behalf of Envisage, welcome. Today marks not only a technological milestone but a turning point in our shared future. What is on offer is unprecedented—an operational model of the Ocular Grid, a system poised to redefine everything from surveillance to supply chain logistics."

Amanda noted the careful phrasing. Surveillance first, infrastructure second, no mention of the ethics Tristan had just invoked. She watched as Governor Hansen took a seat among the press, trying to see if she could keep an eye on which bids would make him flinch throughout the auction.

With that, a staff member stepped forward, carrying a compact case—smooth, brushed black metal with rounded corners and an engraved identifier along the clasp.

"The bidding," the auctioneer continued, "will begin at one billion U.S. dollars."

There was a pause.

Lyla raised her eyebrows. "So much for my casual two billion."

Amanda leaned back slightly, scanning the booths from her new angle.

Tristan set the case in the middle of the table without flourish, as the room collectively leaned forward. Even the aides stared.

Tristan opened the case, revealing the Ocular Grid module, the component that made yesterday's presentation function, but hadn't yet been revealed, nestled in a sculpted bed of matte-black foam. It was the first time anyone in the room had seen the apparatus itself—only its interface and capabilities had been teased in his presentation the day before. The hardware wasn't flashy. It was deliberate. Densely compact and about the size of a hardback book, its surface was smooth, dark, and slightly curved at the edges—more like a polished artifact than a piece of machinery.

Instead of ports or switches, it bore a subtle pattern of filament-thin circuitry across its shell, pulsing faintly beneath the surface like illuminated veins, giving off the impression of something *living*—a hybrid of organic intelligence and engineered precision. Something between a neural network and a weapon. Designed to be untouchable.

Amanda felt Melody stiffen beside her before she saw the look on her face. Her breath hitched. Slowly, Melody turned to her, eyes wide and stunned.

"That's what you were carrying," she whispered.

Amanda didn't answer. She couldn't.

"You knew," Melody said. She wasn't angry, but she spoke with sharp, quiet disbelief. "You knew what it was. And didn't tell me?"

Amanda kept her gaze forward for a moment, jaw set, trying to read Tristan's body language while ignoring the slow unraveling happening next to her. But she could feel the heat of Melody's stare boring into her skin.

"I don't know... I didn't know how... and I still don't know what I'm doing with it," she whispered harshly. "We'll talk, I promise."

Poor Lyla couldn't make sense of anything the two were whispering about and gave Amanda an all too familiar look before all three turned their attention to the front again. Onstage, Tristan began to speak again, the cadence of his voice wrapping around the room.

"For those of you wondering—yes. This is your first look at the working core of the system."

There was a subtle nod between two aides seated on opposite sides of the stage. The auctioneer smiled, "And who would like to open?" The first bid echoed like a starter pistol.

"One billion," the auctioneer repeated. "From Port Ascend Investment."

The second came quickly—two paddles, almost simultaneous. Cerberus Index and Atlas Maritime.

"Two billion. Two point four. Two point eight."

The pace accelerated.

Lyla leaned in and whispered, "This is like watching sharks circle a bleeding dollar sign."

But Amanda didn't reply. She had shifted her attention to Malonga.

He hadn't moved. No notes, no whispers to aides—because he didn't bring any. Just himself and a bodyguard, with a calm expression, and the large armored briefcase resting beside his polished shoes. Its dark shell gleamed under the lights, the biometric clasp glowing a faint green. Everyone in the room had already clocked it. Rumors swirled that Malonga had brought the physical sovereign bonds to back his bid, each one worth hundreds of millions.

But he hadn't lifted his paddle once.

Amanda knew better than to assume disinterest. Malonga's stillness was too deliberate. He wasn't out of the game—he was rewriting the rules. *Was he waiting for a signal? Measuring the room's desperation? Or simply there to remind them all that power could sit silent and still dominate, waiting until the last second to outbid them all?* The bidding roared on.

"Three point two. Three point nine."

At four-point-eight, one of the Gulf State bidders dropped out. At five, Cerberus paused. But Atlas raised their paddle again, and a new player joined—Helion Bridge, whose representative finally shifted in his seat, murmured something into a headset, then made a call. A paddle was raised moments later.

"Five point six."

Amanda leaned forward. Lyla squirmed in her chair, and Melody sat stiff as a board.

Behind one of the booths, a bidder moved once with a sharp, decisive nod.

"Six billion."

The entire room stirred. A slight intake of breath, and everyone shifted in their seats. Even Julius's posture changed, chin lifting like a man watching stocks spike in real time.

But Malonga remained motionless. The auctioneer's voice didn't waver.

"Do I hear six point five?"

There was a pause. Then another bid. "Six point eight."

"Seven billion."

Amanda felt the gravity of the escalating numbers before she could even process it. The room felt hotter, as if the oxygen had been replaced with static. A thin sheen of sweat bloomed across her upper lip, and her temples throbbed with a dull ache.

The auctioneer let it sit, weighted down with an intensity few in the room could fathom. Numbers so large they didn't make sense to most of the world, as if they were just numerals instead of a representation of assets. The whole space felt like it was contracting under the thumb of unspoken stakes—anticipation, dread, ambition—all braided into a single breathless tension. It wasn't fear, but inevitability, and everyone present could sense the seismic shift.

"Seven point four."

Amanda stared at Malonga, waiting for the moment he finally moved. But he didn't. He studied the others—cool and clinical. Hansen hadn't made a move either. He wasn't a bidder, but he sat still as stone the entire time. Her eyes darted back to Malonga. One hand rested on the case beside him, but his fingers never twitched.

She glanced at the screen—bids, names, and flags were all anonymized in real-time for public broadcast.

Cerberus was stalling. Atlas, reaching. Helion wasn't bidding for itself. They were a pipeline. Which meant whoever was feeding them was either incredibly powerful or incredibly desperate.

And still, Malonga sat like a man with no need to play the game.

"Eight billion," the auctioneer declared.

The air was nearly vibrating now—bravado and suspicion colliding under cold lights. Amanda felt the sweat behind her knees. She stole a glance at Julius. His expression was neutral, but his knuckles were white with clenched fists around the sides of his seat.

Then, finally, Malonga moved.

But he wasn't bidding. He leaned forward, unlatched the armored briefcase at his feet, and opened it. Heads turned, and hushed gasps fluttered like insects. Amanda couldn't see the contents, not clearly. Just a flicker of heavy documents, embossed seals, a glint of metal. They were the bonds, and it wasn't showmanship. It was *proof*. What wasn't known was if entire nations had struck a deal, agreed to pay out debts they couldn't guarantee unless indebted for decades, possibly centuries.

He kept his gaze forward, never glancing at the stage or reaching for the paddle resting by his side. Instead, he slid an envelope from the briefcase beside him and passed it, without a word, to an aide who emerged as if on cue.

She crossed the room with quiet efficiency, delivering the envelope to a member of the auction staff waiting near the stage.

The auctioneer faltered mid-sentence, glancing toward the side as muted voices exchanged instructions. A note was unfolded, skimmed, then neatly refolded with care that felt more deliberate than necessary.

The auctioneer straightened, voice perfectly even. "Mr. Malonga would like to acknowledge his presence today as an observer only."

Amanda's breath caught. So that was it. No bid, no challenge—just presence. She felt her pulse spike. He had come not to compete, but to intimidate. To sit in silence and remind every player in the room that his power didn't require applause or winning. It needed only to be seen. And now, everyone who thought they had the upper hand would be second-guessing their footing.

Because if Malonga wasn't bidding, it meant one of two things—neither of them good. Either he had already made his move, meaning he cut a deal behind the scenes with someone powerful enough to bypass the auction altogether. Or he didn't need the Ocular Grid, because he already had access to something just like it.

Lyla blinked. "What? I thought that was the guy to watch."

Amanda stared at the man now calmly closing his briefcase again, like he had done exactly what he came to do.

"He never intended to bid," Amanda said, mostly to herself.

"No," Melody said. "But he just scared the hell out of everyone who did."

That was the genius of it. Malonga's silence was louder than a win. No one knew who he was backing—or if he was backing anyone at all. Was he a neutral observer? A sleeping giant? A threat waiting for someone to step out of line?

A few booths shifted visibly—one bidder stood up to leave. Another gestured to a translator with sudden urgency. Panic wasn't breaking out, but the illusion of control was cracking.

With one simple decision—nonparticipation—Malonga had opened the floor beneath them and shown how little footing anyone truly had.

Then the gavel sound chimed once, crisply.

"Eight-point-eight billion," the auctioneer announced, his voice steady. "Sold to Helion Bridge Group."

For a moment, no one moved. The room seemed suspended, like everyone was silently recalibrating from what had just happened. Then, a single clap rang out, then another followed, and applause broke like a delayed wave, unsure at first, then swelling into a full-scale celebration.

Amanda kept her eyes on the screen, the numbers scrolling in silent confirmation, each digit a tolling bell. The figures blinked with clinical finality, but to her, they pulsed like a countdown to something that couldn't be undone. It didn't feel like a win. The final bid still echoed somewhere in the bones of the building, reverberating faintly as the room began to dissolve around it.

Chairs scraped. Voices rose in hushed urgency. Reporters moved like a tide toward exit points, already reaching for phones. Security teams closed their circles. The air thinned, not with tension, but with the clarity of an irreversible future.

Amanda, Lyla, and Melody got up and headed toward the exits with the rest of the audience. No one lingered. Everyone had someone to meet or call. They didn't even gather around the stage to see if they would get a chance to speak to the Envisage staff.

Tristan found Amanda just beyond the main doors. His expression was pure momentum, his eyes bright, and his jaw clenched with adrenaline. He looked like someone trying to keep still while jolts of electricity ran through his body.

"We did it," he said, breathless.

Amanda offered a soft smile. "Yeah. Eight-point-eight," her expression read as pride mingled with disbelief.

"Amazing," he let out a sharp laugh. "The sale of the century. That's what I heard the reporters saying. I keep waiting for someone to tell me it was a rehearsal."

Behind him, Evelyn Montgomery approached with perfect posture, pearl earrings catching the light. "Tristan, darling," she said, cupping his cheek for a brief, almost ceremonial kiss. "Well done."

Harold stepped forward and offered his son a brisk slap on the back, the kind that looked warm to onlookers but landed just a bit too hard. He wore the faintest trace of a smile, tight and rehearsed. "You stood out in a room full of people trying to steal the spotlight," he said, nodding. "That takes skill."

Tristan's sister Olivia, phone in hand, lifted it briefly for a photo. "Look, it's already trending," she said.

Tristan beamed, and yet—Amanda saw it. Just beneath the polish, a flicker of the boy who used to bring home straight A's but never earned his family's unadulterated pride lingered behind his eyes.

"We're so proud," Harold said. "It's great. Really."

CHAPTER FOURTEEN

Tokyo: Second Day of Summit, 12:30 p.m.

THE ENTIRE AUCTION HAD lasted less than twenty minutes. As Amanda walked alongside Tristan through the private corridor behind the grand hall, the thrum of voices grew louder with each step. He hadn't let go of her hand since he had made a beeline for her when the gavel fell. His grip wasn't possessive—it was tethered, like he needed her to anchor him before the full weight of the moment settled.

She wanted to ignore all of her swirling doubts and accusations. She was increasingly certain he wasn't part of some master plan to control the world. But she believed more and more that he was too blinded by the brilliance of his invention to see what was at stake. "That was…" she began, but her words trailed off.

Tristan turned to her, his expression still somewhere between euphoria and disbelief. "Please. Say it." It was a loaded plea. Amanda could feel the tension and desire behind his words.

She leaned in, smiling, and let go of anything negative. "I'm proud of you."

His breath caught, eyes narrowing for just a moment as if trying to memorize her words. Then he gave a small nod, swallowing hard. "That's all I need. It means everything."

They stepped through a glass doorway flanked by heavy velvet ropes and into a storm.

The lobby had been transformed. Where earlier access had been tightly controlled, now it roared to life with flashing lights, shouted questions, and a crush of bodies angling for position. Cameras craned, microphones surged forward. A wave of reporters swarmed the moment they appeared, and all eyes turned to Tristan.

Amanda blinked against the sudden burst of strobes. The press had been absent from the main event, limited to a fixed feed and a single static view of the auction table. The coverage had erupted, and volcanic media frenzy enveloped everything. Televisions mounted around the lobby displayed the winning bid in bold type, looping images of Tristan behind the auctioneer's desk. The words "Eight-Point-Eight Billion: The Sale of the Century" had already been overlaid on every screen.

"Hey, smile," Tristan whispered, leaning in close without taking his gaze off the cameras. His voice was tight with adrenaline. "Just for a few seconds. Then it's just you and me. Promise."

She slipped her arm through his, projecting calm even as her heartbeat kicked harder. Behind them, Tristan's parents, Lyla, Melody, Julius, and other familiar faces had all found a place off to the side, standing shoulder to shoulder in the filtered shadow of a throng. Reporters pushed forward, the horde tightening around Tristan and Amanda. Lyla had her arms crossed, scanning the crowd with a raised brow and a quiet expression of shock. Melody held her phone loosely in one hand, trying to decide if she should lift and record or keep her focus on the whole room.

A barrage of questions was shouted over the noise. "Mr. Montgomery—do you consider this a victory for open innovation or for privatized power?"

"Is the Grid's code secure?"

"Will sovereign states have backdoor access?"

"Was Malonga's presence a threat or a message?"

Tristan raised a hand, offering a diplomatic smile. "We'll address all questions in the coming hours. But today is about a vision realized. A global step forward."

Security began to close in on the circle around Amanda and Tristan, guiding them toward the elevators behind a row of decorative partitions. He waved at a guard, "My family, make sure they get upstairs," he said.

Julius approached, lifting his hand to the officers. "I'll be with them," he gestured toward Esmé to stay close. " And I'll make sure the room is ready for a board meeting," he assured.

Amanda caught one final glimpse of Melody nodding to her—a look that said, *we saw, we're here, we'll wait*—before the cameras swallowed them again as a guard literally pushed them inside the elevator. One officer held the crowd back as another stepped inside with them.

"Well," he said. "Good call about amping up security today."

Tristan smiled. "Whew," he shook his head, almost incapable of saying anything else.

"Well, congratulations, sir."

"Couldn't have done it without you guys," Tristan said with a slap on the back. Amanda had the realization that the two knew each other outside of Tokyo before he spoke again. "You guys always do such a great job."

"Thank you, sir," the man said.

Amanda could feel the immensity of everything that had converged on this moment—layers of planning, secrets, and unseen forces, all culminating in a single, surreal day. To pull off an event of this magnitude would require months, if not years, of planning. She took a deep breath. If that were true, records would exist—breadcrumbs pointing to who was involved, or at least the chance of finding them. If Governor

Hansen had his hands in trying to take over this operation, surely she could find a connection in a smaller way rather than the most obvious one. *Who else was invited here? When did they secure their invitations? What other events were held where these same players attended?* For the first time since arriving in Tokyo, she had a sense of where to begin.

Tristan noticed the flicker of ideas in her expression. "It's a lot to take in, huh?"

"Gosh, yeah," she said.

"We have a quick lunch planned up here, but I have to leave you with the rest of the VIPs. Rain check on that promise? Just found out I have to meet with the board," he said.

"Oh, okay. I mean, is everyone coming up? I left Lyla down there..." Her voice trailed off before continuing. "Did you know Russell Drake's widow? She's here too. I think Lucien invited her." Amanda waited to see if there was a hint of surprise or knowing in his eyes, but he didn't miss a beat.

"Oh, great. Amazing. What a tragedy, huh? Maybe we can make sure she's taken care of. But I'm sure Julius is the one who arranged it," Tristan spoke quickly as they stepped off the elevator. "He and Russell were good friends, I think."

She was glad he assumed it was a simple gesture from a longtime friend, and his concern was with helping rather than questioning. Amanda had very little spy training, but her sense of reality was unwavering. Something about Melody, perhaps the fact that they were in a similar boat, learning the truth about the world of espionage only recently, made Amanda's trust in her immediate. But where Melody tried to deny and ignore it for years, Amanda had always accepted that the dark underbelly of conspiracies and backroom deals was inevitable, but avoidable. And yet, now she was powerless to keep her distance from it, and so was Melody.

"Yeah, she seems nice. We've kind of hit it off. I could totally be friends with her. And you know Lyla. She's never met a stranger."

"Perfect," Tristan smiled, kissing her on the cheek. "The more the merrier. You'll make a nice little trio."

"And in heels no less." Amanda lifted one foot with a wink as the elevator doors opened, and Tristan was met by another program coordinator who was there to whisk him off to the board meeting.

He winked back at her with a shrug before following the woman through the halls as another staff member said, "This way, Miss Hopkins."

"Oh, thanks, I think I'm going to skip lunch. Too much excitement. Can you excuse me? I just need to find a bathroom," she kept her tone light.

The attendant moved out of the way, allowing Amanda to walk forward. Taking her phone in her hand, she started a group chat with Melody and Lyla.

Meet in the lobby. No time for food.

Both women responded with a thumbs-up reaction.

Amanda couldn't pretend with them anymore—not with the prototype still hidden, Katherine ignoring texts, and questions multiplying by the hour. If there was any hope of making sense of it all, she needed allies who weren't in the spotlight. Not handlers. Not a man she deeply cared about and couldn't come clean with yet. But her best friend, and a woman who she felt understood her like no one else could.

She made it back to the, still buzzing when she saw Melody and Lyla close behind. The auction had taken place in one of the hotel's lower-level ballrooms, repurposed for the summit's highest-security events. The sprawling complex was perfect for anything from small meetings to large-scale productions. Every wing was spilling over with post-sale media, guests, and executives all jostling for space beneath gold-framed signage and bright chandeliers.

They rode in silence to the upper floors, the hush of the suite level a stark contrast to the static-charged frenzy below. As the elevator doors opened, Amanda moved with quiet precision, leading them past rooms tucked behind frosted glass, the carpet beneath their heels muffling every step. They didn't speak until she unlocked the door to her suite.

Lyla glanced around with a head bob and flick of her hands. "Okay. What is it that you two aren't telling me? You brought me here to kill me?"

Amanda didn't laugh. She walked to the minibar and poured herself a glass of chilled white wine.

Melody stood by the window, glancing out at the skyline, clearly waiting before saying a word herself.

Amanda turned, bracing herself against the edge of the counter. "There's something I need to tell you. Something I should've told you days ago."

"Me or her?" Lyla thumbed toward Melody.

"She has a prototype," Melody blurted.

"Of what?" Lyla's voice went from confusion to distress. "That thing? The Ocular Grid?"

Amanda nodded, wordless.

"There better be something stiffer in that cooler than *white wine*," the alliteration on her lips pierced the air as Lyla approached the refrigerator, finding the scotch on a tray close by.

"There's a lot that I need to tell you both," Amanda admitted. "I don't know how much time we have, but I'm gonna need your help."

"Should we sit for this?" Lyla let the liquid sting her tongue before slamming it back and going in for another pour.

"Yeah," Melody's tone sounded more pensive than terse as she left her spot by the window. She and Amanda walked to the couches in the seating area of the suite while Lyla grabbed the whole bottle along with her crystal tumbler and joined them.

Amanda reached for the bottle and set it on the small table next to her side of the couch. "We'll keep the midday whisky to a minimum," she dipped her chin, scrunching her lips together.

"That depends on what else you're gonna say," Lyla sneered, a familiar gesture to her best friend when things went from typical, carefree Lyla, to dead-serious, *I'm not playing* Lyla. The switch was fast and fierce.

"Fair," Amanda responded.

She wasn't sure where to begin, so she thought she'd address the highest point of contention in the room. "Melody. I did know it was a prototype. But I don't know the depths of what it means or how you, Russell, Julius, Tristan, or anyone else is involved. But, Katherine gave it to me, claiming that she thinks I need to be the one in possession of it so that Tristan stays safe."

"Who the hell is Katherine?" Lyla quipped.

"Her handler," Melody replied.

Amanda's eyes widened, surprised at Melody's use of the word.

"Okay, am I the only one in the dark here? Explain it to me like I'm five, okay? Because—news flash—I'm the only one *not* in on this subplot," Lyla said, already feeling the buzz after her second shot.

"My husband was CIA," Melody explained.

Lyla panned her face slowly from one end of the couch to the other, looking at each woman silently.

"I'm not CIA," Amanda said quickly. "I... don't know what I am."

"Isn't that worse?" Lyla quipped.

"Kind of." Amanda took a breath. "A woman approached me in Rome. Before I met you guys for that surprise birthday dinner in June, and... it was a setup. I don't know how, but they must have put some pieces together. I don't know if they want to control Tristan or just his invention, but they blackmailed me to keep close to him."

"Who's they?" Lyla insisted.

"My best guess? Everyone. Katherine, the woman who approached me, the... handler," she choked on the word, "is MI6, Julius is CIA, and Hansen apparently hired Katherine's front company to spy on Tristan and Envisage."

"A spy with a front company of spies?" Lyla huffed, "Convenient. And kinda genius."

"And Russell?" Melody asked.

"He was just a guy at a party for all I knew. I was whisked away to an extravagant retreat, wined and dined, and... I wasn't paying attention to every detail."

"Bullshit," Lyla flicked her head.

"I'm not bullshitting, Lyla," Amanda insisted. "I was so enamored with the scenery, the opulence, Tristan," she barely took a breath until saying his name.

"Fine," Lyla said, "But walk us back. You had to have seen something. I know you. Your mind doesn't just forget details."

Amanda rested her back on the seat, taking a sip of her wine and closing her eyes.

"Where did you first see Russell?" Melody asked.

"At the party, I think," she paused. "No... at the house. He was among the guests who came in before we got on the yacht." She remembered looking just past the stairs of the wide entryway of the Tenerife mansion. "Shit, he was there. I think he was unloading something from the car."

Lyla leaned forward, soberly. "Now we're gettin' some-where," she said, putting her elbows to her knees. "Where else?"

"I... I don't remember," Amanda kept her eyes closed, shaking her head as if trying to jostle a memory loose.

"Okay, so the next time you see him—what?" Lyla asked.

Amanda opened her eyes, painfully aware of what she was about to describe. "It's okay," Melody nodded. "It's why I'm here."

"The next time I see him, we're at the party. I'm with Esmé," Amanda continued, "Everyone seems uncomfortable with his presence. And then... he just... died. People said he had a heart attack, but I knew. I mean, I suspected something wasn't right. He didn't just fall over and grab his heart. He choked." Amanda reached for Melody's hand, tears threatening to rise. "I'm so sorry. He was foaming at the mouth. I couldn't watch it. I just ran."

Melody sat silently, unable to shed a tear about her husband's passing. She thought she'd be the type to cry herself to sleep at night. When you're twenty years your partner's junior, there's an assumption that you'll eventually be widowed in life. And though anytime Melody would think about it in the past, she imagined herself being paralyzed, unable to live or breathe without her partner. But when she got news of Russell's death, she was the exact opposite–mobilized and determined.

Lyla nodded at Amanda, "So, why would they want Russell dead? If Hansen is trying to control things, was he afraid of Russell? Using him?" she asked.

"Russell wouldn't sell out. There's no way he was in bed with Hansen," Melody chimed in. "He was so loyal to his nationalistic ideology that it made him stick out like a sore thumb. He never once told me he was a spy. Me, his wife. He would always say that he traveled on behalf of an insurance firm that assesses geopolitical risk for high-net-worth clients and corporations."

"So, Julius' cover was safe, and so was his," Amanda deciphered.

"Yeah, but then, where does Vivian fit in? Why would they want her dead?" Melody continued to pull at the strings.

"Wait. There's *another* dead person?" Lyla shrieked, reaching for the alcohol and pouring another shot. She slammed it and thunked her body backwards into the cushions. "You're serious?"

Amanda's lips peeled over her teeth with a wince. Melody exhaled through her nose, the corners of her mouth twitching into a faint smile. "Dead serious," she said quietly, her voice steady but without its usual bite.

A wave of laughter caught the air between them, as they all tried to fight back the giggles.

"What is happening?" Lyla finally uttered.

"Who the hell knows!" Amanda said.

"I think I've just found my people," Melody let a soft grin spread across her face.

Lyla put her glass on the end table, leaning in and trying to speak as soberly as possible. "Hey, whatever this is, I got you. We've got you. Damn Jimmy Hansen doesn't scare me one bit."

"Jimmy Hansen?" Melody snorted, staring at the women with a *please tell me you're kidding* look. She couldn't imagine that Lyla would have the balls to go up against the man rumored to be the next United States Presidential candidate.

Lyla shook her head with a sardonic *Yeah, it's true,* grin. "It's fine. We go way back."

"Oh, man," Melody took a breath. "But, what could they possibly have on you?" she spouted, sucking the air out of the room completely.

Amanda gave Lyla a look, and she returned it with the faintest shrug—the kind that said, *"Your move."*

"I'm the one he has something on. I got pregnant in high school," Amanda admitted. "The father was Governor Hansen's son," she tried to let that explanation be enough.

"But..." Melody wanted to protest. To say that couldn't be the reason Amanda would commit to spying or risking her life. But she couldn't say more. Not as a mother, or a woman. She had to let it be, accepting whatever pain was behind that truth without question.

"It's complicated," Lyla tried to deflect, allowing her friend to share only what she was ready to.

"It's okay," Amanda assured. "They took her from me. My baby."

Melody drew in a small, sudden breath, her hand instinctively reaching for Amanda's.

"They separated us, and... Cooper and I were so young. There's so much more to the story."

Amanda hesitated. She wasn't sure how much Lyla could handle. It wasn't only that she'd been keeping the details of the past few months from her best friend; she'd actually never spoken about the accident. The boat ride that changed her life forever. She let a tear escape her eyes.

"When we first met, Cooper and I were only fifteen. His mom didn't like us dating. I mean, *no one* liked us dating, but the only way we could continue seeing each other was if we snuck around. But... since the Hansen men weren't exactly discreet about their affairs, we were allowed to tag along on outings sometimes. Cooper had caught his grandpa and dad more than once with mistresses, so he kind of blackmailed them, I guess."

"Kind of?" Melody questioned.

"Yeah, well, I guess it runs in the family," Amanda said. "So, one night, when we were out on the boat, there was an accident," she threw up air quotes around the word *accident,* so there wouldn't be any confusion. "And Mr. Bubba's girlfriend died. Cooper's dad was already a state rep by then, and everyone acted like their name was too important to be questioned."

She exhaled slowly. "She was so young, nervous, probably barely thirty, now that I look back. They were drinking, and they let us sneak a beer or two, so we hardly paid attention, but then we heard arguing." Amanda's voice lowered. "I remember standing at the railing, hearing the slap of water against the hull, and then—" she glanced at Lyla, then at Melody.

Amanda's eyes clouded over as the memory surfaced. "She went overboard. Mr. Bubba shouted like it was an accident, but he dove in way too late. I was shaking, and Cooper was frozen. Mr. Jimmy didn't have a girl with him that night. He took the dinghy to shore and then showed up like he had rushed in after a call before the sheriff even finished taking notes. And by the next day, the papers called it a tragic fall."

She looked up again. "But I saw Mr. Bubba's hands on that woman's shoulders before she fell. I saw the fear in her face. And I saw how quickly the Hansens covered it all up. They told us to shut our mouths, to remember who we were dealing with. And we did. I mean, what were we supposed to do?"

It wasn't like Amanda didn't know that she had never told Lyla the details of the incident, but the look of shock on Lyla's face made her feel a sense of guilt that she hadn't prepared for. "They can make people disappear," Amanda whispered.

The room stayed quiet for another long moment before Lyla broke the silence.

"So that's why you never had a minute to breathe, huh? Flight hours, school stuff, drama—always running, never resting?"

Amanda gave a small shrug, her expression unreadable.

The three of them inhaled together, as if a single breath might steady the floor beneath them.

"We'll figure it out," Melody said, her voice resolute. "Whatever was born in this room today... I'm in."

"Yeah, same," Lyla added, planting one hand on her hip and raising the other in a half-hearted pose. "Avengers, assemble."

Amanda and Melody just stared at her, eyebrows lifted in quiet judgment.

Lyla sighed and waved her hand. "Okay, fine. We'll come up with something better."

She stood and pulled them both into a tight, impulsive hug.

"You are remarkably chill for this type of situation," Melody muttered with a smile.

"Augmenting real-time trauma with deflective humor?" Lyla said, grinning. "That's literally my job. And it's exactly why you need me on this team."

CHAPTER FIFTEEN

Tokyo: Second Day of Summit, 2:30 p.m.

Tristan texted Amanda from his meeting. *Sorry, the board is still meeting. You okay? Gonna be a while.*

The top investors of Envisage had insisted on immediately discussing what the rollout would look like since Helion won the bid. They expected a massive offer—maybe a few billion at most—but nothing that would jolt the room into silence. This bid didn't just surpass projections; it shattered assumptions about who truly held influence behind the scenes.

No one knew exactly who sat behind the name Helion Bridge Group, but that was the point. They were a syndicate wrapped in layers of corporate obscurity—part investment holding, part geopolitical smoke screen. Officially, they specialized in tech infrastructure for transitional economies. Unofficially, they were a bridge for global interests who didn't want to show their hands.

The group was registered in Liechtenstein, operated quietly out of Zurich, and—if the whispers were true—funded by a sovereign entity whose identity shifted depending on the region you were asking from. No known executives. No public-facing leadership. Just high-stakes assets and a fleet of lawyers. Their bid didn't just win them the Ocular Grid. It secured strategic influence under a layer of perfect ambiguity.

This posed a problem for Tristan and the team he had built at Envisage. Their promise that ethical tech could be scaled, sold, and still do good was what he preached at every meeting since its inception. His board had echoed the stance relentlessly. The vetting process had been multilayered and supposedly airtight. But clearly, something had gone amiss.

Amanda typed back. *I'm good. Hanging with the girls. Should I worry about your parents?*

Nah. They're good. Have fun. I'll see you later tonight. Maybe in the morning? He didn't use emojis much, but he sent a face palm with this one.

Oof. Good luck.

Yeah, thanks. I need it.

The board meeting wasn't celebratory. Tristan had walked into an unexpected storm after basking in the sunlight. Laptops were open, but no one was typing. He saw Julius sitting with his arms crossed, Renée Cho flanked by legal counsel, and Andre de Villiers reviewing a document so closely he hadn't his coffee had gone cold.

No one questioned the sale amount. Eight-point-eight billion was historic. But money wasn't the issue. It was about reputation, control, and legacy. De Villiers started the conversation and went on to list a series of questions for Tristan that the board had been discussing in the few minutes it took him to get from closing gavel to official gathering. *Who authorized the clearance for Helion? What connections, if any, exist between their assets and state actors? Did we just sell our most powerful innovation to a front company for geopolitical leverage? Can we undo it? Should we?*

They were still trying to get to the bottom of question one, and it had been nearly two hours. Tristan was not going to get out of there anytime soon.

"Well, girls, it looks like it's just us for the rest of the day," Amanda said, the room still spinning with a strange parallel universe vibe. "I haven't heard from Katherine in like forty-eight hours, so what do you say we go to one of your rooms and make it a war room?"

"Already on it," Melody said. Lyla widened her eyes, but Amanda only smiled.

"Can't say I'm surprised. Let's go." They slipped out a side entrance of the summit hotel.

Melody had chosen to stay at a boutique inn a few blocks away—stylish, but low-profile. There were no press or security sweeps—fewer eyes on the place. Amanda felt her shoulders ease slightly. Out here, she could let down her guard, if only for a moment. The city's anonymity offered a kind of safety that the summit could not. The walk wasn't long, but it was enough to bolster the energy between them. Amanda took deep breaths of the humid Tokyo air, grateful for the noise and movement of the city—bicycle bells chiming, ramen shops hissing with steam, snippets of conversation drifting past with the recognizable happy greeting, "sumimasen," she'd learned, making her mouth curl upward with appreciation. It dulled the echo of high-stakes tension and gave her a reminder of real life pulsing just beyond the summit bubble.

Melody led them down a quiet street tucked between a wine bar and an alley of cherry trees out of season, then gestured toward an unassuming door with a brushed steel handle. "This is me," she said simply. A minute later, they were climbing a narrow staircase to the third floor, where Melody unlocked her room with a quiet click.

The room was small—nothing like the suites at the summit hotel—but it was functional, quiet, and oddly warm. A single window looked out over the back alley, framed by heavy blackout curtains that had been pulled tight. The bed was made, but pushed to one side, clearly not the room's focus—that honor belonged to the wall across from it. Amanda paused in the doorway, taking in the sight: a map of interconnected names and cities stretched across the enormous papers strung together, anchored by tape, string, and thumbtacks. Scribbled notes—some typed, some handwritten—were layered over one another, curling slightly at the edges as if they'd been moved and removed a hundred times already.

In one corner, a grainy photo of Russell was pinned beside a flight manifest. Vivian Cross's name was written in red block letters. Julius's was underlined. Katherine's name had question marks beside it. And Amanda's name was dead center. Melody stepped in quickly and waved a hand, her tone apologetic. "I was trying to make sense of it all. Russell left me with pieces, but no instruction manual. I didn't think I'd be... showing anyone this."

Lyla whistled low. "Okay, Homeland. This is a vibe."

Amanda stepped forward, studying the notes, then glanced at Melody. "You don't have to be embarrassed. I mean, you were following me the first time we met. Don't think I forgot."

Melody nodded, her mouth twisting upward with a shrug.

"Honestly... It's kind of beautiful. In a deeply disturbing, possibly incriminating way," Amanda said.

Melody laughed under her breath. "Yeah, well, grief and paranoia make excellent project partners."

Amanda walked over to the edge of the map and gently touched a pinned photo of a radar facility. Her fingers lingered, the grainy image stirring a wave of unease. A chill crawled up her spine. She wasn't sure if it was fear, memory, or being in a role she didn't know how to play. "What do you think it means? You know, now that the Grid has been sold and is supposed to be operational."

Lyla dropped her purse on the bed, kicked off her heels, and flopped onto the one chair in the room.

"Okay, let's do it. You two talk, I'll move... erm... this," she said, taking the piece that had Amanda's name front and center and moving it to the side.

"Just tell me what to write. I'll be the secretary," she frowned. "We'll think of a better title."

Melody pulled out a folder from her suitcase and laid it on the desk.

"I've been tracking locations, names, and timing. Some of it doesn't make sense yet. But I think the answers are already here. We just haven't asked the right questions."

Amanda looked at the map again, her gaze sweeping across the network of names and strings like it might suddenly reveal secrets. "Then let's start asking."

"Okay, question one: Julius," Melody said, "Do we think he's gone rogue? What would he have to gain by it?" She wrung her hands slightly. "He's been in the business for decades, and he's not young. I don't want to be blinded by my suspicion and anger that he didn't protect Russel. Do you think he's really after power?"

Amanda shook her head. "Okay, theory one: Julius is CIA, like he told me he was in Tenerife, in full cooperation with England and other allies, hoping to keep control of the Grid. It's not about his power, it's about his job. He's got full government backing, so it's about *their* power."

Lyla took a blank sheet of paper from the stash of notebooks on the desk and taped it next to Julius' name. "Do you have a theory number two?"

"He *is* about power and control," Melody stated emphatically. "He's worked for world powers for too long and wants his legacy to be something different. It's the perfect setup. He's got Katherine's ear, who also has the backing of a major global economy, and no one would suspect his dissent. So, instead of trying to convince Tristan to release his tech to him, he just controls him behind the scenes. Because I'm pretty sure that thing they just sold was more like a licensing deal and not a handover."

"Sinister," Lyla mumbled while writing: *wants money & control,* as theory number two. "But what about a third theory?" she paused. "You said he's in with Hansen, right?"

Amanda nodded.

"And that Hansen thinks Katherine is a private spy?" Lyla asked.

"Yeah, that's why he approached her to protect his assets."

"So, theory three," she began writing, "I think it's sabotage. He wants no one to have it. Sees the danger in all the shit that can—and, if I may, *will*—go wrong when this stuff is implemented."

"That would mean he has a conscience," Melody jeered. "But, okay, sabotage is plausible—whatever the motive."

"Alright, let's talk about Katherine." Lyla moved to another side of the map.

"I can't get a read on her," Amanda said. "This is the second time she's ghosted me since she blackmailed me into this mess."

"And she's playing both sides, Hansen and you?" Lyla asked.

"Literally—being a double agent is supposedly her cover," Amanda confirmed.

Melody stepped up and drew a string from Katherine to Hansen. "But why would a guy who is supposed to start his campaign for the President of the United States next year be involved in this? Won't he be able to have access to the CIA, FBI, and any other intel he wants if he wins?" she asked.

"The operative word being, *if*," Amanda said. "It's leverage. If you're in with the controlling parties, you're in all the way.

So is Hansen part of the Helion Group, do you think?" her voice lowered.

"Well, if he is, didn't he just get what he wanted?" Lyla shrugged.

"Maybe," Amanda said. "So, let's say he's *not* in—who could he use to *get* in?"

"Russell," Melody muttered. She walked to the little desk where more papers were stacked, drawing out a few small labels that had words scribbled on them. "He used to write in code. He taught our boys, too. I used to think it was just a fun game for them—making cyphers and riddles that took them hours to decode. But, look." She pulled out a page that had a few letters circled on it. The red loops on the paper nearly glowed. She pointed to each of them slowly. "H-E-L-I-O-N," she spelled aloud.

"Russell *was* working for Helion?" Lyla gasped.

"I still don't think so. Not directly, but Julius holds a lot of weight in the CIA. If he thought he could use Russell to spy on Helion, he'd do it," Melody said.

"Dang, back to Juliius. Do you think he was acting alone, or was it a mission they were both assigned to?" Lyla then paused, the weight of the implication hitting her mid-sentence.

Amanda's stomach tightened. "So, if Julius had a guy on the inside," she echoed, "then why would he want Russell dead? Katherine told me that Lucien was the one to watch."

Lyla's eyes darted to Melody. "Do you think Russel is about to blow Julius' cover? Was Lucien onto them?"

"I wish I knew," she groaned.

A hush fell over the room, every second stretched longer, with their minds working through the information like puzzle pieces resistant to snapping into place. It wasn't silence so much as a systems-check—internal circuits firing behind thoughtful faces. Lyla took an audible inhale, blowing it out again with even more force.

"What about these other players? Azizi Malonga, the weird guy who hands a note to the auctioneer as a statement. What was that about?"

"Yeah, wait. Let's talk about that for a minute," Amanda said. "He's supposed to be the man with all these secret global influences. He's got these actual paper bonds worth billions from countries who don't want to—or can't afford to—cash them out. Why would his nonparticipation be the thing that causes a stir and sets Helion up for the win?"

"They're bedfellows," Melody spouted as if it had to be fact.

"Say more," Lyla insisted.

"Okay, say Malonga is the guy to beat, so to speak," Melody elaborated. "Everyone thinks so going in, but when he pulls out, Helion's bid is secured. A sure thing. There were no other registered bidders with that kind of capital. So, if Malonga then pays Helion the money, or even better, hands over just a portion of those bonds that someone has guaranteed, it's game over. He gets control without having to be the front man."

"Now, that makes sense," Lyla agreed.

"I don't know... that's not the..." Melody hesitated slightly before she remembered who she was talking to, "It's just not the vibe I get from him."

"Well, it's a theory," Lyla said, writing on the paper next to Malonga's name. *Possible moneybags overlord.* She turned around slowly before looking them in the eyes again.

"But, you guys, we like, have another dead person here on this board, right?" She pointed to the name that caught her eye while she was writing. Vivian Cross was scribbled in bright blue ink over the ocean waters, right near Russell's name.

"Yeah," Amanda sighed. "I think I'll have to put a pin in that one. I can't make heads or tails of her involvement."

"Me either," Melody admitted. "I thought Lucien would give me a clue, but I don't think he has any idea either. Or he's just not willing to dig into anything that would endanger him."

"That's fair," Lyla said.

Amanda felt her phone vibrate and turned to see Katherine's text on the screen. *Had to make a short trip to Chengdu. Will be at the hotel by six. Great results at the auction. Do you have time to meet?*

She turned the phone towards Melody and Lyla without saying anything.

"Great results?" Melody's eyes widened.

"What? She doesn't have flight time wifi? And where the heck is Chengdu?" Lyla said.

"China," both women answered in unison.

"Great, the last thing we need is another superpower to decode," Lyla plopped herself on the bed with a huff. "It's like a geopolitical escape room, and we just triggered a new level."

"Well, before we tackle all of China, let's just act normal," Amanda said. "I think we're onto something here, but I've gotta go meet Katherine, and we have a ball to attend tomorrow, and some pretty badass dresses to wear."

"Ah, it always comes back to the most important things in life, doesn't it? Those little moments that make you say, 'I'm glad to be alive,'" Lyla smirked.

Melody let out a breath she must have been unintentionally holding. "Always," she joined in the banter before taking a more serious tone. "I knew this would be a good thing," she said, nodding at Amanda.

"Well, good or bad, it looks like it's a thing," Lyla said.

"It's *definitely* a thing," Amanda laughed.

As they left Melody's hotel, Amanda hugged both women tightly.

The wind had picked up slightly, brushing strands of her hair across her cheeks as she turned the corner near the summit hotel. The buzz of Tokyo felt impossibly softer and quieter than the little war room she'd created with Melody and Lyla.

She found Katherine waiting near a low stone wall that framed a garden behind the hotel. She wore a slate-gray coat cinched tightly at the waist and a pair of black leather gloves that looked too delicate for actual warmth. She didn't wave when Amanda approached, just tilted her head with that maddeningly calm expression that made Amanda feel both guarded and ten years old.

"I was beginning to think you'd lost interest," Amanda said, crossing her arms.

Katherine gave a faint smile. "Not lost. Redirected. I had a meeting I couldn't postpone."

"In China?"

Katherine's gaze flicked upward, then back. "Yes."

Amanda waited, expecting more—but of course, nothing came. "You could have told me."

"I could have," Katherine agreed. "But I needed you to operate without expecting a safety net. We weren't sure how things would unfold."

Amanda narrowed her eyes. "We?"

Katherine ignored the question. "You did well. Better than projected."

"Are you going to keep talking to me like I'm some kind of case study, or are we going to get real for a second?"

A pause stretched between them, and then—perhaps surprisingly—Katherine gave a small nod.

"Very well. Helion's bid changes everything. Certain parties are concerned that the sale compromised the ethical positioning Envisage built its foundation on."

Amanda scoffed. "You think?"

"That concern now becomes our leverage," Katherine continued smoothly. "We believe Helion is not a monolith. There are factions within it—some driven by control, others by containment. Your job, if you're willing, is to stay close to Tristan. Observe. Keep your instincts sharp."

"Which ones?" Amanda asked. "The ones that say he's too good to be true, or the ones that believe he's just in over his head?"

"I trust you to know the difference."

Amanda exhaled, suddenly tired. "But you vanished again. After all that talk about partnership and trust. You expect me to keep doing this without even knowing what I'm inside of."

"I'm not here to win your trust," Katherine said softly. "I'm here to keep you alive long enough to decide what to do with the truth when it finally lands."

Amanda gave a dry laugh, her voice laced with disbelief. "You always say it like I have a choice. Like any of this is mine to walk away from."

Katherine stepped closer, her tone low. "Then let me be clear. We're in a litmus test for power structures—who wants the Grid, who can be trusted with it, and who's willing to burn down the house to make sure no one has it. You are the one variable no one accounted for. So, just be ready."

"For what?"

Katherine's eyes glinted. "For a signal."

Without another word, she turned and disappeared around the side of the building, her footsteps silent against the stone.

Amanda stood still. Her heart hammered in her chest, unsure whether she'd just been warned or dismissed. The echo of Katherine's final words lingering, she felt the chill of the stone path through her shoes, the sharp edge of night settling. A memory flickered—her first flight solo, the way her hands had trembled just before takeoff. This felt the same. The world watching, the stakes unclear, and no co-pilot. Her phone vibrated.

No dinner. Breakfast it is. See you in the morning.

Amanda's heart sank. It wasn't strategy she craved now—it was presence. Warmth. A quiet, unspoken tether to remind her she hadn't slipped too far from herself. She stared at the screen for a moment, then sent a single emoji: a sad face, small and insufficient.

A moment later, his reply buzzed through. *I'll kiss you when I come in.* Amanda exhaled softly, the breath shaky, one she hadn't realized she'd been holding. It wasn't a promise, but it was an anchor.

CHAPTER SIXTEEN

Tokyo: Third Day of Summit, 7:45 a.m.

"Hey, you're here," Amanda's voice was a drowsy whisper, her eyes still half-closed as she stretched beneath the sheets.

Tristan turned from the tray he'd just set by the window. He moved slowly, barefoot and shirtless, the morning light catching on his collarbone and the faint shadows beneath his eyes. She watched the sharp lines of his torso as he moved, a flutter rising in her chest.

"I've been trying to wake you," he said softly, crossing to her side. "You wouldn't budge."

She smiled, stretching out her arms to him. "You should've tried harder."

"I thought about kissing you awake last night," he murmured, sitting beside her and brushing a fingertip along the slope of her shoulder. "But it got so late. And you looked too peaceful. Too perfect."

"Liar," she said, reaching out to slide her hand around the back of his neck, pulling him gently down toward her. Their lips met slowly, sleep-warm and unhurried, a kiss between dreams and daybreak.

"What time did you come in?" she asked when he pulled back, her fingers still curled into his hair.

"After two," he said. "I didn't want to startle you."

"But you said you'd kiss me when you came in."

"I know," he whispered, forehead resting against hers. "I hated not keeping that promise."

Amanda tilted her head, brushing her lips against his again. "You can make it up to me."

He smiled. "Room service is part one."

"Tell me there are raspberries," she murmured.

"Fresh," he lifted his palm as if he was going to serve them to her right there.

She stretched languidly beneath the sheets, then patted the space beside her. "Bring them over. I'm suddenly starving."

He smiled, leaning down to press another kiss to her collarbone before slipping off the bed to retrieve the tray. "Okay, coming in hot."

He wheeled the cart beside her and eased the silver domes open, each movement unhurried, as though savoring a secret, uncovering their contents like a magician mid-reveal. Amanda sat up, wrapping the sheet around her as she peeked under the silver dome.

"God, that smells incredible," she said.

"Raspberries, croissants, eggs so perfect they should be illegal," he announced, pouring the coffee.

"Are you serving it or selling it?" Amanda joked as he handed her a cup and settled beside her, one leg folded beneath the other.

They ate in easy silence for a few moments, the quiet broken only by the clink of forks and the occasional sound of the city waking up beyond the windows.

"So, how was your day yesterday? We don't need to talk about mine," Tristan's eyebrows lifted with over-emphasized drama.

Amanda glanced at him, eyes lifting above the rim of her cup, her smile easy. "It was good. Low-key."

"You and the girls hung out?"

"Yeah. Lyla, Melody, and I spent some time at Melody's hotel. Nothing fancy."

He tilted his head, curious but not pressing. "What'd you do there?"

She took a bite of a croissant, chewing thoughtfully. "Honestly? We just talked. Got to know each other better."

"About what?" he asked, grinning. "World domination? Facial serums? Secret pasts? Tell me there was a pillow fight."

"Exactly," she replied with a smirk. "You're four for four."

Tristan laughed, reaching to brush a crumb from her lip. "I like knowing that Lyla is here. I wish Kyle could've come, but

I get it. He used to be my ride-or-die in college, you know. I kind of bailed on him for a few years, though." An atypical moment of reflection seemed to hit Tristan without expecting it. He dismissed it quickly. "Anyway...What's Melody like?"

"She's surprising," Amanda said softly. "There's more to her than you think."

He watched her for a beat longer, his smile fading as he curled his bottom lip under his teeth. "Honestly, I don't think about Melody much... but you? I think about you a *lot*," he smiled, tugging at the sheets, watching the fabric slip off her body. "There's more to you than I think, too."

Amanda looked down at her plate. "That's probably true," she tilted her head, mimicking his lip bite. He slowly reached over and took her plate, setting it gently back on the tray without a word.

"That was part one of my apology," he said, his voice soft and low.

"Oh?" she asked, arching a brow.

As his hands rested lightly on either side of her hips, he leaned into her. "Part two," he murmured, "requires fewer napkins."

Her breath caught, but she didn't move. "Is that so?"

"Mm-hmm." He kissed the inside of her wrist, then her shoulder, slow and deliberate. "And we don't have to be anywhere until this evening."

Amanda tilted her head, letting her fingers drift lazily through his hair. "So you're saying I finally get your full attention?"

"All of it," he whispered, brushing his lips just beneath her jaw.

Tokyo, Third Day of Summit: The Envisage Gala 5:30 p.m.

Music slipped through the halls like perfume—low, smoky jazz curling from a quartet tucked beneath a ceiling of crystal and candlelight. The notes weren't loud; they didn't need to be. They threaded through the room, seductive and slow, reminding every guest that luxury had its own language.

Amanda stepped forward, her heels clicking softly against the marble of the hallway to the main ballroom, the train of her slate-colored gown brushing the floor behind her. She walked alone. Despite his best efforts to avoid them, Tristan had spent most of the day locked in meetings. While she got ready, their messages had been brief—short check-ins between obligations. Even the girls had gone mostly quiet, saving energy for whatever performance the evening required of them.

"Damn," Lyla murmured at Amanda's side, her voice low but unmistakably amused. "You clean up nice."

Amanda turned slightly. Lyla stood radiant in a black satin jumpsuit with a plunging neckline and sequined cuffs, her curls swept back in a way that struck the perfect balance between glamour and rebellion.

"You're not so bad yourself," Amanda winked. "Seriously, though. You look like you just stepped off a Vanity Fair cover."

Lyla kissed the air toward Amanda with a wink before her eyes flicked around the room. "Too bad this place is crawling with future dictators and polished liars," she kept her voice low. "Otherwise, I might even enjoy myself."

Amanda's smile lingered, but her gaze drifted. She spotted Esmé in a crimson sheath dress, floating through a small circle of admirers like a woman born to command attention. Julius, as expected, was absent, whether tucked away in another closed-door meeting or hurrying to get ready, she wasn't sure. Her last text from Tristan said that he'd make it before cocktail hour ended.

"I think I'm going to make the rounds," Amanda said quietly. "You want to see if Melody's here yet?"

Lyla tipped her head. "Copy that. I'll check the bar. I mean—it's where I'd be."

They entered the room, Amanda gliding deeper into the crowd while Lyla stayed along the sides. A delicate chime of crystal on glass echoed through the space, with ripples of laughter and light conversations filling each corner.

"Looking for someone?" came a voice near Amanda's shoulder.

She turned to find Anton Filby in a sharp navy tuxedo, raising his champagne glass in greeting. His silver hair gleamed under the chandeliers, and his smile was laced with knowing charm.

"Hey, Anton," Amanda replied, her tone light. "Just making my way around the room. Wouldn't want to miss the chance to congratulate the lucky winners."

He chuckled and offered a slight bow. "Don't forget to find Clarisse tonight too," he said, tipping his glass once more before disappearing into the crowd.

Amanda pressed on, skimming the edge of conversation clusters, feeling both watched and invisible all at once. When she saw Esmé, she lingered at the periphery, letting her gaze drift to the sculpted folds of her gown—an architectural silhouette in shimmering bronze, catching the light like molten metal. Esmé turned, and her face lit up.

"Amanda! Finally. I was beginning to think I wouldn't get a proper word with you at all."

Amanda's smile came easily. "It's been nonstop."

Esmé reached out, her fingers warm and steady on Amanda's forearm. "You look radiant, my dear. But of course, you would. Tonight feels like something of a coronation, doesn't it?"

Amanda laughed softly. "Not sure there's a crown involved."

"Oh, please," Esmé waved a hand with theatrical flair. "You're luminous. I crown you myself," she said, the words almost sung in her signature melodic cadence.

They stepped away from the swell of conversation with others. "If Tenerife hadn't ended so abruptly," Esmé continued, her voice dipping with a trace of regret, "I think I might have talked you into staying longer. We barely made it past introductions."

Amanda's expression softened. "I would've liked that too. It already feels like a different lifetime."

"It was supposed to be restful," Esmé said with a wistful smile. "Instead, we were left with ghost stories no one dares to repeat."

Amanda caught the phrasing, hesitant to point it out. She knew the powers that be didn't expect talk of the deaths at the summit.

"I'm going to grab a drink," she said gently. "I didn't get one when I came in. Just wanted to say hi."

"Of course, darling. But don't disappear for too long."

Amanda gave a grateful smile as she turned toward the entrance where waiters floated by with trays of sparkling wine. But she didn't take more than a few steps before she saw Tristan. The notable shift in the room should have told her that the night was just about to begin.

He walked in like a spark in slow motion, his bowtie slightly loosened in that intentional, effortless way that made him look unrehearsed. His eyes found hers without hesitation, and, after crossing the room with quiet purpose, he took her hand in his, as though it belonged there.

"You're stunning," he said, his voice low and certain. "I don't care who else is in this room."

She felt the weight of the crowd's eyes land on them. The spectacle wasn't lost on her.

"Careful," she murmured, lips barely moving. "I might start believing you."

He leaned in, brushing a kiss across her cheek. "I hope you do believe it. I'm done with stress and strategy—tonight, I'm celebrating."

He twirled her into his arms, and the music seemed to rise to meet them—an elegant waltz wrapped in jazz improvisation. Amanda followed his lead, their motions instinctive. She let the warmth of his hand at her waist and the soft pressure of his palm against hers pull her into the moment. As if on cue, a dozen couples or more began to join them, striding toward the luxurious marble dancefloor and elegantly jiving with partners.

She let the moment carry her, matching his rhythm without thinking, the scent of his cologne clean and dark, familiar to her now. He held her a little closer with each step, his voice just above a whisper.

"There's no pitch tonight," he said. "No press, no presentation. Just dancing, food, wine... and you."

She looked up at him, surprised by the simplicity in his tone.

"I'm really glad you came," he added, his eyes not leaving hers. "You could've disappeared, and I wouldn't have blamed you. But you didn't."

Amanda's breath caught, not from surprise, but from how quickly his words bypassed her defenses. She didn't answer right away. Instead, she let her cheek rest lightly against his shoulder as they turned with the music.

"I almost did," she admitted.

He nodded. "But you didn't."

"No," she said. "I didn't."

They danced in silence for a few bars more, the noise of the room fading behind the velvet layers of the music. She could feel the steadiness in his chest, the subtle way he adjusted his hold, guiding her without pressure. Just as Amanda was beginning to forget the room entirely, a familiar voice cut through the music with perfectly timed irreverence.

"Well, well, look at you two. I leave you alone for five minutes and suddenly it's a frickin' movie scene in here."

Amanda laughed softly as she turned to see Lyla, a champagne flute in one hand and a mischievous glint in her eye. Her jumpsuit shimmered with each step like a well-timed spotlight.

"I'm just saying," Lyla continued, lowering her voice theatrically, "the lighting is suspiciously good, the music's way too romantic, and you," she pointed at Tristan, "are officially making the rest of us look bad."

He grinned but didn't let go of Amanda. "I'll take that as a compliment."

"You should... but, I gotta steal your girl here for like, five minutes, okay?"

He let Amanda go with a nod and a playful protest. "Five."

Amanda followed as Lyla looped her arm through hers, steering them off the dancefloor and toward the quieter edge of the ballroom, where the lighting dimmed and the crowd thinned around ornamental planters and diplomatic small talk.

"You okay?" Amanda asked as they walked. "You've got that face."

"What face?" Lyla countered, eyes forward.

"The one you make when you're about to say something but wish you didn't have to."

Lyla gave a noncommittal shrug. "Maybe. But not here. I need five minutes where no one's eavesdropping."

Amanda's brow lifted. "Did you find Melody?"

Lyla slowed. "It's not about Melody."

Amanda stopped walking. "Lyla, what's going on?"

But before Lyla could answer, a crisp voice interrupted them.

"Well, if it isn't Amanda Hopkins and Lyla McCafferty."

They turned simultaneously, as if the motion was suspended in time, finding Mrs. Elizabeth Hansen standing just a few feet away, perfectly composed in a sleek burgundy gown, her tone familiar, plunging them into the memory of being caught climbing through her son's bedroom window when they were fifteen.

Amanda's artificial smile came automatically. "Mrs. Hansen. I wasn't expecting to see you here tonight."

"Neither was I," she replied smoothly. "But my husband insisted. Flew the whole family here yesterday. Still battling a little jet lag, but he said it was a can't-miss evening. And apparently, he was right."

Lyla cleared her throat. "So good to see you, Mrs. Hansen. But we were actually just on our way out for some air."

The Governor's wife tilted her head, still smiling. "Of course you were, girls. I'm gonna find my husband with that drink he was supposed to fetch me. Ya'll enjoy the night, okay?"

As Mrs. Hansen turned away with that signature half-smile—poised, dismissive, and dangerously sweet—she blended back into the swell of the ballroom without another word.

Amanda released the breath she was holding, turning to face Lyla. "Well. That wasn't terrifying at all."

Lyla didn't laugh. In fact, she hadn't budged. Her gaze remained fixed just over Amanda's shoulder. Amanda began to follow it instinctively, but Lyla caught her arm before she could turn.

"Wait."

Amanda blinked. "What?"

Lyla took a deep breath, her voice suddenly too soft for Amanda to hear without leaning in. "This is what I was trying to tell you before we bumped into her."

The confusion on Amanda's face didn't need elaboration. She just shook her head with a *what are you trying to say* look as she tried again to turn towards the ballroom.

Lyla's eyes were gentle now, bracing. "He's here, Amanda."

"Who?" Amanda stopped.

Lyla hesitated before saying it. "It's Cooper."

The name hit harder than she expected. It was a jolt low in her ribs, like a muscle remembering that it once ached—that it even could.

"What?" The word came out breathless, smaller than she meant.

"He just walked in over by the bar. Melody and I had been chatting, and Lyla paused. "I saw him. It's him, and he's not exactly blending in with the crowd."

Amanda swallowed, suddenly aware of the weight of her own heartbeat. "Why didn't anyone tell me he was coming? Damn Katherine."

"I don't know," Lyla said gently. "But I didn't want you to have a jump scare in, like, the middle of a champagne toast or something."

Amanda nodded, eyes unfocused. Her voice barely carried as she fought back tears. "Thank you."

She took a moment before finally turning. But as she did, she couldn't help scanning the room, searching for a glimpse of someone she wasn't sure she was ready to see. But as if all other objects had fallen away, across the ballroom, and just beyond the soft golden haze, Cooper Hansen was smiling, sipping his drink, and chatting with people around him.

He looked older. Sharper around the edges. His jaw was more defined, carrying the weight of adulthood in the way that he stood, not rigid, but confident. His tux was classic black, understated compared to the room's gold-drenched decadence. And yet, Amanda couldn't take her eyes off him.

Each second stretched impossibly wide as her stare clamored to finally meet his. He took a step forward. Amanda's breath caught in her throat. Another step, and then he smiled. It wasn't a press smile or a polite, political nod. It was the smile she hadn't seen in eighteen years. With each stride, the room fell away. Lyla had moved to the side—her instinct to run interference completely vanished. It was as if there was a silent understanding; the three kids of yesteryear were gone, their comprehension of what had taken place matured. With one glance, their shared trauma was replaced with a forgiveness that sought answers and inner peace.

Cooper finally met Amanda, extending a hand without a word. Her lips parted, but no sound came out. There was no script for her to perform. Just the past, suddenly, impossibly—standing right in front of her. Amanda stared at his hand for a beat too long. Then—almost involuntarily—she reached out and took it.

The moment their palms met, a thousand memories surged forward at once: the way he used to loop pinky fingers with her during chapel, how he'd once traced the curve of her collarbone like it was sacred, how they'd sat in silence the night before everything changed. They ambled into the party pretending like they weren't in a ballroom built for empires and lies.

He gave her hand a gentle squeeze. "Hey, Mandy."

The name hit her like an open palm to the chest. He was the only person on earth whose voice made her nickname sound precious instead of provincial—like it belonged to a girl who was loved, not forgotten.

"I—" she started, then stopped. Her voice had caught somewhere between her stomach and her heart.

Cooper searched her face like a man who wasn't sure she was real. "You look…" He gave a quiet laugh and shook his head. "You look exactly like you. Just—all grown up."

Amanda kept her eyes glued on his. "You too," she finally spoke, heat rushing through her spine and making her scalp tingle.

Lyla finally stepped in. "Hi! Sorry," she said in a voice that wasn't sorry at all. "Cooper! What are the odds, am I right?" she said, pinching Amanda's arm as if to awake her from sleep.

Cooper offered her a small, respectful nod. "Hey, Lyla," he didn't say it, but Lyla hadn't changed a bit either. "I didn't mean to intrude," he returned his attention to Amanda. "I just… wasn't expecting to see you here."

"Yeah, I could say the same," Amanda exhaled.

"Well, Dad wanted the whole clan here. You know, buddying up with the stakeholders is never a bad idea for a campaign." Cooper spoke matter-of-factly.

That moment, Amanda realized she was still holding his hand, as she dropped it swiftly at the mention of his father.

"Wouldn't expect anything less," Lyla said, placing her other hand on Amanda's arm, trying to turn her away from him.

"I heard you went into politics," Amanda said, more neutral than she felt.

"I heard nothing after you disappeared," he replied, gentle but pointed.

The words stung—not because they weren't true, but because she had no choice. His parents had made sure of that. They cornered her, threatened to destroy her future—no MIT, no chance at having them give her school or aviation recommendations. And when they told her they could track his phone, she believed them. Every message, every attempt he made to reach her, she ignored—because answering him might have put them both in more danger. She hadn't just disappeared. She'd been silenced. Forced to protect him in a way he'd never understand.

And yet, out of everyone from her past, his disappointment was the one thing she still couldn't bear.

Lyla huffed, shifting beside her. "That's rich coming from you," she said, unable to articulate anything else.

Cooper deflected Lyla's comment, "Look, I didn't mean to throw ya'll off. I am just... surprised to see you," he nodded cordially with a smile.

"Me too," Amanda said. "I thought—" She shook her head, stopping for a moment. "I don't know what I thought." She gave Lyla a look that let her know she was okay. She wanted to talk to Cooper in the strange, magnetic way that a need for closure demands.

"I'm going to... grab us more champagne," Lyla said, eyes flicking between them. She pulled Amanda's ear to her mouth before whispering, "Yell if you need rescuing."

Amanda nodded with a smile, "Promise," she whispered.

"You look good," Cooper said quietly once Lyla had taken a few steps away.

"So do you."

A dense silence settled between them, the low thrum of the room filling the interval.

"I have so many questions," Cooper said.

"I don't know if I have answers," she replied.

He nodded. Then, almost like an afterthought: "You're happy?"

Amanda hesitated. The answer was yes. And no. And *don't ask me that here.*

She smiled instead. "I am. And you?"

Cooper looked at her for a long moment. "You know how it is," he smiled. "I'm definitely happy to see you. It's been so long."

"Eighteen years," Amanda said it like a reflex.

Cooper nodded, looking at the floor. It was the first time he had taken his eyes off her.

"Yeah, it's been a lifetime. And it took an occasion like this to bring us together again," he said. "I won't keep you, though. I'm sure you have obligations... and if I know Lyla, she'll be around in about three-point-five seconds.

Amanda exhaled a laugh, smiling.

Cooper leaned in, close enough that only she could hear.

"You still hold your breath when you're scared," he said, his voice gentle, almost wistful. "I used to know what that meant."

Before she could respond, a warm hand slipped around her waist.

"There you are," Tristan said, smiling as he appeared beside her. "I was starting to think I lost you to champagne and the girl squad."

His energy was radiant, proud, and electric. He pressed a kiss to Amanda's temple and turned to Cooper without pause.

"Hey there. Tristan Montgomery."

Cooper offered his hand, calm and neutral. "Cooper Hansen."

Amanda watched them shake hands—two men from very different phases of her life, one etched into her history like a scar beneath the surface, the other unfolding around her like an uncertain horizon.

"Good to meet you," Tristan said. "You here for the summit?"

"Something like that," Cooper said easily. "You two enjoy your night."

He gave Amanda one last look—measured, unreadable—and then walked back into the crowd, swallowed by silk and light.

Tristan turned to her, oblivious. "He seemed... intense. Friend of yours?"

Amanda smiled—soft, distant. "The Governor's son. We went to school together."

"Small world," Tristan said, pulling her back onto the floor, the music swelling again, rising not just in tempo but in the intensity that throbbed in her mind with every beat.

And just like that, like the world around her, she was spinning.

Chapter Seventeen

Tokyo: Third Day of Summit, 9:15 p.m.

THE GALA SHIMMERED LIKE a dream as it drew to a close—music softening, conversations thinning, and people excusing themselves to retreat for the evening. Amanda coasted through it all in the rhythm of someone half-removed, as if watching her own life through glass. She kept each step calculated, each smile a careful artifact of poise.

She had come face to face with the only boy who had known her before her life turned into a secret. Not just before the dossiers and disappearances, but before she had abandoned a version of herself she had no interest in reviving.

Amanda had gone through the night, pretending to be unbothered, tethered to Tristan with a smile that wasn't entirely false—but didn't feel quite as true as it had just an hour before, either. The effort of keeping her expression calm, her spine straight, and her voice steady was more exhausting than she expected any covert operation to be.

Amanda sat at a table, dangling her strappy heels from her fingers as she chatted with guests, a glass of untouched champagne nestled in the other hand. Inside the clutch at her side, her phone gave a buzz. She had almost forgotten she had it, the vibration kicking her thoughts towards Katherine, the only person not in the room who would text at this hour. She set her glass on the table and looked at the screen.

Possible compromise. Leave tonight. Instructions to follow.

Amanda tucked the phone under her palm without flinching. Peeling away from the conversation she'd been in, she drifted toward the far side of the ballroom, catching Lyla's eye across the bar. She tipped her head to the right, signaling Lyla to join her.

"Hey, what's up?" Lyla asked. "Did Tristan leave?"

"No, he's still stuck with that group of people over there trying to find out what the board was doing all day yesterday and today."

"What *were* they doing?" Lyla asked.

"You know, if I were better at this, I would have asked..." Amanda widened her eyes, "But... we didn't exactly talk much before they called him away again." She bit her lip.

Lyla gave her a knowing look. "That's my girl," she smiled.

"Shut up," Amanda chuckled. "Look, I think this is serious," she said, tilting her phone for Lyla to see.

Lyla moved her eyes from Amanda's to the phone and back. "I'll text Melody."

Come to the hallway. Near the terrace. Need to confab.

The words showed up in a text thread the women shared, a second notification appearing immediately after, which read: *Lyla Grant named the conversation: "Spyce Girls."*

Amanda looked at her screen, flipping it abruptly back to face Lyla. "Really?" She couldn't stifle a small laugh. "At a time like this?"

"Look, if I can't bring my whole self to this death-defying shindig, you're gonna have to find yourself another Posh, okay?"

Amanda let out a full laugh. "There's no one else I'd rather die with."

Lyla put her arm around Amanda with an affectionate tug as Melody reached the heavy velvet curtains near the terrace doors. "Hey, what's going on?" she asked.

"Just discussing our Spyce Girl names, I'm Posh, she's obviously Ginger, so the rest are up for grabs," Lyla offered.

"Spice Girls?" Melody couldn't hide her confusion—she hadn't noticed the second notification on their text thread.

"Yeah, you know, Spyce. Girls. Get it?" Lyla said, punctuating each syllable with a little wave of her hand in the air. "Spyce. With a 'y.'"

Melody pressed her lips together, unsure whether to laugh or be annoyed.

"Hey, I wasn't going to suggest *Scary* for you, but it *is* still available," Lyla flashed a toothy grin.

Melody's mouth cracked fully open, her lips curling up-ward. "Clever. No one will ever suspect," she mocked, giving Amanda a side eye. "And I'll be Sporty, thank you very much," finally committing to the bit.

"Okay, now that the pressing agenda is out of the way, ladies, I need your help," Amanda said, voice low, moving from teasing to somber. "I have to leave. Tonight. I mean, I think I do. Katherine says she's sending instructions, but that I have to get out. I just don't know if I should trust her—or run," the last word came out in a whisper.

She looked between the two women beside her, glancing first at Melody, steady, composed, and intense. Grief poured out of her in strange directions, not dramatic or loud, but sharp-edged and sudden, like something brittle cracking beneath pressure. She offered her collected information easily, as if it hurt more to keep it in than to give it away. That was what made Amanda nervous. She couldn't tell if Melody was sincere to a fault... or if Russell had inadvertently trained her better than even she realized.

And Lyla? She was there because no matter how far Amanda fell into this double life, she knew she could count on Lyla to keep herself tethered to the person underneath. She didn't flinch. She didn't ask for proof. She just rode the wave of movement like she brought along her magic carpet for the ride.

Amanda's jaw tightened. "I don't know what Katherine's really playing at. But if she says I have to leave, then something's about to give. And I'm not waiting around to find out what."

She caught Lyla's eye. "If I go, you don't have to come."

Lyla rolled her eyes. "Try leaving without me. I dare you."

Amanda let out a breath that was almost a laugh. Her pulse still raced, but her footing felt steadier. Something about having them beside her—Melody's cryptic loyalty, Lyla's unwavering presence—had drawn her back to center. This was the closest she'd felt to clarity in days. Her pulse still raced, but her footing felt steadier.

Melody nodded. "I'm in. Now, what about the prototype?"

Amanda hesitated. "It's still in the locker," she whispered.

"I'll go," Melody said. "No one will be watching me."

Amanda opened her mouth to protest, but stopped herself. She knew Melody was right. They couldn't leave without it, and she couldn't be the one to get it.

"Okay, let's just go to the lobby. I'll just tell Tristan that I'm tired and going to the room. It won't faze him."

Lyla nodded. "Alright. Here we go," her tone serious as ever.

They scurried along the hall, not saying another word, but before they reached the doors, Amanda spotted a familiar silhouette lingering just beyond the terrace archway, as if waiting for a chance to reemerge. Cooper was standing alone, waiting for the right moment to get her attention again.

"Amanda?"

She let go of Lyla's arm, waving her on before turning to face him. He stood with hands in his pockets, bowtie slightly loosened, the same quiet intensity in his eyes.

"I was hoping I'd catch you again before the night ended," he said, stepping closer, but carefully weighing the distance. "Can I... could I get your number?"

Amanda's eyes flickered, caught off guard by the question. "I—" she hesitated. "I heard you were engaged. Congratulations."

His head bowed low for a moment before looking at her again. "Thank you," he said. "That means a lot."

She offered a small smile. "I hope it's everything you wanted."

Cooper grinned wordlessly. "And for you?" he asked carefully. "Is this the life you imagined?"

"Hardly," Amanda scoffed. "But, here we are," she said.

He studied her for a moment before responding. "Yeah... It's something, seeing you again. After all this time. It feels like more than coincidence."

She didn't reply—there was too much history for one moment to carry all of its weight.

"I'd like to stay in touch," he finally continued. "I mean... if that's something you'd want too."

Amanda's eyes met his as she let out a breath, steady and calculated. "You take care of yourself, Cooper." As she walked swiftly away, she ignored his last glance, the pain in his eyes, and felt her heart stop. She paused. She wasn't about to let her quest for answers about someone else's puzzle be more important than her own. She turned on her heels and rushed back to his side, touching his elbow before putting her hand out.

"Your phone," she said quietly. He took his telephone from his pocket and placed it in her hand, fingers slightly brushing her palm. The touch made his skin quiver.

"Give me a few days. Don't text before then."

She lifted her gown with a turn and ran as quickly as she could in her eveningwear, down the steps and into the evening, hoping to disappear completely.

The hotel lobby glowed with oversized floral arrangements and a chandelier like a cluster of frozen stars, as Amanda moved through it with her head high, gown flowing behind her like the final note of a song. Her shoes now back on, she willed herself into an apparent calm, ignoring every burning emotion inside her that threatened to ignite like a powder keg.

She caught up with the women already perched on the edge of a velvet sofa near the cocktail bar, flipping through a digital menu like they'd simply decided on a nightcap.

"Hey," she said, somber as ever, taking a seat. "What do we do now?"

"We get the hell outta dodge," Lyla said flatly, like it was both a punchline and a battle plan.

"But how?" Melody asked.

Amanda took a breath. Her fingers moved quickly over her phone, opening a hidden app and logging into the offshore account the company had wired her when she first signed on. She hadn't touched it until now—because once she accessed it, there'd be a record. She figured she had one move, maybe two, before someone flagged the withdrawal.

The balance stared back at her. It was enough to vanish a dozen times over.

"I'll charter a jet," she said. "I've filed ghost flights be-fore—executive repositioning, no manifest required. We can launch out of Chofu or Yokota before sunrise. No customs. No delays."

"Just us?" Lyla asked.

Amanda looked up, eyes steady. "If you're still in."

Lyla smiled with a brave, irreverent tilt of her mouth, which Amanda had come to count on. "You think I packed this jumpsuit just to flirt with strangers?"

Melody cracked a smile. "Great," she said, glancing between them. "But where are we going?"

Amanda opened her mouth to answer, then closed it again. The question stuck in her throat, tangled in uncertainty. A flicker of unease rose in her chest—she hated operating without a plan, without knowing the next three moves. But maybe that was the point now: to follow the thread and trust her instincts, even if they were shaking. She hadn't thought that far ahead.

"I don't know, but if I fly us out, and we stop once to refuel, I can take the route solo—file it as repositioning, executive discretion. No one will look too hard if I get the timing right."

Melody took a breath. "I think I know where we can go. I have a phone... It was Russell's. I think it's a burner, but I've never powered it on. I wasn't sure if it was traceable."

Amanda's eyes narrowed—perhaps Melody did have a trove of information she was still clinging to. "And now?"

Melody exhaled. "Now seems like the time. Before he died, he told me that if anything ever went sideways... There was one person he trusted. Anywhere in the world."

"Who?" Lyla asked.

"Andrei," Melody said. "A Romanian friend. I don't know his full name, but Russell said if he was ever in a bind, Andrei could get him out. I'm guessing there's more in this phone—contacts, messages, maybe even coordinates."

Amanda studied her face. "Then we start with a name," she said. "I'll make sure we're heading for Bucharest."

Lyla lifted her eyebrows. "Romania?"

Amanda nodded. "It's as good a place as any to disappear. And if Russell trusted this man, I'm willing to find out why."

Melody smiled, satisfied. "I'll grab the case, and we should all get separate cabs to the airport. What time?"

"I'll text," Amanda said. "But only once. After that, I'm off-grid. And if anyone's tracing flights, they won't find this one till we're gone."

Melody nodded, standing to make her way back to her hotel as Amanda turned to Lyla.

"I need to save a few contacts from my phone before I leave it here. Can I AirDrop to you?" she asked, already tapping and scrolling.

Lyla handed her phone over. "You got it. Want me to do anything special with them?"

"Yeah," Amanda said. "When they land in your Contacts, just rename them to something boring. Bank guy, dry cleaning—anything that doesn't look like names."

A soft *ding* signaled the transfer.

"No one will see an AirDrop history," Amanda added, "but turn off Wi-Fi and Bluetooth after—just in case anyone is running a trace nearby."

Lyla nodded, already moving through her settings. "You sure you're okay leaving your phone?"

"I have to be," she shrugged.

Lyla left, disappearing into the elevator without looking back.

Amanda lingered for a moment in the polished stillness of the lobby, her phone tucked beneath her palm like a secret already slipping from her grip. Every instinct in her urged her to run, but she walked instead—slowly, deliberately—crossing through the corridor with a practiced calm. She nodded once at a bellman, barely meeting his gaze, and wove past staff and late-night guests, her heels clicking softly across the marble floor before the carpet at the elevator swallowed the sound like a hush before a storm.

The moment her suite door closed behind her, she exhaled, dropping her clutch on the bed, as she powered off her phone and slid it on top of the minibar cabinet, beneath the stacked snacks. Someone would find it eventually. Just not soon enough to stop her.

She let her gown drop as it pooled around her feet in a silent surrender. Changing quickly into black travel pants, a soft sweater, and flats that wouldn't make a sound on tile. She hurried around the room, taking only what was needed, and pushed it into her carry-on bag.

Suddenly, the door clicked open behind her. Amanda's spine straightened, her breath locking in place. She turned just as Tristan stepped inside, his keycard still in hand. He paused on the threshold, eyes scanning her from head to toe.

"Hey. I thought you were going to bed. But..." he scanned what he could see of the room, "you going somewhere?"

He looked half-drunk on the night's adrenaline with his collar undone and hair slightly mussed. His jacket was draped over his shoulder, and there was still a trace of laughter in his eyes.

"I didn't think you'd be up," he continued without giving her a chance to say a word, closing the door behind him. "I figured I'd come back to find you passed out face-down in room service."

Amanda smiled, warm and disarming, her voice smooth despite the way her heart pounded against her ribs. "Ha, no. I couldn't sleep."

He chuckled and moved closer, slipping his jacket onto a nearby chair. "What's all this?" He nodded toward the open bag, the travel pants, and the shoes by the door.

She shrugged, zipping her carry-on with casual precision. "Just getting a jump on tomorrow. I have a flight, remember? I told you I have to eventually go back to work."

He crinkled his nose in a way that made Amanda's knees go weak. "Ah, that's right," he said. "Bummer."

Amanda smiled. "I wasn't sure how late things would run tonight, so I figured I'd pack while I still had brain cells firing."

Tristan sat on the edge of the bed, leaning forward with his elbows on his knees. "You probably left just in time. You missed a whole third wave after you left. They brought out some kind of rare Japanese whisky. Julius practically started a fireside chat."

She laughed, letting it glide across the room like it belonged. "I guess I always miss the fun stuff."

He smiled but didn't move. "My parents want to have breakfast in the morning. Just a quiet thing. Us, Olivia, and a few board members. Can you come with me?"

Amanda paused long enough to make it believable. "Of course," she said, walking over to him and brushing a hand over his shoulder as she bent down to press a kiss to his temple. "I wouldn't miss it."

He looked up at her, eyes softening, voice low and reverent. "You're amazing, you know that? Like, I can't believe you're real sometimes."

"I've heard rumors," she teased.

He exhaled, then stood. "I'm gonna rinse off. I feel like I've been wearing this tux for a decade."

"Yeah, of course, go ahead," she said, gesturing toward the bathroom with a smile. "Take your time."

He kissed her once, sweet and unhurried, then closed the door behind him. The nearly immediate sound of running water filled the space behind him.

Amanda stood still for a moment, waiting for the steam to curl into the air, a signal that the shower was running full and hot—her window to leave. She placed a note on the nightstand, as her fingers hovered above the zipper of her bag, pulse quiet but insistent, like her whole body was holding its breath. She didn't cry. She didn't shake. She just paused—one suspended heartbeat—before leaving the room, the hotel, and slipping into the stillness of the night.

Chapter Eighteen

Bucharest, Romania: 12:42 a.m.

"I'm never flying again," Lyla muttered, stepping onto the pavement as if it might swallow her whole. Amanda didn't answer right away. A dull pressure curled along her spine and up the back of her skull, her eyes stinging with sleepless grit. The cold Romanian air scraped at her throat like sandpaper, waking her nerves just enough to feel the hollow ache of exhaustion settling into her bones.

"You always say that," she finally replied, fatigue halting a full smile from forming on her lips. Amanda's muscles ached with the strain of solitude in the cockpit, the pressure of twelve and a half hours of decision-making pressing on her like the weight of the sky itself. Her thoughts felt sludgy, her limbs stiff from vigilance, and not even the crisp air could fully chase away the fog in her head.

The sky over Otopeni Airport glowed lavender with the promise of dawn as they made their way away from the chartered jet. Feet hitting the tarmac with a quiet finality, each step echoed louder than expected in the early morning hush.

The air was cooler than Tokyo, a chill biting at Amanda's exposed neck despite the sweater pulled tight around her. Breaths came out in short, visible puffs. She welcomed the sting; it made everything feel real.

Melody stayed quiet, her expression unreadable, but Amanda noticed the subtle tremble in her shoulders. Lyla tramped along the asphalt, her oversized sunglasses already in place—an absurd but comforting layer of armor. She tugged her phone from the pocket of her coat and tapped out a quick message, thumb moving with practiced speed.

"Just letting Kyle know I'm alive," she muttered. "Still can't tell him where I am, but at least he knows I haven't been kidnapped by pirates."

Amanda nodded. "Time to blend into the crowd," she said, pointing to a door leading to the main terminal.

Melody turned her head. "You sure it's a good idea to enter the country with our passports?"

"I don't think we have a choice. I don't know how to side-step passport control."

"Makes sense. If only Russell had told me he was a spy while he was alive," Melody exhaled. "Maybe I'd be able to handle some of it too," she let her shoulder drop. "Or maybe if I had lived with my eyes wide open before now, I'd be more help." She spoke as if voicing her regret made it real, its weight threading through the quiet.

"Hey, we do what we can with the information we have, right?" Lyla assured. "I don't think anyone will have had the time to track us yet. Let's just get in and see what magic this guy Andrei can work for us," she suggested.

Amanda pushed open the glass door and winced as the sterile brightness of the terminal struck her like static. The fluorescent lights buzzed overhead, sharp and unrelenting, jarring her senses more than she'd expected. The air inside was colder than the morning outside and smelled of cleaning solution—an antiseptic jolt that made her stomach twist and her grip tighten on her bag. It was surprising how many people formed the early throng of travelers, the setup perfect for surveillance to be muddled and overwhelming. For now, they were invisible.

The three women moved through customs without a word. Passports were stamped by a disinterested officer who barely looked up. Though the line was long, there were no questions or delays. Just the mechanical sound of another floodgate of passengers emerging behind them.

In the arrivals area, Amanda scanned for signs of transportation options.

"Let's sit," she said, guiding them toward a row of vinyl chairs under a glowing screen showing arrivals and departures. She dropped her bag to the floor and rubbed her temple. It was noon in Tokyo, and she'd been awake for over twenty-eight hours.

Melody hovered for a moment, then slowly sank into the chair beside her. Her fingers traced the zipper of her purse, hesitating before tugging it open.

"I haven't touched this since the day I emptied Russell's safe deposit box. But if we're counting on Andrei... this is all I've got."

She pulled out the phone—an outdated model, matte black, the kind that looked both cheap and indestructible. It didn't have a case or a lock screen. But it was a weight in her hand that suddenly felt heavier than before.

Lyla leaned in. "You sure it won't ping anyone? Like, light up some tracker in Siberia?"

Melody shook her head. "I don't know. I feel like it's not connected to anything. I didn't find a SIM. I think if I turn it on, I can maybe find something stored on the device itself. I have the charger, so it's got battery, I think. It's been a while since I left, so it's not full, but I think it should have some charge still. I just want to find a name, or number—anything." She held her breath as her thumb hovered over the power button.

Amanda watched her, running scenarios in her mind. "Wait," she said gently. "If it's a burner... then whatever's in there, it could be something he didn't want anyone to find. You ready to do this?"

Melody nodded, her jaw tightening, "Yeah," she said as she pressed it.

The screen lit up with a dull blue glow. No logo, no boot animation—just a flicker of life, followed by a stark home screen and a battery indicator barely holding at twelve percent.

Lyla looked at the device carefully. "Looks like something Russell rigged himself. Stripped down OS, no tracking, no logos—just the basics. Perfect if you don't want to be found."

They all leaned in closely as Melody tapped into the contacts. There were only a few, and one of them read: *Andrei—RO—Safehouse*. Melody tapped the name to call.

A man's voice came through, low and precise. "Alo?"

"Hello, is this Andrei?"

"Who gave you this number?"

Melody swallowed. "My husband. Russell Drake?"

There was a long beat of silence before he spoke, "Where are you?" Andrei said abruptly.

"Bucharest."

Another pause followed, even longer than before.

"Do you know the spot?" he asked.

"The spot?" Melody choked out the short syllables.

"Check the notes. I'll be there in twenty," he said before the line went dead.

Melody lowered the phone, eyes meeting Amanda's. "Check the notes?" she almost panicked, "Does this thing have notes?"

Lyla crossed her arms. "Guess we're about to find out. Here, give it to me."

Of the three of them, Lyla was the most adept at digital literacy. She took the phone in her hands, pressing buttons until the small screen illuminated a few lines of text.

Hanul Românesc. "That's gotta be Romanian," Melody pointed to the words.

Lyla connected the phone to the WiFi, Googling the words quickly. "It's a restaurant," she reported.

"Let's find a taxi," Amanda said, standing so quickly that she almost toppled over.

"Woah, hey. You've done a lot today." Melody said, grabbing her elbow. "We'll navigate, you just take it easy, all right?"

"Yeah," Amanda whispered, finally feeling the ache of ex-pired adrenaline.

They stood outside the restaurant's massive wooden door tucked beneath a sandstone archway on a main Bucharest thoroughfare. The windows were dark, save for the orange flicker of a streetlamp that caught on the carved trim of the shutters. The scent of yeast and coal smoke lingered faintly in the air, like someone had been baking bread in stone ovens before sunrise.

Amanda stood slightly in front of the others, her posture relaxed but ready, her tired eyes finding the strength to sweep the street. Melody held the old phone like it was still vibrating.

A key rattled in the lock, and the door creaked open just wide enough to reveal a man in a dark coat, mid-fifties, sharp-eyed and stoic. He looked them over once, slowly—Melody first, his eyes narrowing with a flash of calculation or distant memory; then Amanda, whose guarded posture and unreadable expression made him pause for a beat; and finally Lyla, her sunglasses still perched atop her head, adding a Bond vibe to the dim, shadowy entryway.

"You said you were alone," he said in low, accented English.

Melody didn't cower. "I said I was coming. I never said I'd be alone," she confirmed.

He studied her for a moment, then stepped aside. "Come."

They entered a dark, hushed space. The tables were set with folded linens, copper lanterns unlit. The restaurant remained cloaked in shadow, just enough to see the thick wooden beams, the heavy tables, the embroidered runners laid out like relics of an older world. It smelled of wood smoke, garlic, and yesterday's wine. Andrei didn't offer them seats. He simply closed the door and turned, arms folded, blocking the exit.

"You say Russell sent you."

Melody nodded. "He didn't *send* me. He never said what he did. Not directly. But now that he's gone, I found this phone. I just remember him saying that if anything ever happened, if he or I ever needed help, we had a friend in a man named Andrei."

Andrei's face didn't change. "He told many people many things."

"I have children," Melody said, her voice cracking but her spine straight. "I don't care what he did or didn't tell you. I know he trusted you. And he knew something was coming. He didn't say it out loud, but I saw it on his face. I felt it in the way he tucked this phone into a safe without telling me why."

Andrei stared at her for a long moment. Then he asked, "What's his code word?"

Melody blinked. "What?"

"He told me if anyone came in his name, they'd know a phrase. A code. One phrase."

Melody exhaled, panic flickering behind her eyes. Then—like a thread unwinding—she closed her eyes and let the memory surface, uncoiling slowly from some hidden recess of her mind where she'd buried it for safekeeping.

"Every night, when he kissed the kids goodnight, he'd say the same thing: 'Watch the wolves, count the stars.' I asked him once where it came from. He said it was from a military story where someone didn't make it home. It sounded almost like a lullaby, but I think it was a warning in disguise.

She opened her eyes. "That's the only line he ever repeated that didn't sound like his—the one he acted like we had to remember if we ever got lost."

Andrei's face didn't change, but he gave the smallest nod. "That's it."

The stillness that followed wasn't silence—it was something heavier. A pause filled with grudging acceptance. Andrei turned, pulling out a chair at one of the back tables, and sat.

"Sit down," he said gruffly. "All of you. If Russell trusted you—even a little—I'll hear what you came to say."

The women exchanged glances, then together sat down without a word.

Andrei leaned forward, steepling his fingers. "Before he died, Russell contacted me. He said someone had found him. Said the world was about to shift in a way that no one saw coming. He asked for my help. I said yes. But now he's dead. And you're here."

Melody swallowed. "I don't know what he got involved in. But I think whatever it was... It's not over."

Andrei nodded once. "Then let's start at the beginning. I was a friend to him while he was stationed in Eastern Europe."

"You worked with him?" Melody asked, voice lowering, almost breathless.

Andrei nodded. "During the early days of the Ukrainian resistance," he said, "Russel watched Russia take Crimea in

2014. He requested to be assigned a post in Ukraine. Our intelligence worked hand in hand with yours, but America... they are fickle. They don't like Putin, but they don't fight him."

Melody nodded, not familiar enough with the conflict or her husband's role in it to digest the extent of what Andrei was saying.

"They moved him out to Ukraine as requested," Andrei clarified. "But Russell was loyal, not ultimately to country, but to people. He wanted to aid citizens instead of superpowers. He was precise. Lethal when he had to be. Too curious for his own good." He paused, then gave a faint, sad smile. "And too soft when it came to his family."

Melody exhaled, her eyes shining with the hint of tears.

Andrei folded his hands together. "But he visited me here a week before he died. He said someone had come to him—someone from Africa. Said there weren't only regional tensions anymore, but global ones. He called it *the matchstick moment*." His eyes cut to Amanda. "You wouldn't know anything about that, would you?"

Amanda leaned in slightly, speaking for the first time, not confirming, not denying. "Well, if it means we're all here because something's burning, you're not wrong. And you just might be our only lead."

Andrei smiled slyly. "I watch the news. I know what global shifts are happening." He let the tension sit for a moment, shifting in his chair, before leaning back slightly. His gaze sharpened on Melody. "Russell didn't come to Romania by accident," he said. "He was sent here by someone who doesn't leave a trail."

Melody's brow furrowed. "Who?"

Andrei blew a sharp breath threw his nose. "Azizi Malonga. He does not belong to a government, a company, or a cause. He doesn't exist on paper. But the world knows his reach. Oligarchs fear him. Politicians hate him. And people like me—well, we still wonder if he's real."

Amanda tilted her head. "And Russell trusted him?"

"He did more than trust," Andrei replied. "He worked for him."

Melody's hand tightened around the edge of the table. "Are you saying my husband betrayed his country... left his post?"

"I'm saying he was working for the only man brave enough to look Julius Babb in the eye and say no."

Lyla let out a low whistle. "Didn't think that was possible."

Andrei gave a dry smile. "Malonga saw what was happening with Mr. Montgomery and the prototype. He told Russell it was too perfect—too seductive. Malonga believed Julius was grooming Tristan to be the unwitting front man for a new kind of control. Not a weapon, but worse."

Amanda's jaw clenched. "Information."

Andrei nodded. "The most powerful commodity on the planet. Manipulation of reality itself. Control what people see, what they believe, what they buy. Malonga understood that the technology was not only advanced—it was dangerous. And he didn't want to steal it or buy it. He wanted to make sure it never made it to market."

Melody sat very still. "And Russell...?"

"Was supposed to observe. Infiltrate. Get close enough to see if Julius could be stopped. If he couldn't stop Julius, then he was to find someone who could."

Amanda's breath caught. She felt the weight of the case she had hidden—the only version of the prototype that hadn't been corrupted, burning a hole in her suitcase. Katherine's words came rushing back like smoke curling around a lit fuse: *"The prototype, the one Tristan built himself, is the only model that contains the complete hardware."*

But Andrei wasn't finished revealing the unbelievable facts he possessed. His expression darkened. "There's something else you need to know. Before Russell died... he made a switch."

Melody's brow furrowed. "A switch?"

"He got access to the prototype. The real one, when he was on a trip."

Amanda leaned in, her voice low and measured. "Are you saying he stole it?"

Andrei confirmed with a head bob. "Yes, he replaced it with a copy. Julius believed he still had the working model. But he didn't."

Silence filled the space with a deafening boom. Amanda sat back slowly—the full weight of what he was saying beginning to settle. "So the case I was carrying..."

"The one Katherine gave you?" Lyla asked, her voice just above a whisper.

"Was already a decoy," Amanda finished.

Melody looked down at her hands. "But that means..."

"That means the real prototype is somewhere else," Amanda said. Her eyes flicked to Andrei. "You're saying Russell had it."

"He did," Andrei affirmed. "But he also knew the danger of what he was carrying. He didn't trust anyone enough to hand it over. Maybe he meant to pass it along eventually—maybe he was waiting for the right moment, the right person. But that moment never came."

Amanda sat forward, connecting dots out loud. "So if Katherine swapped out the case behind Julius's back... and Julius didn't call her out, he couldn't have known, and they both had fakes. Maybe someone else figured out that Russell had the real one first."

She took a long breath before her voice sharpened. "Jimmy. Hansen. Just as I thought on that damn boat in Tenerife. Katherine said she switched Julius's out for a fake one on the island, and Russell was already dead by the time she showed up."

Melody blinked. "You think the Governor did it?"

"Oh God," Lyla muttered.

Melody's tone shifted, heavy with realization. "So we've all been chasing shadows. And he might have the real prototype."

Andrei let their realization hang in the air for a moment before pushing back from the table. His chair creaked, but he didn't stand. He recalibrated, resting one arm along the back.

"Maybe ghosts, maybe not. There's one more thing you should know," he said. "Russell had a place. A retreat."

Amanda's eyes narrowed. "What kind of place?"

Andrei's lips curled, a rare glimmer of pride in his otherwise guarded demeanor. "A cabin in the mountains. A collection of them really. It is very old, very quiet. No neighbors. No tourists. It's where he'd go when things got... complicated. When he needed to think. Hide. Work."

Melody tilted her head slightly, a flicker of anticipation tightening the muscles above her brow. "You mean like a safe-house?"

"More than that," Andrei replied. "A vault. Not for money—for secrets."

He glanced toward the windows, now glowing with streaks of orange as the rising sun began to fill the sky. "Even the royals know the value of those mountains. The Prince—well, now he's the King, I suppose—he's come to Romania for decades. He once said, *'There is a sense of age-old continuity here. A virtuous circle where man and nature are in harmony.'*"

Andrei gave a small shrug, proud of himself for memorizing the King's words verbatim. "And... he is not wrong. It was good enough for Russell and fit for a king." His eyebrows lifted, showing obvious pride for his nation.

Lyla blinked. "Wait, are you quoting King Charles—you know, the actual King of England?"

Andrei smirked. "He's not just a figurehead. The man bought property in the village of Viscri, and he visits Transylvania more than some of our own politicians. He said it's one of the few places in the world where he can breathe. You think that's a coincidence?"

Amanda exchanged a glance with Melody. "So Russell chose it for the same reasons."

Andrei nodded. "Isolation. Natural barriers. And a network of old forestry roads no GPS will ever get right."

Melody leaned forward. "Do you know how to get there?"

"I do," he said. "He trusted me more than most." His voice was flat but carried an edge of something deeper, it could have been a memory, perhaps even grief. "I can take you myself, though it would be better if I stayed to monitor things here. I'll have someone I trust drive you—it's not far, but it's not an easy road. You'll want someone who knows every turn before the forest swallows you. The last hour is all serpentine roads and silence."

Amanda's hand tightened around the edge of the table. "Then that's where we need to go."

Andrei gave a curt nod. "Good. Eat something. Rest if you can. You'll want a clear head when you arrive. That place doesn't tolerate distraction. I have a few cots in the back. The driver can be here in an hour."

Chapter Nineteen

Carpathian Mountain Range, Romania

Amanda fought to keep her eyes open, watching the landscape transform, the last signs of city life dissolving in the rearview mirror as the mountains drew them forward. Romania stretched before them, wild and unapologetically ancient—a land not so much seen as felt, like stepping into a dream that had never needed to wake. Rolling hills gave way to jagged cliffs, forests that seemed untouched by time. She thought about how much the world tried to tame itself with cities, glass towers, and surveillance grids. But here, only a few miles outside of the city, nothing bowed to modernity. Lit only by moonlight, it was the starkest contrast to the future vision of the world she had just witnessed in Tokyo. These mountains simply existed, vast and untamed. The farther they drove, the smaller she felt—and the more she welcomed it.

In the front seat, their driver remained silent, his eyes fixed on the road with a focus that felt more like devotion than duty. Every so often, he muttered something in Romanian—maybe to the road, maybe to himself. None of them asked for a translation.

Lyla had dozed off against the window, her sunglasses still perched like a shield even in sleep. Melody was quiet, too, her gaze fixed on the passing trees like she was memorizing the pattern of branches.

The road to the Bucegi Mountains unraveled like a ribbon pulled from the earth, winding through mist-laced valleys and pine-drenched silence. As the car climbed, the forest stooped in close on either side. Branches reached like fingers as if to shield travelers from sight, or to silently judge all humans as trespassers.

She tried to hold on to the mountains, to her drifting thoughts, to the hush outside that seemed to press gently against the windows, but her grip on wakefulness loosened with each breath.

The forest eventually thinned, giving way to a sweeping ridge where the line of trees fell back like drawn curtains. The car slowed to a crawl on the uneven dirt path, tires crunching over gravel until the final bend revealed a clearing perched on the shoulder of the mountain.

Just before the final bend, the car jerked slightly as the driver slowed, then rolled to a stop beside a crooked wooden sign faded with age.

He turned in his seat. "You must walk from here. The road ends for cars. It takes you to the cabin."

Amanda blinked. "How far?"

"Not far. Five minutes?" He said it like a question. "You can see it from here." The driver pointed to a small structure in the distance, barely visible.

The women exchanged glances—tired, dubious, but too curious to stop—and began to gather their things.

As they all began to step out, he added, "You came at a good time. After the first snow, this path is gone. Buried for weeks. We say the forest decides who comes and who stays."

Amanda looked up at the sky, gauging the temperature. "It doesn't snow in September, right?" she asked hopefully.

She began walking towards the cabin as the women trudged behind her, grateful not to have taken more than a small suitcase and a handbag, her boots sinking into the soft earth.

The safe house wasn't a modern cabin; it was older, hand-built, and utterly unpretentious. Weathered stone and dark timber framed its shape against the rising spine of the peaks. Moss crept along the roof's edges, and the windows paned with thick, imperfect glass reflected a warbled sky. A slanted porch leaned toward the view like it, too, had surrendered to gravity.

Amanda took the key from the door's ledge as Andrei had instructed, the door creaking open under her hand, revealing a space that smelled faintly of cedar and iron stove ash. Two bedrooms flanked a narrow hall. A single bathroom, clean but spare, split off the back. The kitchen was functional, its cupboards stocked with preserved goods, its sink plumbed and working. Electricity hummed faintly through the light fixtures overhead. The home had old-world bones with a modern pulse.

"This is... not what I pictured," Lyla said softly, running her fingers along the rough wooden counter. "Cozy bunker vibes, but surprisingly bright."

Amanda smiled faintly, dropping her bag. "I guess Russell knew how to disappear."

They all explored the interior, peeking into closets and lifting woven rugs as if secrets might be stashed underneath. From the window, Amanda noticed an outbuilding.

"Hey, look," she pointed.

"Can we look later?" Melody murmured as she paused in front of the back window. "Surely we've bought ourselves enough time to rest."

The weight of the day—no, the past *week*—caught up all at once. Sleep wasn't a desire; it was a demand.

"I'll take the far room," Melody said, already moving toward the bedroom on the right.

Amanda and Lyla exchanged a glance before ducking into the other. Two twin beds with patchwork quilts sat beneath a window that framed the tree line like a painting. They didn't even speak as they dropped their bags, shoes thudding softly against the wooden floor.

Lyla sank into her mattress, pulling out her phone. "They said there's no signal here, right?" she murmured, eyes already closing. "I sent Kyle a message from the airport while I was on WiFi. I'm sure he won't worry. He won't be up for hours anyway."

Amanda collapsed into the opposite twin, which carried a faint scent of smoke and soap, grounding her in something oddly comforting amid the disorientation. She turned towards Lyla, smiling. "You picked a good one, didn't you?"

Lyla's smile was almost invisible, half-conscious. "Yeah."

Neither Melody nor Amanda had made any attempt to check in with anyone. There was no one expecting Melody—no one watching the skies. Melody's boys thought she was off-grid on a month-long European cruise with girlfriends. In a way, it was true. Just not the kind of adventure they'd ever imagine. Amanda imagined that Tristan found the note she left, saying that she had to leave early and was probably too tipsy to remember asking her to join him and his family for breakfast. He likely only expected her to check in after a flight, and she hadn't given him details on that. It would be a few more hours before he would sense anything. Or she hoped, at least.

Sleep took her before the next thought could form.

Melody stood in the small kitchen, barefoot, pouring coffee into one of the handcrafted ceramic cups she'd found tucked behind a jar of lentils. The moka pot—a small stovetop coffee maker that brews coffee by passing boiling water pressurized by steam through the grinds, especially known for producing strong, espresso-like coffee without the need for an electric machine— sputtered its last bit of steam on the stove. It filled the space with warmth and a smell that soothed as much as it awakened Amanda.

She lumbered to the kitchen doorway, hair tousled, her shirt falling off one shoulder.

"What time is it?" Amanda asked, her voice husky from sleep.

"Little after four a.m.," Melody said, sliding the mug across the table toward her. "Wish we could've slept more than a couple of hours. I woke up half an hour ago and couldn't fall back asleep. I figured I'd poke around a little."

"You find anything?" Amanda asked, eyeing the counter, where a neat folder sat beside a half-burned candle.

Melody nodded. "Notes. In the room where I slept. The file's labeled with an *R*. Not sure what it means, but maybe Russell meant for someone to find them?" Her voice trilled upward at the end as if looking for an answer.

Before Amanda could respond, a throaty rumble echoed from the hall. "Tell me I'm not dreaming and that coffee is real."

Lyla approached in mismatched socks, pajama pants, and one of Amanda's sweaters that she must have fished out of an open bag while still half asleep. The cabin had gotten bitingly cold in the black of night, and one of Lyla's core principles was doing everything possible to stay warm. She complained about the cold more than anyone Amanda knew.

"Yes, it's real," Amanda said, nodding toward the small pot. "And hot. Melody just made a fresh one."

Lyla grunted in approval. "Did we time travel or just nap like the dead?"

Melody cracked a smile. "Somewhere in between."

By five a.m., after their fourth round of coffee from the sputtering moka pot, the women had already sifted through the folder Melody had found in the cabin. Its contents were eerily familiar—names they'd come across before, dates and places that had surfaced in Russell's notes. There was nothing new yet. But it confirmed they were tracing the right path.

They explored the cabin further to find a cedar-lined closet with coats, wool-lined boots, gloves, and scarves—neatly arranged sets, as if Russell had not always been alone when here. After being a little disappointed in the contents of the papers they found inside, they tied their hopes to the outbuilding.

Stepping outside, Lyla waved the women forward.

"Nice and easy; the guy said there were bears up here," Melody said as they crept along a gravel path.

Lyla sucked air in through her teeth. "Bet this wasn't on anyone's bucket list."

The air was sharp, numbing their fingertips through gloves and painting their breaths into thick ribbons. The flashlight beam cut a narrow path through mist that hovered close to the ground, while in the distance they heard an owl hooting.

"Perfect ambiance, my guy," Lyla said, maneuvering as gingerly as if she were a real-life spy, avoiding a web of laser beams. "The last thing I need is a mountain owl dive-bombing us in the dark here."

Amanda shushed her briefly. "We can probably pick up the pace," she suggested.

The small sister cabin was farther than it had looked. By the time they reached the structure, the smallest hint of dawn turned the sky into a dark midnight blue, rather than a *can't see your hand in front of your face* kind of dark. The building appeared deceptively small, an angular silhouette crouched against the cliffside.

Amanda pushed on the door, heart thudding with the weight of their last hope and the cold air pressing in around them. Her breath formed a soft cloud in the dim light as she tried the handle again, feeling a spike of anticipation. It didn't budge, so she began feeling around the door frame for a key. Melody spotted a small urn on an exterior ledge and looked inside. She shook her head. Nothing.

"Hey, look," Lyla said, touching a small metal plate under the handle. "There's a keypad. Any guesses?"

"Our anniversary? June 13," Melody replied.

"Zero, six, one, three," Lyla stated the numbers aloud as she pressed until hearing the sound of the bolt turning. She swung the door open, letting her fingers trace the wall for a light switch. "Wow, this is cool," she said.

The interior opened up into a room much larger than they'd expected, neatly furnished, cozy, almost. Bookshelves and traditional tapestries lined the back wall. In the corner was a desk, a long table with maps pinned beneath a pane of glass, and several crates marked with initials and dates.

"Oh my gosh," Amanda whispered. "Russell was running a one-man CIA archive."

Not needing to discuss a plan, they split up, each woman drawn to a different corner of the room. Melody flipped through folders labeled with regions: Sudan, Qatar, Belarus, Japan. Amanda ran a hand along a low row of cabinets, noting names she didn't recognize—aliases, maybe.

Lyla lifted the lid on a box marked: *Cross – V.*

"Vivian Cross," she said aloud. "Isn't that the name of the other lady? The one who died on the dive trip?"

Amanda turned, "Yeah."

Melody was already reading over her shoulder. "Hedge fund manager. She traveled between cities, countries. Looks like she coordinated the movement of capital. Not just legal."

Amanda scanned the paperwork. "Broker deals for people like Malonga. Asset shielding. Transfers without records."

Lyla exhaled. "So she was helping him move money around to fund operations?"

"Or sabotage them," Melody said. "Maybe she was part of the plan to stop Julius. Stop the Ocular Grid."

Amanda's voice dropped. "If Russell and Vivian were working together... then that's two people close to the truth. And now they're both dead."

Lyla folded her arms. "So, who found out? Katherine? Julius? Hansen?"

A hush fell between them, tense and expectant, as if the air itself was waiting for the next name to be spoken. They were no closer to answers.

"Do you think they are loyal to their countries?" Amanda asked, her voice barely above a whisper. "Or something else?"

Her question hung in the air as they kept searching, the hours slipping past without them noticing. It wasn't until the light behind the frosted glass shifted from steel blue to a soft ochre that they finally turned to see the wall opposite the shelves—glass from floor to ceiling. It was so clean and precise that it had blended into shadow. But now, as dawn broke over the horizon, the view was impossible to ignore.

The room jutted out like it had been carved from the mountain itself, one side suspended over the valley. Morning mist clung to the Carpathians, rising and dipping in waves, dark, primal, and breathtaking.

But what stole Amanda's breath was not the house itself; it was the sudden feeling of exposure, of being seen by the vastness around her. A quiet reverence settled in her chest, laced with a twinge of grief. It reminded her of everything she'd lost, and everything she was still running from, perhaps what she was still hoping to gain... or escape. This was the world beyond all of it.

The cliffs stretched out in all directions, a kingdom of jagged rocks and velvet shadows. Clouds hung low, spilling over ridgelines like misted silk. She felt a strange kind of kinship with the land, like it spoke in a language she hadn't heard in years but somehow still understood. The familiarity felt innate, as if her beloved Smoky Mountains had a mirror on the other side of the planet, holding a rope between them, one steadying the other. She could see why Russell would choose this place. It was unsearchable. Sacred, in its own way. A place where the truth behind hidden secrets could breathe.

Lyla moved toward the glass slowly. "Okay. Russell wins. Coolest hideout ever."

Amanda didn't speak. She pressed her palm to the glass, her breath catching as she again absorbed the vastness before her. The mountain cold bit at her skin, but she welcomed it, anchoring her, reminding her she was still here, still searching. The distance below was dizzying, a reminder of how far they'd come and how little they still understood. Yet, in the hush of morning and the silence of stone, something stirred in her—a sense that this place had waited for them, and that the truth might finally be ready to rise.

A low thrum shivered through the floorboards of the cliff-top lookout. Amanda stilled, a half-unrolled map in her hands, and looked toward the ceiling.

"Do you hear that?" she asked, frozen.

Melody was already moving toward the glass wall, her eyes narrowing. "Look, it's a helicopter."

Lyla stood in the corner, hands deep in a crate of radio parts. "Well, that's not ominous at all."

They formed a huddle at the glass, deciding whether it was safer to stay inside or investigate what was happening.

"It's not like we can hide," Lyla shrugged.

The women stepped outside and into the icy dawn as the noise grew louder—rotor blades slicing the sky like a warning. From their vantage point, they could see the helicopter cresting the ridge, a matte black silhouette against the brightening sky. It circled once before descending toward the clearing between the cabin and the smaller building.

Dust kicked up in all directions as it landed. The trees bowed with the gust, and for a moment, the noise swallowed everything.

A thick-shouldered man bumbled out first, moving casually.

"Andrei," Amanda muttered.

Melody took a step back. "This was a trap?"

Lyla jabbed a thumb toward the landing chopper. "Great. He's an executioner with a mountain Uber. Amazing," she said with her signature flippant tone.

Andrei approached, glancing once towards the cliff's edge, then back at them. His mouth opened, as if he wanted to shout an explanation, but before he could say anything, the helicopter door opened again.

Azizi Malonga stepped out in a long wool coat that fluttered from the sharp gusts of wind the heavy chopper blades left in its wake. He adjusted his gloves slowly, surveying the mountaintop like it belonged to him.

Amanda's stomach churned. The man she'd watched from a distance in Tokyo, a name whispered across every lip there, was somehow in the remotest part of the planet she could find.

"The network these people have is staggering," she thought.

As Malonga and Andrei made their way closer, Amanda stepped forward, finding her voice. "Mr. Malonga," she said simply.

"Miss Hopkins. It's a pleasure," he said, extending a hand. His expression remained stoic and unreadable. "Shall we?" he gestured for them to enter the cabin.

No one else spoke; they simply followed his signal. The few yards' walk to the building felt like a dramatic film scene played in slow motion, everyone walking in step, no one speaking, fabric and hair floating endlessly. But Lyla couldn't bring herself to laugh or make any more quips about the craziness of what was happening. She loved her best friend. Would do anything for her, and she had proven it. But this was over the top. Even for her.

"What do you want?" Amanda finally spoke when the door closed behind them.

Malonga paused. Then smiled, his bright teeth revealed gradually, in a slow-moving arc.

"To stop Julius Babb," he said. "Before the world bends at his feet."

Chapter Twenty

Bucegi Mountains, Romania

The safe house had warmed slightly since sunrise, but the chill in the room had nothing to do with the mountain air.

Malonga stood at the head of the table, gloves off, hands resting on the wood. Amanda, Melody, and Lyla sat like students waiting to hear whether they'd passed a test.

"I owe you context," he said. His voice was low and composed. "And perhaps, apologies."

Amanda didn't speak. She only nodded.

Malonga looked to Andrei, who leaned against the doorframe like he'd rather be anywhere else.

"I know you want answers, and this could be lengthy," he began.

"It looks like we've got nothing but time," Lyla blurted.

Malonga pursed his lips. "Russell was more than a source," he said. "He was a partner. Quietly, for years. When he stopped reporting a few weeks ago, I knew something had happened. I contacted Andrei, his most trusted source, and then you showed up," he looked at Melody, "We were on high alert. We knew we couldn't participate in the auction without knowing if he had confided in you, and our group had a mole. And so, we've been watching."

Melody's arms folded across her chest. "And who exactly is your group? Are you not involved with Helion?" she asked in a way that sounded more curious than accusatory.

"I am not. We have a little bit of *everyone* in our cohort," Malonga replied, without defensiveness. "Men not unlike Julius with power and influence, but perhaps with more scruples. It takes a global effort to impede a global takeover, wouldn't you agree?"

Melody nodded.

"So when you came to Tokyo, I assumed Russell had shared his work with you," Malonga explained. "But then you disappeared, and before I left Tokyo," he shifted his gaze to Amanda, "I was able to suppress a bit of Tristan's panic because my surveillance at the airport saw you all leaving together."

Amanda looked up at him, trying to keep her own panic hidden. "Oh," was all she could say before he continued.

"After you left, Tristan found your phone. He found the note you left, saying you had to leave for an earlier flight. He was... unsettled."

Amanda narrowed her eyes. "So, he did find my phone?"

Malonga nodded. "And pinged your passport through internal channels. He now knows you're in Bucharest. He believes it's a coincidence. Romantic, even."

Lyla snorted.

"He also accessed your flight records," Malonga added. "You were smart to choose a layover, but you used your real name. The rich don't need warrants, dear. Just curiosity and power. I'm the only one who knows your precise location. So, for now, you are safe."

Amanda leaned back, her jaw tight.

"Bucharest is one of the Ocular Grid build sites," Malonga continued. "A key node for Europe. Each location is undergoing last-phase evaluation to mimic the successful model used in Tokyo. Tristan and his team will arrive in less than twenty-four hours."

"So you want me to meet him? Act like none of this happened?" Amanda asked.

"Yes. Seamlessly. Convincingly. He expects you now. It would raise suspicion not to appear."

"And what's the cover story?" she stammered, unable now to keep her voice from trembling.

Malonga gave her a knowing look. "Simple. Log in somewhere—anything public—and send him a message. Tell him you left early, forgot your phone, meant to call but couldn't. Apologize. Be casual. This is not unlike you and your job that you've returned to. You're fulfilling a role, correct? Someone hired you."

Amanda said nothing.

"Russell was trying to stop the rollout," Malonga took the opportunity to go on, voice gentle. "He embedded hardware chips at different build sites—circuit-level delays. Not destruction. Sabotage."

"And Vivian Cross?" Amanda asked.

Malonga's expression darkened. "She acted as my broker, but made the mistake of trying to sell state bonds to Hansen. They are uncommon and made him nervous. He put the pieces together too quickly. He realized that many other interested nations—that are about to release the wealth tied to their bonds—are invested in what your country didn't take seriously. The American government hasn't shown much of an interest in what we do in Africa, Europe, or Asia. Not if it doesn't line their pockets."

"But he's running for president."

"Yes. And if he wins—if someone hands him access to the Grid—he'll hold a blueprint to every nuclear defense system on the planet. Not just where they are. How to preempt them."

A long silence fell.

Amanda's voice was hoarse. "And Katherine? Do you know her?"

Malonga finally smiled.

"The British," he said, "are excellent at letting the Americans do their dirty work. She may just be who she says she is. But Julius has been in the game just as long, and he's compromised. So, I don't put it past her either. But I have not spent much on intel to find out. She hasn't raised many concerns."

"So Julius *is* corrupt," Amanda said breathlessly.

Malonga crossed his arms, the edges of his mouth spreading into a subtle grin. "Corruption is in the eye of the beholder," he said, squinting his eyes momentarily. "I have the sense that you are not accustomed to political work."

Amanda scoffed. "You know, Katherine gave me a prototype, right? And Andrei tells us that it's a fake because Russell took the one Julius had before Katherine could get to it. What am I supposed to do with that?" She spoke rapidly, as if not expecting anyone to answer her questions before pausing and meeting Malonga's gaze intensely. "Did he give the real one to you?"

"He did not," Melonga answered. "But there are a few versions around the globe. Each site, even though tampered with, has a variant of the original. The idea that Tristan's original prototype could be the only uncorrupted device may be wishful thinking."

"And why should we trust you?" Lyla finally asked, exasperated by the whirling facts and accusations.

Malonga met Lyla's gaze and didn't flinch. "You shouldn't. Not blindly. But ask yourself—has anything I've said contradicted what you already know?"

No one answered. The silence wasn't trust, but it wasn't rejection either. It was the space between, where alliances were formed out of necessity.

Outside, a rustle passed through the trees like the mountain was exhaling after a long night's rest. The sun had risen higher, casting long gold bands across the table, across their faces. The safehouse had warmed since sunrise, but the chill in the room remained—a cold that had nothing to do with air or altitude.

Amanda stood, the scrape of her chair sharp in the stillness. Her eyes didn't leave Malonga's.

"Thank you," she said finally. "For the context. I wish I could ask you a thousand questions right now, but my mind is spinning. I don't even know where to begin. It's hard to know who to believe—you have to understand that, right?"

Malonga simply nodded. "I do," he said.

Amanda turned to face Melody and Lyla.

"We need to talk."

They both gave a silent look of agreement.

Malonga straightened his coat and glanced toward the door. "I'll give you some time, but you'll need to come with me, Miss Hopkins," he said. "Andrei will remain behind and ensure your friends are taken safely down the mountain. My pilot will see them home—quietly, and without record."

He looked to Melody and Lyla with a nod of reassurance. "You've done enough. Let us take it from here."

The women shared whispers, standing outside the cabin door, luggage at their feet. The helicopter sat idly, giving the driver time to make it up the steep hills before they took off.

Melody and Lyla wanted to protest, but they knew they couldn't.

"You can't go with me," Amanda said, her voice low but firm, her gaze steady.

Melody didn't flinch. "I know." It was the calmest kind of heartbreak. No arguing or desperate appeal—just the quiet erosion of two people reaching the limits of how far they could walk side by side.

Amanda exhaled slowly, the cold air stinging her lungs. "If anyone else suspects that we left together—"

"They'll come for all of us," Lyla finished.

Melody's voice was resolute, but her eyes shimmered faintly in the morning light. "I've got three boys at home. I can't say I have all the answers I came for, but it'll be nice to be invisible for a while."

Amanda stepped closer. "You won't have to run forever."

Melody's laugh was dry, almost amused. "We all run forever. The trick is not forgetting who we are while we do."

Amanda reached out, and Melody leaned into the hug like an old habit—tight, familiar, and full of things they didn't have time to say. Lyla draped her arms around them both.

"Is this a bad time to mourn the breakup of the Spyce Girls?" she teased.

"You're incorrigible," Amanda snorted, Melody letting out a low moan that turned into a strained laugh.

"Yeah, but you love me," Lyla demanded.

"True," Melody responded first, making the two women smile. "I'm glad we met," she said before plunging into the group hug again.

"Us too, and we'll miss you," Lyla giggled.

"Wait," Amanda turned to Lyla. "You need to go home, too."

"Oh, do I?" Lyla said, arching a brow. "Just like that? Back to Kyle, my extremely important business, and boring networking events like I didn't just survive a spy movie with a murder subplot and a possibly haunted cabin?"

"You heard Malonga. Someone has to go home and show that this was just an extravagant girls' trip. It'd be more dangerous for me if you didn't."

Lyla looked down, kicking at a patch of gravel with her foot. "You know, I hate it when you make sense."

Amanda reached for her hand and gave it a squeeze. "I always make sense... you, however..." She could bring the light-heartedness when necessary, too.

Lyla sniffed. "You better not die, Amanda Hopkins. Not without me. Because we would make an epic scene. You can't do it alone, okay?

Amanda smiled, nodding emphatically as if she agreed wholeheartedly. "I'll do my best."

Lyla pulled her into a quick, fierce hug and, when she stepped away, pressed something into her palm. A worn lucky coin—one Amanda had given Lyla back in college.

"I kept it," Lyla said. "Now it's your turn."

Amanda swallowed hard. "You're such a pain in the ass."

"And you're ridiculous. But I love you."

"I love you, too."

Melody cleared her throat softly. "The driver's here. We have to walk down the path a little bit, remember?"

"Yeah, you guys good?" Amanda choked out the words.

Melody's eyes communicated her calm assurance. "Yeah. We'll both vanish in opposite directions."

Amanda watched them go as the pines curved in around them, then she turned to Malonga. "You said I need to check in with Tristan."

"There's a laptop in the archive building," he said. "Air-gapped. You'll use an encrypted WiFi portal we've arranged. It will make it seem as if you borrowed a computer at an airport lounge."

Amanda gave a wry smile. "So, no admissions, no forever goodbye explaining why this is way too much for me?"

"Correct. Just guilt, charm, and casual affection. In other words, lie like you mean it."

Amanda nodded once. "It won't be hard to act like a perfect girlfriend," she let her mouth droop, heaving with regret.

Malonga's gaze didn't waver. "Just remember who you're pretending to be—and who you actually are."

"I wish I knew the difference," she said, looking at the trail that led back to the archive building, then toward the ridge where the helicopter still waited.

She felt split down the middle—half tethered to the women she loved, half already walking into the future she hadn't asked for but couldn't escape.

Amanda stepped inside the room alone, her footsteps muted by the heavy wool rug. A laptop sat on a shelf, just out of the line of sight, inconspicuous among the maps and folders. She opened it slowly, not needing a password as the screen blinked to life.

She clicked the portal labeled *KLM Lounge – OTP* and waited.

A basic browser opened, and there was a single window with a blinking cursor in the search engine. She typed in *TikTok*, the only social media account she knew Tristan viewed. She looked up his user name, *The_OG_guy*, and opened a DM.

She flexed her fingers. Then began typing.

So sorry. Had to dash out early in Tokyo. Hope you got my note about the flight change. Long story, all fine, but I didn't want anything to go wrong on my first day back to work. Lol. Realized I left my phone at the hotel. :FacePalm: Borrowing a computer in the lounge, will grab a new SIM at my next stop.

She paused, staring at the blinking cursor.

It sounded casual. Harmless. Normal. And a complete and utter lie. She had been great at lies of omission and lies wrapped in truth, but this was going to take the cake.

She hovered over the *Send* button, then hit it. The message zipped off into the ether, pixels masquerading as connection. For a long moment, she sat there, her hands resting flat on the wood. Not moving. Not breathing. Then she closed the laptop, slow and deliberate, like sealing a vault.

Behind her, the wind howled lightly against the glass. The mountain remained unmoved.

Bucharest, Romania

The bustling city struck Amanda like a fever dream, far too deafening after the quiet of the mountains. The ground pulsed beneath the taxi as it rolled through Revolution Square, the golden light of sunset mirroring the marble facades of old palaces. New glass towers cast spines of reflection over cobblestones and rusted balconies. The air was rich with autumn warmth and the faint tang of diesel, the chilliness of the peaks now distant.

Amanda sat back, sunglasses on, lips slightly parted—the studied poise of someone who looked like she belonged, but carried secrets in her bones. She'd packed in a hurry, but she'd calculated one outfit with care—cream trench, boots she could run in, and a silk scarf tied loose around her neck, a touch of softness to look like she was in love. Now was the time for this outfit.

The driver dropped her at the InterContinental. It's where Tristan would be staying and holding meetings for the day. She found him standing near the elevator, backlit by a row of chandeliers, speaking with someone. He turned the moment she walked in, breaking off mid-sentence.

Amanda's heart skipped, caught in the thrum of recognition and the ache of uncertainty. She felt like she might tip off balance, her legs suddenly feeling more like liquid than appendages. His presence was so familiar and desired, but it clashed with the jagged knowledge of all she'd endured and now internalized.

"Amanda," he said, his voice low and threaded with relief. His stride was quick and unguarded.

She allowed a genuine smile to spread across her lips as he approached. The irresistible desire to touch his skin was quickly rising in her chest.

"You're here," he smiled, pulling her close.

"I'm here."

He leaned in, brushing his lips against hers in a kiss that lingered a fraction too long to be casual. "I was starting to think I'd have to send a search party. Or that you'd ditched me for a backpacking trip through the Carpathians."

Amanda laughed, letting it sound natural. "You wouldn't believe the story if I told you."

"Try me." His smile broke wide.

She reached for his hand. "Let's get upstairs first."

He didn't let go when they entered the elevator, when they stepped aside to allow another guest to join them, or when the doors slid shut again. He just turned toward her and pulled her face to his, unembarrassed to kiss her deeply in public, his hand at the base of her neck, thumb brushing her collarbone.

"I'm so glad you're here," he said. "Because I have something to ask you."

She smiled, wrapped in the comfort of him, even as the world around her felt bent and distorted. "Oh, you do?" She tried her best not to think about anything but him.

"I do, and I want to make sure I don't miss my chance before you fly away again." He tugged her hand as they stepped out of the elevator, making their way to a suite gilded by twilight, the heavy curtains drawn halfway open.

Tristan walked ahead of her, tossing his coat on the back of a leather chair, and loosening his collar like a man finally alone with someone he trusted. He turned slowly, as if feeling the weight of the moment before it arrived.

"I had this whole big thing planned," he said, gesturing vaguely toward the view. "Dinner on the balcony. Champagne. You in one of your slinky backless numbers."

Amanda raised an eyebrow. "Sorry to disappoint."

He smiled, stepping toward her. "You never do."

She tilted her chin, reading him—he was nervous, hands in his pockets, his foot tapping feverishly. It wasn't the confident, stage-ready Tristan Mongomery. This was the version who whispered in bed at night about wanting something real. The one who didn't want to build the future alone.

"I've been thinking about this since Geneva," he said softly. "And every second since you left Tokyo without a word only made it clearer."

Amanda's breath hitched in her throat. He reached into his coat pocket and pulled out a small velvet box.

"I know the world is a mess. I know I'm in the middle of building something that terrifies half the planet and excites the other half. I know your life is... layered. And complicated." He spoke quickly, spewing out a cascade of feelings he couldn't contain. "But I also know I want you in it. All of it."

He opened the box, revealing a delicate vintage ring. A massive diamond framed by sapphires. It was kind of their thing at this point. The midnight blues and sapphire sparkles.

Amanda was speechless, mouth agape.

"I'm not asking for an answer tonight," he added quickly, holding her gaze. "You don't owe me anything. I just want you to know that wherever you go, I'll be there when you land."

Amanda stared at him, at the ring, at the man whose world was about to become far more dangerous than he understood. And yet, he was still here, offering his future like a fragile and fearless gift.

She couldn't say a word. Instead, she walked to the window, her back to him, resting her forehead onto the cool glass. Outside, the city was alive and yet unobservant. Oblivious to who was watching, who was scheming, who was controlling.

Because somewhere, war plans were being written in code. But behind her, right there sharing the same oxygen, Tristan waited for a simple answer. Waited for her to remind him he was loved. Waited with his love for her in return.

She didn't say yes. But she didn't say no—only turned to look at him. A soft smile curved at her lips, and she walked into his arms.

"I just need a little time," she said.

Tristan kissed her hair and whispered against her temple, "I've got all the time in the world."

About The Author

Shelly Snow Pordea is a storyteller at heart, known for her exciting novels that connect, heal, and spark meaningful conversations. She first captured readers' imaginations with *Tracing Time*, a time-travel romance series that remains a fan favorite in its category. In 2021, Shelly and her brother placed in a top screenwriting contest for a co-written family drama based on their experience growing up in a cult—an exciting step into the world of film storytelling.

Her 2024 novel, *The Cheating Wife*, was inspired by a real incident of public shaming—a woman's property vandalized with the words "cheating wife" scrawled in graffiti. "After witnessing graffiti on a woman's property, blatantly accusing her of being a 'cheating wife,' I knew I was going to write a story about how far we've come—or haven't—from the days of public shaming and scarlet-letter-wearing," Shelly says. "The patriarchy is alive and well, and this book is my attempt to remind us all to take a look at our part in it."

Shelly is also the author of the *Flight Risk Spy Series*, which follows a high-flying heroine who stumbles into the world of espionage. She has based the travels of her protagonist, Amanda, on locations she's been lucky enough to visit. She and her family maintain a residence both in Brașov, Romania and St. Louis, Missouri.

Beyond her professional pursuits, Shelly is a dedicated mother to three incredible adults, loving wife to her favorite guy, George, for nearly three decades, and Buni (boo-nee) to one enchanting, magical granddaughter. She invites you to join her journey on social media, where she shares her insights and creative endeavors. Follow her @shellysnowpordea for a glimpse into the world of a multifaceted storyteller and advocate.

Also by

Shelly Snow Pordea

"A fun, engaging travel adventure with a female James Bond vibe that keeps you turning the page."

Books in *The Flight Risk Spy* Series:

The Night We Met – One encounter changes Amanda's life forever. March 2025

The Last Flight from Tokyo – Amanda's hunt turns deadly as she races against a ticking clock in Japan. June 2025

The Flowers of May – Back on American soil, Amanda discovers betrayal blooms closer to home than she thought. September 2025

Unfollowed – When everything goes offline, Amanda's past is sure to catch up with her. December 2025

From chance encounters to near-deadly escapes, this high-stakes series takes Amanda across continents, through smoky backrooms, and in a race against time. Each book peels back a layer of deception as Amanda learns that flying under the radar might just be the hardest thing of all.

Fasten your seatbelt! This spy series is a trip you won't want to miss.

★ ★ ★ ★ ★

"So original, imaginative, and captivating."

Book 1 in the *Tracing Time Trilogy*, Anna Wright grapples with the effects of her depression while living a secluded life with her young family abroad. When her husband disappears, she is faced with accepting the assumption of his death or uncovering the truth behind his work.

Anna returns to the only thing she knows, her Midwest family, but life on the farm isn't like what it was growing up.

Times and people have changed, and her quest to find herself again turns into a burning desire to know the truth. Her husband's colleague, Christopher, and the distinguished Professor Trinkton reveal secrets behind their studies, leaving Anna with the impossible choice to either join their efforts or lose David forever.

While she is an involved and loving mother, she does the unthinkable, choosing to travel through space and time without her children, justifying to herself that she's on a mission to help save the planet and return her husband safely to his family. Her tenacity and determination lead her to successfully embark on an unfathomable journey. And what she finds is unthinkable: her husband, stuck in a time period in which he was unable to access the technology needed to return, has been betrothed to another.

The Victorian British era in which David had been trapped for nearly eight years left him all but hopeless until Anna arrives. Overcoming the epic trials their true love story must face, along with a mystical guide, together they make a way to return. But things aren't simple when toying with the fabric of time.

Book 2 in the *Tracing Time Trilogy*. Fourteen years after the disappearance of David and Anna, Christopher Mack is imprisoned for their murders. Maggie Sturgeon, the young daughter who was left behind had been raised by her mother's brother and Turkish-born auntie, Ami.

Now an adult, Maggie finds that Trinkton, who she knew to be the lawyer involved in the murder case, was actually her parents' former Professor at UCLA. Following in her father's footsteps and being accepted into their science program, she too finds herself uncovering secrets she was never meant to know.

Connecting with a fellow student, and son of a prominent professor himself, Maggie and Rowan join forces to unearth every mystery about the past. What they didn't expect was to be entangled far more than they could have imagined. Rowan finds that his parents were also participants in the infamous time travel program as they uncover a convoluted string of events that led them to become deeply involved in a network of people in *The Program*.

Arriving in 1970s England, they reunite with their parents only to be plunged into a world from which they only wished they could escape. Maggie and Rowan ultimately believe they can make a difference by trying to thwart the growing effects of climate change, but their compromise is being fully controlled by *The Company.*

The family drama an absentee parent must face with their adult children takes on new meaning once Maggie confronts her parents as their paths cross in a time period none of them were meant to experience.

Book 3 in *The Tracing Time Trilogy.* After years in *The Program,* two generations of parents who had struggled to make sense of the lives they built were forced to reveal secrets to yet another generation. Young Maisy had a peaceful life growing up in England as the daughter of expats in the 1990s, but her stoic personality and stunning looks always drew attention. Thinking it was her weirdness that made her feel like she never quite fit in and determined to find herself, she set off on a backpacking adventure that would change her life.

Antonio was unlike anyone she'd ever met. Dropping her a secret note in an airport lounge, he leads Maisy to a startling discovery of who she really was, no spiritual self-revelation involved. Coming to terms with the fact that she was the third generation in a family of time travelers, Maisy conspires with Antonio to blow the whole thing up. She finally feels like she has answers for her misfit life, yet she has only scratched the surface.

Being involved with *The Company* has taken its toll on everyone, and Maisy is the young blood needed to lead the charge for this family to regain their freedom once and for all. While not fully abandoning the initial mission of trying to help save the planet, she, her parents, and grandparents set off to do collectively what one could not accomplish alone. One problem remains for Maisy, Antonio isn't part of the family.

Leaving the past behind, all three generations duly return to the twenty-first century as Trinkton and Christopher are finally able to share the truth about what had transpired during their absence. Both happy endings and love lost are inevitable.

★ ★ ★ ★ ★

"A story that stays with you long after you've finished."

Morgan Conner had it all—until the words *cheating wife* appeared spray-painted across her property, turning her world upside down. Suddenly, her picture-perfect life is in pieces, and the whispers of her community grow louder by the second.

Caught in a storm of judgment and betrayal, Morgan must dig deep to fight for her truth and her survival. In a society where appearances often mean more than facts, can she rise above the scandal and find her own voice?

Dive into this powerful story of resilience, redemption, and breaking free from the expectations of others.